*Don't let your boyfriend
keep you from finding your wife*

THE LOVE GALLERY

K.B. CASIMIR

First published in the United States 2025

This edition published 2025

ISBN: PB: 979-8-9914031-2-2

Cover and formatting by Books and Moods

For Amber.

My love, without you, none of this would be possible. I started to dream again when I met you. You are my muse, my sunshine, my smile on a bad day.

You rescued me when I was drowning. Nobody will ever compare.

I love you.

Wind whipped through Lucy's blonde hair as she stared at the shrinking scenery of Port Canaveral. She ignored the hum of the ship's engine, the boom of the horn signaling they were embarking on their week-long journey to the Bahamas.

Lucy Price did not want to be there. There was nothing fun about being confined in open waters with her boyfriend for an extended period of time. Being confined in an apartment together on land was suffocating enough.

"It's just water," the boyfriend in question, Chris Ford, whined as he nudged her in the side, pulling Lucy from her reverie. "Come *on*. Let's go explore the ship."

Lucy looked over at him and regarded his face, then waved her hand. "I'm enjoying up here. You can go without me. We still have cell service. Text me if you need me."

Chris hesitated, as if he were going to say something, but eventually turned and left her in peace.

This whole vacation had been Chris's idea, and though

Lucy appreciated the effort, she knew it was hollow.

They had been in a relationship for six years now and she wondered if things would always be so... *stagnant* or if they would turn exciting again. Gone was the endearingly awkward yet somehow charismatic boy she'd met in her algebra class those years ago. She had only been taking the class to complete her pre-requisites, as had he, but they had hit it off immediately.

Originally, Lucy came from a small family in Daytona Beach, Florida. She had big dreams of becoming a writer when she grew older, and joined the journalism program at the University of Central Florida in Orlando to achieve that dream.

Chris, while chatting to her instead of doing his assignment, told her he was from Orlando and was getting a degree to join his father at his tech company. He wanted to make software, just like his dad. This was all just a 'stepping stone' to him.

Lucy had never been overly popular with boys growing up. She had had a boyfriend here and there throughout high school, but nobody had ever stuck. They had just been means to ends: prom dates, homecoming dates, someone to take pictures with over the summer. Nothing of *substance*.

Which was probably why she fell hard and fast for Chris right out the gate.

Things hadn't been all bad at first. She wouldn't have stayed with him otherwise. But as they neared graduation, and Chris faltered in his studies and began relying on his family's money, he had grown complacent in life. Lucy had no help from her parents — they would have if they could, but they didn't come from money and had none to spare for her studies. She had gotten a full academic scholarship, thankfully, but still needed to have a job all four years of college. She hadn't minded, hard work wasn't foreign to her. She had been taught at a young age to have a strong work ethic, and that nothing ever came for free.

She just wished Chris had been taught the same philosophy. It would have saved her a great many headaches over the years.

After graduating — or more accurately, her graduating summa cum laude and Chris barely squeaking by with a D average, they stayed in Orlando to pursue careers. Lucy had secured an entry-level position for a fashion magazine within the city, and Chris had been employed by his father. But after a few months, Chris reverted back to not showing up, slacking off, and eventually his dad fired him.

Things hadn't really been the same since then.

That was two years ago.

Chris had not adjusted well to being cut off from his family, and resorted to spending what he had left in his accounts at local casinos. He had won big the first weekend he was there and… that was it.

Now Lucy was paying for their apartment, utilities, groceries, and working overtime, all while Chris either slept in, played video games, or passed out in the casino. He had promised to get it together, and had even gone to rehab for his gambling addiction for a few months, but as everything else went in his life, his commitment hadn't lasted long. Lucy was just too exhausted to fight it anymore.

And now, to make up for his transgressions with blackjack tables and slot machines, they were on a cruise. Because *that* would magically fix everything and they would come back from the beach ready to be married.

Please.

Lucy squinted through the burn of the gusts around her, and soon, she could no longer make out the shore. Only the deep blue and white crests of waves crashing against the ship's exterior.

She took a deep breath and told herself she would have a good time. It was a big ship and Chris had no problem wandering around without her, so hopefully a couple of cocktails and an all-you-can-eat buffet would take away the burdens of her regular life and put her in a state of grace for the next seven days.

Turning from the ship's railing, she waded through people and went back inside. She pulled out her phone and tapped the screen to wake it up, but found no notifications. Pressing her lips together in a thin line, she locked it and tucked it into the pocket of her dress.

She'd go exploring on her own.

ucy strolled along the smooth floors of the ship, having taken the elevator down to the main deck from the outside area. She eyed the rest of the cruisegoers mingling around her, and was glad she looked the part. She joined many others in her floral dress and sandals, all complete with a white, linen hat that flopped with every step she took. She scanned each room she went through. There was a dull roar of chatter, laughter, bartenders shaking drinks, shipworkers asking families if they wanted pictures, and other employees trying to sell everyone something. There was music bouncing off the walls, faint noise from every corner with the multitude of events packed into the ship's schedule.

She had never been on a cruise before. Her family couldn't afford something like that and this was the first vacation she'd ever really gone on with Chris.

So far, it wasn't too bad. Probably because there was a distinct lack of Chris.

She continued through another wide threshold of the

ship and bright, colorful lights and loud noises assaulted her senses. Her eyes widened as she observed the flashing games with people's backs to her as they smashed buttons and pulled down on levers. Her stomach turned and she abandoned her exploration of the ship to make a lap through the casino.

And, as expected, she found a familiar back-of-the-head sitting at a card table.

Irritation feathered in her jaw as she quickened her pace. She put her hand on Chris's shoulder, forcing the man to turn around. "Are you serious, Chris?!"

"Ummm…" was all Chris said. Lucy shook her head and stormed away from him.

"Lucy, wait," he said from behind her, having abandoned his post at the blackjack table. "Come on, we're on a cruise and it's what everyone is doing. I was just going to play one game, get it out of my system. You're the one who didn't want to come with me when I asked you to earlier. What else was I supposed to do?"

"You're in *recovery*," Lucy said, ignoring the looks they were getting from passersby. This was not the first time she'd made a scene over this. "This trip is supposed to be for *us*. Not you trying to get lucky," she said, her voice low but shaking with anger. "I leave you alone for *ten minutes* and you're already ruining everything."

"I'm not *ruining* everything. I played one game. Actually, I didn't even *finish* the game because you interrupted it. Now I'm definitely losing money. So thanks," Chris said, folding his arms.

"I can't believe you," Lucy said with an incredulous laugh.

"You know what? Go enjoy your game. I'm *so sorry* for getting in the middle of it," she said, putting her hands up.

Chris frowned and reached out, but she took a harsh step back, as if she'd be burned by his touch. He reached up and adjusted his black, square-framed glasses, then shook his head. Strands of brown hair fell down around his face. "Look, it's a stupid game. It doesn't matter. Let's go get something to eat."

"I'm not hungry," Lucy muttered. "Just leave me alone. I'll find you later," she added, before turning to leave him.

As usual, he did not follow.

Lucy walked away from the casino, but eventually sunk into a chair near a closed-off area. It wasn't overly busy and the noise of the ship's welcoming events faded around her. She assumed the boat would come to life later that night when cell service got knocked out and there truly wasn't anything left to do but enjoy the trip. She closed her eyes and rested her elbow on the arm of the chair, propping her head against her fingertips. Her eyes burned and she felt a balloon inflate in the base of her throat. Gritting her teeth to stave back any emotion threatening to burst from her, she squeezed her eyes shut even tighter.

"You okay?"

Lucy blinked her moist eyes open and trailed them upward to meet the eyes of a woman she did not recognize. She was tall, had dark hair, and some of the prettiest brown eyes she'd ever seen. Again, Lucy blinked, and a traitorous tear ended up escaping.

"Oh no," the mystery woman said, her voice thick with an accent — English, maybe? Lucy watched dumbly as she quickly looked around, then frowned at her. "I don't have anything to dry those tears."

"Oh," Lucy finally said, sniffling as she wiped her cheeks with the back of her hand. "No, it's okay. Really. Thanks for worrying about it though," she said. She pushed her blonde bangs away from her eyes and subconsciously brought her curls over to one side.

"I like your hat," the woman said with a smile.

Lucy mirrored the smile, though it was a bit more half-hearted, and brought her hand up to touch the hat. "Thanks. When in Rome and all," she laughed, rolling her eyes.

"For sure," the woman laughed. She glanced over as people began walking by, and she shot Lucy an apologetic glance. "Sorry. One moment," she whispered, putting a finger up. She turned her back to Lucy and side-stepped to a black table that Lucy hadn't even noticed was there. There was a big piece of artwork standing atop it and a few stacks of little cards and brochures. Lucy's eyes raked over the back of the woman, who was clad in all black, and it dawned on her that she must work on the ship. Why else would she be giving some spiel about whatever art was next to her in a full pantsuit?

Lucy took a deep breath and stood up, smoothing the wrinkles out of her dress. She pulled her hat off her head and cradled it in her hands, waiting awkwardly for... whatever her name was to finish with this couple that, admittedly, looked like they couldn't have cared less about anything she was saying.

Eventually, they left, and Lucy forced a smile as the woman turned back to her. "Sorry about that," the woman said. "Occupational hazard."

"It's okay," Lucy said, waving her hand dismissively. "So you work on the ship? Is that yours?" she asked, gesturing to the grand painting of a river winding around a snow-fallen village.

The woman glanced back at the work and laughed. It was a laugh that consumed Lucy in a way that caught her so off guard, her thoughts blurred for a moment. "That? I wish. This is a Bolotov piece. It's beautiful, eh?" she smiled, turning her gaze back to Lucy. "I work in the art gallery."

"Gotcha," Lucy nodded, her eyes roaming to the name tag on the woman's lapel. It was oval-shaped and white with *CHROMA* at the top and a named printed below it on what appeared to be a clear label strip. "Scarlett?"

The woman looked down at her name tag and laughed, pinching it. "That's me!"

Lucy couldn't help but smile. Her rosy cheeks darkened, but she put it down to the crying. "I'm Lucy," she said, outstretching her hand. Scarlett shook it, and Lucy felt… off. Strange. She swallowed and dropped the raven-haired woman's hand. "Chroma?"

"Yeah, that's the art gallery I work for. We partner with DreamWave to sell art on the ships. Lots of cruise lines do it. We work with a few different companies, but this one is our moneymaker."

Lucy nodded. "Do you like working on the ship? You must see so many different places."

"I like it, yeah," Scarlett said, nodding. Her eyes would go from Lucy to scanning the room again. Lucy understood she had a job to do, and felt a little bad about distracting her, but… she didn't have anyone else to talk to. "I don't see as many places as you'd think," Scarlett continued, snapping Lucy's attention back to her. "We usually work on port days. Sometimes we'll have a day off to go explore, but being on this ship, it goes to the same place almost every time. You get tired of it after a while."

"I didn't think about that," Lucy said, tilting her head. "How long have you worked on cruises?"

"This ship, just a couple of months. But I've been contracted with DreamWave Cruises as a whole for two years now," she explained.

"How do you even start working on a cruise ship?"

"Like any other job," Scarlett laughed, shrugging her slender shoulders. "I applied and never thought I'd get in. I was working in interior design at the time back home. But they responded, I went to the interview, and here I am."

"Where's back home?" Lucy asked, a few of her questions slowly being answered organically.

Scarlett gave an impish smile and narrowed her eyes. "Guess."

"Hmm," Lucy hummed, tapping her chin. "England?"

"Clever," Scarlett laughed again, then nodded. "Yes. London. Boring, I know."

"Yeah, right," Lucy scoffed. "I'd love to go to London, much less be *from* it."

"Where are you from?"

"Florida. Orlando, specifically. Boring, I know," Lucy said with a smirk.

Scarlett raised her eyebrows. "Oh, so this cruise wasn't

very far for you to travel then. I like Orlando. When we dock for boarding, sometimes I can sneak away and go shopping."

"Do you ever go to the theme parks?"

"No," Scarlett sighed, slumping a little. "I don't have *that* much time, unfortunately. I've never been before."

"Wow, really? Ever? Anywhere?"

"Nope," Scarlett said, shaking her head. "I'd love to go someday though. There are a few in Europe that I wanted to visit as a child. Are they fun? They *look* fun."

"They're fun," Lucy nodded. "But like you feel with seeing the same destination over and over, sometimes you get tired of it. There's a lot more to Orlando than theme parks."

"You'll have to give me some recommendations then," Scarlett smiled, then looked over as a slew of people made their way down the hall. She sighed and looked back at Lucy. "I have to talk to these people. I don't want to keep you. Look, come to this," she said, handing her one of the little flyers stacked on the table next to her. "It's in two hours. We're doing a gallery presentation. There will be free champagne."

Lucy pinched her fingers around the paper and glanced down at it, then started to decline. "Oh, I don't... I don't think I'm quite an art connoisseur," Lucy started, but trailed off when Scarlett shook her head and insistently pushed the flyer back in her hands.

"You don't have to be. Just come look. I'll have a little more free time to talk. Hopefully," Scarlett said. The people drew nearer, and she gave her a smile that nearly knocked Lucy over with its radiance. "Did you come here with anyone?"

Lucy hesitated, then nodded. "My boyfriend, yes."

"Bring him along, too," Scarlett said. But at the look that flashed across Lucy's face, she tilted her head. "Or… don't?"

"He's not really into this kind of thing," Lucy sighed.

"Then just you," Scarlett said. Their time was up though and her attention was starting to be pulled elsewhere. However, as Lucy started to walk away, Scarlett gently touched her arm. "See you later?" Scarlett asked.

Lucy, unable to refuse, nodded. "Yeah. I'll be there." The blonde felt a little better about her decision with the smile and wink Scarlett gave her, before the taller woman turned her attention fully back to the guests vying for her attention. Lucy looked her over one more time, before turning to go check out the rest of the ship.

At least she had *something* to do other than mope.

ucy had not been back near the casino and had not seen Chris since their fight.

Nor was she sad about any of that.

In the two hours she had to kill between saying goodbye to Scarlett and going to the art show, she had ventured back up near the top of the ship and indulged in the food they had to offer.

All of the options were overwhelming. On the upper, outdoor decks of the ship, a pool centered the floor and was surrounded by a sea of blue, folding chairs. The chairs extended on each upward floor, giving everyone plenty of space to find a spot to bask in the sun. Around the pool were varying bars and places to stand in line and grab a quick bite: burgers, tacos, burritos, even soft-serve ice cream.

She walked past the pool and outdoor restaurants and into the buffet area. There were people in line piling their plates with food. Craning her neck, Lucy tried to take inventory of the buffet's options as she wandered by. It all just looked like the usual things: meats, salads, pastas, desserts, and probably a thousand other items Lucy could never eat all at once.

The inside was lit up and each wall was lined with large windows that looked out to the passing water. She noticed some passengers just sitting and enjoying the view. Lucy passed by a few more standalone windows for food and eventually landed on ordering a chicken wrap.

Crowds began to slowly die down around her as she sat alone by a window and ate her food. She assumed everyone else was now hitting the bar or the pool, or had already stuffed themselves the second they got onto the boat.

She had considered changing into a different outfit, something a little more formal that would be appropriate for an art gallery, but she hadn't wanted to run into Chris in the room and risk another fight starting up again. For all she knew, he was passed out at one of the slot machines. She hated that she didn't really care either way.

Often, she went back and forth from mourning their relationship — as if it were already over — and thinking of ways she could still fix it, fix *him*. It was taking everything out of her, to the point where her friends had told her that she didn't smile the same as they remembered. She had gone home to visit her parents recently and her mother had sat her down privately and tried to get every detail she could out of her. When Lucy confronted her about prying, her mom simply said she 'didn't have her spark anymore' and was deeply concerned.

It had cut through Lucy like hot water on snow.

Lucy had hyper-fixated on old pictures of herself on her social pages, trying to find where the light had left her eyes.

There were so many happy pictures of Chris and her together, being the 'power couple' all their friends affectionately described. Where was *that* Chris and Lucy? What kind of sad, twisted version were they now where she didn't even *like* to take pictures together anymore?

Lucy physically shook the thoughts out of her head, her hat shifting a little atop her blonde curls. She threw her food away and pulled out the small flyer Scarlett had given her and her phone from her dress's pocket. Tapping the phone, she eyed the time and decided it was now or never if she didn't want to be late.

She wandered around on the deck the paper had described until she finally found a sign above the door that matched the flyer. She spotted Scarlett at the same time, manning the table at the front.

"Table duty again?" Lucy greeted with a smile as she closed the distance between them.

"Lucy! Hi! You made it," Scarlett gushed, a beaming, pearly-white smile gracing those pretty, sharp features on her face. "I'm so pleased. Look, we're doing a raffle, take some tickets," she said, tearing off a few for her. "Don't tell them I gave you more than one," she whispered as she leaned forward.

Lucy smiled and held the tickets tightly in her hand. "I won't," she promised quietly. "Are you going to be out here the whole time? I guarantee I'm going to have a *ton* of questions about all this art you teased me about."

"I won't be out here the entire time, no, just until it starts," Scarlett reassured. "I'll come find you. But go in, grab a glass of champagne, have a seat." She gestured toward the door.

Lucy nodded and did as she was told. The room was rather large, and she wondered if it was converted to a club during some of the time. The floor was tiled, but all different color squares, and there were high-top counters circling the rainbow. The center of the floor with the colors was lowered, while the rest was raised up. It *definitely* reminded her of a dance floor in a sticky bar back home.

Chairs lined the lowered floor, but Lucy decided to stay hidden at one of the high-top tables in the back. She glanced around, unable to count how many framed canvases were displayed all throughout the room. There were even some not on easels that were propped up against the wall and railing. She wondered if there were even more stowed away in another room somewhere. There *had* to be.

"Alright everyone, let's get started. If you'll take your seats," a man called out from the front of the barrage of chairs. He was clean-shaven, in a well-tailored suit, and had blonde hair styled back. Lucy assumed he was the person in charge. Maybe Scarlett's boss.

"My name is Gavin, I'm the art director here on the ship. Nice to meet you all," he said with a smile, looking around at everyone. Lucy smirked to herself. Definitely Scarlett's boss. He seemed nice enough, but maybe she could get some details on him from Scarlett when she saw her in a bit.

She half-tuned out what Gavin was explaining, her thoughts elsewhere. She was sure he was just detailing how to buy art and what they would be giving away for the raffle, neither of which she really cared all that much about. She wasn't planning on buying anything and how good could a cruise ship art gallery raffle really be anyway?

People getting up to move and wander around eventually grabbed her attention, and she followed suit. Lucy's eyes scanned the room and finally she spotted Scarlett, but... she was talking to someone else. Shoulders drooping, Lucy decided to busy herself with actually looking at the art. It was like a museum. She walked through the makeshift aisles, her head on a swivel as she admired the artwork. There were no prices on them, of course, which immediately signaled to her that she would *not* be able to afford any of this. It would look nice in her home, but...

"Wow," Lucy whispered to herself, practically gliding to a painting that completely took her breath away. It was a vibrantly colorful oil painting that featured two silhouettes walking down a cement pathway in the center of the canvas. They were in a park, the leaves of the trees a brilliant mixture of oranges, reds, yellows, blues, and greens. There were benches lining the pathway and it looked like it had *just* rained in the scene. The cement glistened with the puddles' reflections, and Lucy couldn't help but feast her eyes on every detail.

"That one's called 'Spring Night.' It's nice, isn't it?"

Lucy jumped a little at the voice, and turned to look at Scarlett, who was standing next to her now. She shook her head at the woman's apologies, then looked at the painting again. "I've never really spent time looking at fine art before, but... this is amazing."

"I know what you mean. Being an interior designer, I had connections to the art world, but it never really interested me. It wasn't until getting this job that I truly began to appreciate the finer things in life," Scarlett responded, admiring the artwork with her. "Would you like to take it home? I can reserve it for you and you don't have to pay until the end of the cruise. It'll ship straight to your house."

"Oh, I... I don't think I can splurge on something like this. Chris would go bonkers," Lucy murmured, shifting her gaze down.

"Chris is your... boyfriend?"

"Yes."

Scarlett regarded her carefully, then tilted her head. "Why didn't he come with you? I know you said he wasn't into this sort of thing, but... usually couples who go on cruises together can't stay away from each other."

"We... got into a fight," Lucy sighed, looking over at Scarlett. "A big fight. I don't even know where he is. This cruise was supposed to be a fresh start, a... bandage on the situation, but... I don't think that's going to happen."

Scarlett frowned and glanced back as Gavin began calling everyone back to their seats. She paused for a moment, then turned back to Lucy. "Well, for right now, while you're in here with me, you don't have to think about any of that stress. You can just enjoy yourself. I'll get you another glass of champagne," she reassured with a smile. She squeezed Lucy's arm again, then fluttered away to do as she said.

Lucy took another look at the artwork, then went back to her seat. Quietly, she thanked Scarlett when she zoomed by to drop the fresh glass off, then she focused on Gavin at the front.

"We'll start off with a raffle. Who likes raffles?!" Gavin called out, waving his hands for people to start cheering. Lucy resisted groaning. She understood he had to be a showman to work on a cruise, but he was laying it on *pretty* thick. The blonde woman slowly dragged her gaze around the room, noting everyone's excitement. They were definitely drunk. She was *not* drunk enough to be doing all that, and thanking every power above that she had decided to sit in the back. With her visual sweep of the room, she eventually locked eyes with Scarlett, who widened hers, then cut them quickly to her boss. Lucy hid her giggle behind her champagne glass, then bit her lip as Scarlett went so far as to roll her eyes and mimic a yawn. Lucy mouthed 'stop' with a smile, not wanting her to get caught and get in trouble. She felt like she was in high school again.

"Going twice for number two-eight-four? Anyone? That's strange," Gavin said, double-checking the ticket in his hand.

Scarlett jabbed a finger toward her from across the room, causing Lucy to look down at one of the tickets in her hand. She read the number. *284.*

"Uh…" Lucy blurted out, raising her hand. "I have that one."

"Great! We have a winner!" Gavin said as he basically skipped over to her. "For you, a one-hundred dollar voucher toward any piece of artwork you'd like. Word of advice, wait until the end of the cruise to use it. We have some pieces hiding away that you'll want to see before you lock into anything yet," he grinned, winking at her. For whatever reason, Lucy was annoyed by that wink. She liked it better when Scarlett did it.

After she was left in peace, she felt a presence by her. Lucy looked over at smirked at Scarlett. "You're going to get in trouble," she whispered, sipping her drink.

"What have I done? I'm just standing here innocently next to my *favorite* raffle winner. Now you have a discount on that pretty artwork," Scarlett grinned, her voice hushed.

"You're just trying to sell me something," Lucy teased, setting the glass down. She leaned a little closer to where Scarlett was standing, then toyed with the leftover raffle tickets laying on the countertop. "Did you rig that?"

"What? *Me*? I'm wounded," Scarlett said dramatically, clutching her chest. "I am nothing but *fair*, Lucy... What's your surname?"

"Price."

"I am *nothing* but fair, Lucy Price," Scarlett repeated, narrowing her eyes. "But I may have tripped and fallen into the little box with the tickets. What's it to you?"

"Nothing, nothing," Lucy laughed, shaking her head. "What did I do to deserve such special treatment, Scarlett... What's *your* last name?"

"Sinclair."

"What did I— Wait, *Scarlett Sinclair*?"

Scarlett frowned. "Yes...?"

"Why do you have the *coolest* name ever? All I have is lame, boring Lucy Price."

"Lucy Price is a cool name," Scarlett laughed quietly, shaking her head. "But yeah... my name is cooler. You got that right."

Lucy stuck her tongue out, then folded her arms. "What did I do to deserve such special treatment, Scarlett Sinclair?"

"You showed up to my doorstep *twice* looking like the saddest person ever. You basically forced my hand," Scarlett smiled. "You're on holiday. You should be happy all the time."

Lucy's chest ached at that. She *should* be happy all the time. She had plenty of things to be thankful for: her career, her home, her friends… but her relationship was soul-sucking.

Lucy was about to say something else to Scarlett, but everyone in the middle of the floor began getting up and moving out of the room. She frowned a little, then looked over at the woman next to her. "When is the next event you have?"

Scarlett sighed and looked down at the tablet in her hand, poking and swiping a few things on the screen. "Nothing else today, but we have a gallery down on Deck Three. Come see me. Or— the art, I suppose," she said with a smile. "It's near where dinner is served, if you want to have a sit-down meal instead of the buffet. Maybe you could come on your way."

"Okay," Lucy smiled, nodding. "I'll come say hi to the art," she teased, looking over her face once more. "See you later."

carlett stared at Lucy's back as she walked out of the room. Her eyes roamed over the way that pretty, white, flowery dress hugged every curve and how those gorgeous blonde waves bounced with each step—

"Scarlett."

The woman jolted a little and looked over at the voice, meeting eyes with her boss. "Gavin. Hi. I'm about to start breaking everything down."

"Good," Gavin said, his bubbly persona gone now. He was strictly business. "I need to go get coffee, but I trust you can handle this by yourself?"

"All of it?" Scarlett asked, looking around with her eyes wide and concerned. "This will take me all day."

"Better get started then," Gavin said, pinching her chin, before he left the room with everyone else.

Scarlett sighed and put the tablet down, then slowly spun in the room to survey where she should begin.

As she began pulling canvases off their easels and putting

them to the side, her thoughts went to this American girl that had completely captured her attention.

Scarlett didn't have many friends aboard the ship, other than a few of her coworkers and some of the other workers on the ship. Anyone who flitted into her life as a passenger didn't last long, and most of them only chatted her up to get a discount on some piece of art they wanted. Or they wanted to leer. It was a lonely career, but she enjoyed being able to look outside and see the ocean, or go out to a beach once a week, or see how many different walks of life people came from.

She thought about how sad Lucy looked and wondered if that's what she looked like when she'd been back home in London. She hadn't left her job as an interior designer because she had a 'passion for art,' she had left because she *had* to escape that country. Getting on a boat that sailed around the world seemed like a viable option for that choice.

She felt like a different person now than who she'd been just a couple of years ago. Back then, she was out partying, drinking, hanging off the arm of her rich boyfriend, having the time of her life… but now she realized she was just stuck in a revolving door of burying her sadness and anxiety.

She had met Raphael Martin through work, having been hired to decorate one of his properties in London. He was a French businessman, came from a wealthy family, and was expanding some of his company to England. He primarily worked in corporate law and ran a firm for banking officials. A lot of money flowed in, but there were also a lot of shady dealings coming in and out.

Raphael had been a flirt from the start, something Scarlett

was used to. She was a saleswoman at heart, and working with higher-income clientele meant putting up with a *bit* more flack to close the deal. She used her looks to her advantage and it worked. Most of the time.

It worked *too* well for Raphael and once she finished the job, he had immediately invited her to his housewarming party. He had guised it as enjoying her work, but she knew it was deeper than that.

But then again, who was she to turn down such a powerful man?

So, Scarlett went to the party, meeting Raphael's bigwig friends, all of whom had no qualms in making remarks about her appearance that made her stomach turn now. Back then, she had just giggled and thanked them. She didn't even recognize that poor girl in her memories.

Servers floating around the large, immaculate home had forced drink after drink in her hand, and after a few hours, she... didn't know what happened. Even now, she just remembered waking up in Raphael's bed.

He had been kind at first, making her breakfast after a night together, hiring a driver to take her to the office, spoiling her with lavish gifts and trips, but... the more she got from him, the more controlling he became over her. He would be forceful in the bedroom, he would grab her arm when she did something he didn't like in public and scold her in private as soon as he could manage. Eventually, she felt like she was his child or toy, not a partner whom he claimed to love.

When she tried to leave the first time, Raphael had gone berserk. He had threatened to kill himself, then threatened to sue her company and blacklist her from working anywhere else. The next day, he had sobbed to her and told her he wouldn't do anything like that again.

And like the naive, 20-something fool she was, she had forgiven him.

It happened just like that. Over. And over. And over.

Until one day, she'd had enough. He had raised his hand to her, for the first time in their toxic merry-go-round, and she had convinced herself to be brave and leave. It hadn't happened right away, there were many, many bruises and cuts made and healed again and again until she had finally gotten out. She had told herself that even if he ended up killing her, death was better than the prison she'd found herself in.

There were days when she feared with every new set of cruise passengers that Raphael would show up and find her. She scanned the faces of everyone who walked past, making sure the devil in her nightmares wasn't here to drag her back to hell.

Scarlett came back to the present, and thankfully, through her dissociation, she had gone into autopilot and had cleaned up the majority of the room. Another hour passed before she actually finished, and by the time she got everything back into either the storage room or displayed in their gallery down a few floors below, it was nearly dinner.

And for the first time in a while, she was looking forward to standing in that tiny room full of canvases, if only for a few minutes' worth of conversation with her new friend.

ucy trekked through the ship down to a lower deck where her and Chris's room was. There were still some bags parked outside doors, but when she got closer to their room number, she didn't see anything. He must have brought everything in.

She scanned her keycard and pushed the door open once the lock clicked and turned green. She let the door swing shut behind her and she looked around. The room had two separate beds, which made her confused. Had they not gotten one bed? "Chris?"

"Finally," a voice scoffed nearby. Chris was standing in the tiny bathroom adjacent to one of the twin beds, fixing his hair in the mirror. He was dressed nicer than when she'd left him. Now he was in a pair of dark jeans, a black polo, and it looked like he was putting quite a bit of effort in his hair. He didn't have that much to style, and he'd been doing the same thing with the top of his head since she'd known him, so she wasn't sure why it took him so long some days. It was a short, normal, masculine cut with no length on the sides and sometimes *too much* length on the top. It just looked messy most of the time.

"What do you mean 'finally?' I was barely gone for two hours," Lucy said with a frown, her things from the art gallery still in her hands.

"More like three," Chris said, glancing over at her. He did a double-take at her hands and jerked his chin up at her. "What's that stuff?"

Lucy looked down at the papers. "Oh. I went to one of the art shows. One of the workers had a table and she invited me to the event. I got a voucher for a discount on a piece of art."

"We're not getting any stupid art," Chris laughed, shaking his head. "You might as well just throw that away."

Lucy's frown deepened and she bit back her quip back at him, and settled for going across the small room to look at herself in the mirror. She set her things down on the tiny vanity desk and began combing her fingers through her curls. She sighed almost silently to herself, then took her floppy hat off. Setting it down, she smoothed her hair over again and tried to ignore the gnawing feeling consuming her insides. She tried to remind herself constantly that people had it worse than her — Chris didn't physically abuse her, they had a roof over their heads, and he was fine... most of the time. He wasn't outright *cruel* to her, he just... didn't really believe in compliments that went deeper than how her ass or boobs looked in an outfit.

"Are you almost ready?" Chris asked as he emerged from the bathroom and looked at her.

Lucy didn't look at him. She couldn't. She would get irritated all over again. "I *just* got back. Give me just a second to fix my hair and I'll change into something different. What time is dinner?"

"Seven."

Lucy tapped her phone to life and noted she had a little less than an hour. She frowned to herself, wondering if they'd have time to swing by that gallery beforehand. Would it even be open afterward? She turned her attention back to her reflection and leaned forward to check on her makeup. She never wore too much, just a little eyeliner, some strokes of mascara, and some powder to smooth her face out. Honestly, she wasn't even that *good* at intense makeup. She left that to the professionals. Though, she *did* enjoy watching tutorials online, not that she'd ever tried anything like that. Clothes and fashion were where she shone.

As she walked past Chris to go to the bathroom to touch up her face, she noticed his completed look. He'd thrown on a sport coat over the polo. He looked nice. His hair was styled back neatly and she could smell her favorite cologne on him. Obviously he was trying to get on her good side. She *hadn't* forgotten how he'd completely ruined the beginning of the trip just a few short hours before.

She had barely been in the bathroom for a minute before a nasally voice interrupted her focus.

"Babe, how long do you think it's gonna take?" Chris called out. She could sense the annoyance in his tone.

"Not long. Fifteen minutes," Lucy called back. "Why are you in such a hurry?"

"I'm not, you know I just hate wasting time. There's no point in staying cooped up in here if we're both ready. If you had come back a little earlier instead of going to that art thing or running off to pout, we could have made better use of our time."

Lucy clenched her jaw at this, her grip tightening on her mascara tube. She took a few deep breaths and pulled the wand out, carefully brushing it along her lashes. She would not take the bait, she would not take the bait, she would not take the bait…

"Plus, I won some money for us and I wanted to buy you something pretty," Chris went on.

At this, Lucy capped the mascara and stepped out of the bathroom so she could see him. "Are you serious?"

Chris looked at her and frowned, putting his hands up. "What? You mad I actually *made* money? Figured you'd be happy."

"Happy?" Lucy scoffed, shaking her head. "I don't care if you won a million dollars off those stupid slot machines, you still *lied* to me and went against your word. You're in *recovery*, Christopher! How could you be so stupid? Why aren't you taking this *seriously*? You don't take *me* seriously. *Us*."

Chris's jaw fell slack. "You did *not* just say that to me. I take us *very* seriously. I didn't do anything bad. I *made* money, you never *listen* to that part. You always stay focused on the little shit," he swore, throwing his hands up in exasperation. "I have always taken care of us, even when my parents decided to abandon me."

"They didn't *abandon* you," Lucy laughed. Even though they had this conversation a hundred times over, she still couldn't believe the nonsense he came out with sometimes. "*I* take care of us. You do not have a job, Chris. I pay the bills for the apartment."

"I paid for this trip!" Chris exclaimed.

Lucy *barely* resisted rolling her eyes. She could have choked on his narcissism. "I didn't ask for this trip, Chris. I asked for you to be better. You *have* to get better."

Chris shook his head and folded his arms, his cheeks red with what Lucy assumed was either embarrassment or anger. She could see the glint of his emotion behind the lenses of his glasses.

"My therapist says I deserve better than this," Chris went on.

"*What* therapist?"

"At rehab. She says you don't believe in me. You're always breathing down my neck, expecting me to act perfect, and the second I slip up, you freak out and start a fight just like this. It's not *my fault* there's a casino on board. How was I supposed to know that? And you have to walk right by it to get anywhere. It's a bunch of temptation. And I only played *five* games. It wasn't even that bad. I don't know why you're getting so worked up about it. And if you'd *listen* to anything I ever said, you'd hear me tell you *again* that I won money. Two hundred dollars. But now I'm not buying you anything, since you're being mean to me."

"Mean?" Lucy repeated, her eyebrows up to her hairline. It was like talking to a cement wall sometimes. All the time. She took another deep breath and closed her eyes for a moment, then composed herself. "I do listen to you. I'm sorry that I come across as mean. That's not what I try to do. I just want you to be healthy, Chris. Better. I want your parents to be proud of you and not be upset with you. Do you understand?"

"Now you're not *proud* of me?"

Lucy blinked and ran back through the last words she said. *What?* She swallowed and put her hands together to avoid pulling her hair out. "I'm always proud of you. I love you and that's why I want to help you. I want to keep you on track."

"You always *do* that," Chris said, shaking his head. He turned from her and folded his arms.

"Do *what*?"

"Talk to me like I'm some little kid. I made more money than *you*. All you do is work for a magazine. My dad could *buy* your entire building, you know that, right?"

"This isn't about me. At least I *make* money. Present tense. Not past. You don't make *any* money right now."

"I *just* made—"

"Yeah," Lucy interrupted while waving her arm at him. "Whatever, Chris. I'll be ready in a little bit." She walked back to the bathroom to resume fixing her makeup.

"I'm not even hungry anymore," Chris said. Lucy heard some rustling around in the main part of the room, but she didn't poke her head out to look. The next noise she heard was the door opening, then closing loudly.

Her hands trembled as she slowly set down her mascara and closed her eyes. She could feel the wet paint getting on the tops of her cheeks, but she didn't care.

She just cried.

S carlett smiled at the man in front of her telling her... whatever on earth it was he was saying. She hadn't listened to a word that came out of his mouth. She was in the ship's art gallery, the sound of people chattering as they walked by filtering into the room. It wasn't a huge room and it was crowded with easels of artwork and sculptures in every corner.

She was a little disappointed that the minutes, then hours, had ticked by and Lucy hadn't shown up.

Okay, maybe more than a little.

Scarlett knew she shouldn't expect anything from anyone on a cruise, given she didn't know them and there were a million other more fun things Lucy could do on the boat than come look at art she had already seen earlier that day, but... she had thought they shared a moment. She was worried about Lucy. Was she okay? Had she just forgotten?

"What do you think?"

Scarlett focused back on the present and her eyes darted

to the painting the man in front of her was pointing at. It was forest-themed piece with a regal tiger staring down whomever looked at it. She cleared her throat and snapped back into her professional persona. "I believe if you have the space for it in your home, it'll be a conversation-starter. You'll want it to be the center of attention in whatever room you intend to hang it. But it's an excellent choice. Shows you've got good taste."

The man seemed satisfied by that answer and she directed him to Gavin to be checked out. Her smile dropped as soon as she was left to her own devices, and she rubbed her forehead. Was she so desperately lonely and craving human interaction that she got borderline *upset* over a woman she just met not showing up to her art gallery? She hated taking things so personal, and knew there was a likely and reasonable explanation for Lucy's absence. Not that she was owed an explanation in any case.

Scarlett's anxiety was running rampant in her brain, shooting all sorts of worst-case scenarios to every corner of her mind. She was very sure they would have heard about someone either falling or being thrown overboard, and even if that *had* happened, it was highly unlikely it would be Lucy. She probably just got caught up at dinner, or with her *boyfriend*, and was occupied with something else.

Scarlett also knew she was antsy just because she was jealous of all the fun things other people got to do on the ship while she was stuck at work. She definitely envied all the happy faces, the laughter, the *good times* the shipgoers always seemed to be having. She got a copy of the ship's activity schedule every morning and often just skimmed it, but every now and then, something — usually a form of trivia — caught her eye and she grumbled about having to get dressed for a damn art show.

Slowly, she wandered across the room, which was small and filled with easels holding canvases, sculptures on various tables, and way too many people. She stood by the door, content with simply greeting people as they came in, rather than trying to sell these pieces to someone who was too drunk to even consider purchasing something. She forced a smile and nodded her 'hellos' and 'welcome ins' to everyone who either found themselves lost or just looking for something to eat up the 15 minutes between the last event and the next one on an upper floor.

Nine o'clock hit and she closed the door to the gallery, leaving her, Gavin, and their other art dealer, Olive, in peace inside the room. Scarlett walked over to Gavin and was desperate for a distraction. "What do the numbers look like?"

"Yours are... fine," Gavin said, his eyes never leaving the laptop screen in front of him. "You started off strong then tapered off. Olive did well moving the sculptures though. She sold four. You didn't sell any."

"What about the bloke wanting that tiger painting?" Scarlett asked with a frown.

"He was interested until he heard the price. Said he'd have to talk it over with his wife, but... we both know he isn't going to come back. You couldn't tell he was poor just by looking at him?" Gavin asked, making a slight face of disgust.

Scarlett bit the inside of her cheek to remind her to watch what she said. "Sometimes it is difficult to tell. Everyone is dressed in their cruising outfits. He seemed to show a lot of interest in interior decor and artwork when I chatted him up. I was sure he would be a closed client."

"Well, he wasn't," Gavin said, finally looking up at her. "You're on tabling duty tomorrow."

"I thought Olive was…"

"She *was*, until you tanked your numbers tonight. Now you get to make up for it by getting more people into our next auction and running the price game," Gavin explained, shifting his eyes back down to his laptop.

Scarlett *hated* the price game. She had to give people little pieces of paper and they got to guess what price a displayed piece of artwork was. The person who got the closest — only revealed at the art auction *and* if they were present — didn't even get the art in question. They just got a voucher or a free bottle of champagne. One time they even gave away a light-up pin with the ship on it. It was a joke. They had had plenty of cruisers get angry with them for 'misleading' them, which she didn't blame them at all. She just hated being on the receiving end of it when it wasn't her fault.

At least maybe she'd catch Lucy walking by.

Scarlett swiped into her cabin and looked around, noting she was alone. Her roommate and coworker, Olive, usually didn't filter in until late. It was against the rules for them to have any sort of relation with a passenger, or really even a coworker, but Olive somehow always found a way to keep herself from being lonely. She had an on and off relationship with their boss,

Gavin, and Scarlett couldn't keep track if they were together or broken up at the moment.

Honestly, she was thankful for the solitude.

Scarlett trudged over to her bed and flopped down onto it, pantsuit and all. Letting out a large breath, she closed her eyes and tried to get her body to relax. It had been such a long shift, as was always the case on the first day of each cruise round. She preferred the cruises that lasted a week, like the current one, because it gave her more of an opportunity to get the galleries set up the way she wanted. The shorter cruises, like four or five days, were always a little more difficult and fast-paced. During the week, she'd try to learn faces and some names, only to help with her sales.

Lucy was different though. Scarlett didn't care so much about sales. She just enjoyed talking to her.

God, she *was* lonely.

Scarlett covered her face with her hands and groaned loudly. Leave it to her to find a pretty girl she got along with and made ample small talk with and be actually *upset* she hadn't seen her when they'd agreed. She was so out of touch with the dating scene that she wouldn't even know where to start, *not* that that's what was happening with Lucy. She barely knew anything about her and she had an entire *boyfriend*. Albeit a boyfriend she wasn't happy with, but… Scarlett didn't like to share and she certainly didn't like competition.

It saddened her to think about how miserable Lucy had looked the two times she'd encountered her. Scarlett knew all too well being brought to tears by a man who didn't know how to treat her. She was thankful to have escaped that life.

Scarlett slowly heaved herself up off the bed, finally, and walked to the bathroom. She grabbed a makeup-remover wipe and cleaned off her face, then tossed it in the small trash bin. The employees' cabins were a little nicer than the normal interior staterooms. They had a small porthole window and had a *little* bit of a bigger bathroom, but everything else was pretty much the same. It made her feel like she was in school again, sharing rooms and trying to ignore bed partners when they'd stumble into the place drunk and fail to be quiet. Scarlett had not been so inconsiderate in her time rooming with Olive, keeping her infrequent flings to herself and *off* the boat, but Olive flouted the rules constantly. It was a wonder she hadn't been caught yet.

Scarlett pulled off her clothes and tossed them in the small laundry basket nestled at the foot of her bed, just outside the bathroom door. She started up the shower and waited for the water to warm up, before stepping inside.

This was her favorite part of the day. It was always nice to get some time to herself when Olive wasn't barking at her to hurry up. She could actually *enjoy* some relaxation time and wash her hair as thoroughly as she wanted to.

Scarlett leaned her head against the shower wall and let the water rain down on her. The streams caressed her body in a way that pulled apart every taut muscle from the never-ending day she'd had. Sighing to herself, Scarlett finally forced her arms up to get her hair products.

She was starting to feel better about not seeing Lucy. It was just the first day, and getting attached to a passenger was *never* a good idea. She would just continue doing her job and that would be that.

Scarlett turned the water off after finishing her nightly routine and took her time with her skincare regimen. Once she felt completely rejuvenated, she settled into bed and began scrolling on her phone with the limited internet access she had. Hopefully Olive wouldn't wake her up when she eventually did come to bed.

Lucy stood in line at one of the coffee shops on the boat, trying not to feel sorry for herself.

Chris had eventually returned that night while Lucy was in bed in the dark. She had had to push the two separate twin beds together to make one big bed. It annoyed her all over again about the trip and reminded her *why* she was always the one who planned things. Any time she had ever left Chris in charge of something, whether it be a vacation, concert tickets, or even a fast food order, he found a way to mess it up. When they first started dating, she put it down to him just having bad luck, but as the years went on, she realized it was just because he was an idiot.

After she had been long asleep the night before, Chris had crawled into bed next to her, smelling of alcohol and cigarette smoke.

There was only *one* place you were allowed to smoke on the ship.

It had taken everything in her to stay quiet and keep her

breathing even so he didn't suspect she was awake and rehash their fight. Honestly, she was certain he was too drunk to notice *anything* that night. She was happy he hadn't started groping her and making her feel like a 'bad girlfriend' for rejecting any physical advances.

Lucy stepped forward when it was her turn and ordered an iced vanilla latte, hoping it would bring her back to life. She had gotten up early to go to breakfast and watch the sunrise. Chris had eventually found her on the deck and asked to eat, but she informed him she already had. Surprisingly, he hadn't been upset, and merely said he'd find her later.

She didn't *want* this trip to be a disaster. The very last thing she desired in her life was stress. She wanted to be happy on that boat, making memories with the love of her life.

But as each day passed, she was less and less sure that's what Chris was to her.

"Thanks," Lucy murmured, curling her fingers around the cup the barista handed her. She swirled the drink inside as she stepped out of line and started to make her way to the casino. She didn't *want* to see Chris there, but… it was the logical first place to look. She wondered if she could talk to anyone at guest services and get any gambling transactions blocked on their keycards…

"Lucy."

The blonde stopped and came out of her daydream when she heard her name from a now familiar accent. She blinked and turned to face a dark-haired woman, looking completely pristine as usual.

"Oh, Scarlett. Hi. Sorry, I was in my own little world,"

Lucy said, turning to face her. "Do you ever sleep?" she teased, gesturing to the table with her cup, the ice sloshing inside.

Scarlett laughed under her breath and shook her head. "Not as much as I'd like. I live off that stuff," she said, pointing to her coffee. "What do you drink?"

"Vanilla iced latte," Lucy said, looking down at the cup. "Boring, I know."

"Not boring. I like those. I'm a matcha girl myself," Scarlett said with a smile.

A slightly awkward silence settled between them as they both shifted on the spot and looked around at some of the people walking past them. Finally, Scarlett broke the tension.

"How was your night? Do anything fun?"

Lucy sighed and sipped her drink. "No… I didn't. It was a long—" she started, then her blue eyes widened. "Oh my *God*, Scarlett, I didn't come to the gallery last night. I… I am *so* sorry. I was going to but I…" she trailed off, unsure of how to continue.

"It's alright," Scarlett said. Lucy could feel her gaze roaming her. She made a mental effort to relax her body language. "You doing alright now, though?" Scarlett continued, her tone laden with concern.

Lucy barely restrained telling her every minute detail of her fight with Chris from the night before. "I'm doing alright now," was all the blonde could manage.

Scarlett pressed her red-painted lips together in a thin line and arched an eyebrow. "Well… unless you're going to elaborate, all we have to talk about is your guess for how much this painting is."

Lucy's eyes wandered to the grandiose painting. It was another landscape, one in a field with a lone tree. There were all sorts of colors blended into the sky, and Lucy could imagine herself reading a nice romance book under the branches and enjoying the breeze around her. She took in the beauty, then looked down as Scarlett held a small piece of paper out to her and a tiny pencil. "Oh. You're serious?"

"Unfortunately. The closest guess will win a prize at the end of the cruise," she explained.

"The artwork?"

"You'd think that, wouldn't you?" Scarlett said with a tight smile. "But no. I don't know what the prize is yet. Probably a bottle of champagne."

"That's it?" Lucy laughed.

"Well, it's free," Scarlett said while shrugging. "Beggars can't be choosers, I suppose."

"Guess not," Lucy said with a smirk, then she set her coffee down on the table. Cupping the small piece of paper in her hand, she pressed the tip of the pencil against it. "Do I get any hints?"

It was Scarlett's turn to smirk now. "That's cheating."

"*No*, it's *hinting*," Lucy retorted, holding her glinting gaze. "Please?"

"You're going to get me in trouble. I can just buy you a drink, you know, you don't have to jeopardize my job to get some champagne," Scarlett said.

Lucy blushed and cut her eyes back down to the paper. "I'm more of a wine girl anyway," she said quietly, scribbling a number on the paper. She folded it up and handed it to her.

Scarlett reached out and took it, their fingers brushing against one another. Lucy's blush darkened and she swallowed, then took another therapeutic sip of her caffeine.

"There you are. I must have made two laps around the whole ship."

Lucy dropped Scarlett's hand and looked over at an expectant Chris. He always looked so… bewildered. As if he didn't know what was going on half the time. She wished she could be so *simple*.

"What're you doing?" Chris asked, glancing at Scarlett, then the painting. "More art?"

"Um…" Lucy stammered, then came back to herself. "Yeah. Chris, this is Scarlett Sinclair. She works with the gallery on the ship," the blonde said, watching her boyfriend shake hands with her… with *Scarlett*. "And Scarlett, this is… my boyfriend, Chris Ford."

"Ah," Scarlett said, shaking Chris's hand.

"'Ah?'" Chris laughed a bit awkwardly, shooting his girlfriend a glance. "Not usually the reaction I get when I meet someone for the first time."

Lucy smiled reassuringly at Chris, then when he turned his attention back to Scarlett, she shot a pleading glance her way. Scarlett's eyes seemed to soften and she gave a nod that only Lucy would have noticed.

"I just mean… Lucy told me she was here with her boyfriend and I didn't have a chance to meet you at the art show yesterday. Good to put a face to a name now. That's all," Scarlett said, her smile not reaching her eyes.

"Got it," Chris said, then he looked at the materials on the table under the canvas. "You running some kind of giveaway or something?"

"Yes," Scarlett said, her voice snapping back to the professional tone she'd greeted Lucy with that first encounter yesterday. "Guess the price and win a prize. We're running it the duration of the cruise. We'll announce the winner at our final gallery show on our final day at sea."

"Cool," Chris said, grabbing a small entry card and one of the pencils. He scribbled his answer down, then popped it into the slit of the box resting on the table. "I'm good with numbers."

Scarlett merely smiled in response.

Lucy hated this entire interaction. She hated that she'd been interrupted, that she hadn't had the chance to properly *explain* what had happened the night before, why she hadn't been there like she promised. She knew she didn't owe this woman anything, given they barely knew each other and had only just met the day before, but… Lucy hated lying to anybody. She just hoped Scarlett had been busy enough the night before at the gallery to have not really noticed her absence.

"Well, come on, babe, there's an EDM trivia happening in ten minutes. I want to see if I can win," Chris said, tugging on Lucy's arm.

Lucy sighed and looked at Scarlett. "How long are you going to be here?"

"Until noon. Then I have to help get the ballroom ready for another show for the people who didn't attend yesterday. Then I'm off."

"What time is the show?" Lucy asked, ignoring Chris's

insistent pulling. She felt like a mother more than a girlfriend most days.

"Three. You should come," she said, then caught herself. "Both of you."

"Yeah, we'll see," Chris answered before she could. "*Babe*."

Lucy knew she was out of time. She sighed and met Scarlett's pretty dark eyes again. "See you later."

"Bye," Scarlett said softly, and Lucy finally let herself be pulled away.

Scarlett watched Lucy walk away with her boyfriend and felt her stomach twist. She had never really *seen* that look on someone else before; she had only been *told* that's what she looked like when she was with Raphael. Her friends had always told her to dump him and move on, but they hadn't known the hell she was going through the entire relationship.

She hadn't wanted things to end the way they had between her and Raphael. There was a time when she really thought she'd marry him. Then when things started to go bad, she felt trapped, like she would never be able to *escape* him.

Raphael's family had never believed her when she had plucked up the courage to divulge details about what their son was doing to her. They had never believed that *their son* could *possibly* put his hands on someone, and if he had, she had done something to provoke him. Only her friends had believed her, and had been the driving force behind her getting out.

Scarlett had never grown up with *much*. She hadn't been poor, by any means, but didn't have unlimited wealth like

Raphael. She had had to work for what she had, but her family had helped her get through school and supported her when she was finding the right career. It was a luxury she knew a lot of people didn't have, and she was so thankful. She had never told her parents about what happened with Raphael, one, because she'd been ashamed, and two, because she'd been so scared about what Raphael might do to them that she hadn't wanted to breathe a word.

It sounded dramatic, and sometimes she felt like she had been sucked into some thriller, but it was true. She had *seen* things with him, things that she thought only existed in cheap mafia films and books, that made disappearing the only option for her when she managed to get out. Raphael had been cruel and sadistic and hadn't wanted to relinquish control over her or anything else in his life. He had money from his business and parents, which made him feel entitled to *anything* he wanted.

Unfortunately, what he wanted for a long time was Scarlett.

There had been days when she could barely get out of bed from how either being too sore to move or too petrified with fear that she'd see Raphael downstairs. They lived in a grand penthouse flat in the heart of London, not the property she'd helped decorate initially, but another separate property he had bought not long after they started dating. She had always worked for everything in her life and took her career *very* seriously. She had never had much handed to her, other than some help from her parents to get her through school. They hadn't been well-off, but they hadn't been poor either. She understood the value of a good work ethic and getting things done the right way. She respected anyone who did what they had to do to make ends meet. The world was brutal and unfair. Who was she to judge anyone based on the path of life they were on?

Raphael had not had the same sentiments. He looked down his nose at *anyone* lesser than him, which was pretty much the entire population of Europe. Scarlett often used to travel with him to different corporate events around the continent, and sometimes in the States. There was a time when she got excited to go with him somewhere, but after a few years, it turned to dread. Each trip bred a nastier fight. There was one trip when things had gotten so heated between them in a hotel room that she couldn't be seen for the rest of the week. People would *talk*, as Raphael told her.

More like he'd get arrested for beating the shit out of her and 'ruining her pretty face.'

She had spent many of her teenage years partying with her friends, as any young girl did, but all that came to a screeching halt when things got worse with Raphael. She had gone from enjoying time with her friends, with *their* friends, to becoming a hermit holed up in a lavish property she could never call home.

When she broke up with Raphael, or rather, ran away without ever explaining or looking back, she vowed she'd never let herself get trapped like that again. No man, woman, *anything* would make her feel smaller than an ant *ever* again.

It had been just about two years since she'd laid eyes on Raphael. He had been out of town for a business trip, just for a few days, and she'd taken it as her moment to strike. Scarlett had a secret bag packed with all her essentials tucked away in a corner of her wardrobe behind a shelf of shoes. The day Raphael left, she took the bag, her approved credentials for DreamWave, hailed a cab, and never looked back.

This was her life now. Was she content? Sure. Happy? Enough.

She wouldn't say she was living the dream. But anything was better than the nightmare she'd been trapped in with Raphael Martin.

Passersby pulled Scarlett back to the present, a few of them asking about the contest. They grabbed a few small pencils and scraps of paper and began scribbling their guesses against the table. Scarlett knew the answer, and always kept her poker face strong when different guests would try to get her to give them a hint.

Instead of her thoughts drifting to Raphael, they resumed focusing on Lucy. She didn't know *why* she was so transfixed on this girl. She chalked it up to seeing the worst parts of her past in Lucy's *present*, and knowing that she wished she had had someone who saw right through everything to fight in her corner.

"Scarlett," Gavin said as he approached the table the woman was dutifully stationed at. "Good news. You're off the hook for this afternoon."

"What?" Scarlett asked, tilting her head. "Am I in trouble?"

"No, but I felt I was too harsh last night. Seems like you did well with the price game today," he complimented, picking up the small box which was practically overflowing with folded up guesses. "Olive and I can handle things today."

Scarlett opened her mouth to protest the change in schedule, but stopped herself. What was she supposed to say? That she *wanted* to work more? They weren't going to pay her overtime and she wouldn't be able to explain why she just *had* to be there in case two passengers decided to show up. Instead, she nodded and forced a smile. "Thanks. I'll get this broken down and help you both set up, then I'll be on my way."

"Sounds perfect," Gavin said, putting the box back down on the table. "See you in a bit."

The rest of Scarlett's shift had been uneventful. She had gotten a few more guesses and eventually packed everything up on her table. Gavin came by to help her transport the art on display for her game, and she followed him to the ballroom to get their event ready to go.

After she finished helping, she returned back to her room and took the opportunity to get caught up on her scheduled social media posts for the company's pages. Most of their job was setting up various galleries for passengers, but another chunk of it was coming up with marketing strategies. She had never been *great* with promotion, focusing more on her creative side, but she had been taught a lot in the last few years she'd been on cruises. Her coworkers had helped her, and luckily, she got along fairly well with Olive. She had been with the company for a *little* longer than Scarlett had, but had welcomed her with open arms. Scarlett had desperately needed friendship when she signed her contract. Being alone *wasn't* an option for the mental state she'd been in.

Scarlett laid on her side in her bed on one end of the room, staring at the same graphic design app that had been opened on her phone for the last 20 minutes. She wondered if Lucy had gone to the show. Had she brought Chris? Had she noticed her absence? Had she felt disappointed?

Olive, who was due to go in for her shift in a little bit, came out of the bathroom dressed to the nines, her hair bouncing with every step. She was a short, curvy Black woman with a big smile and pretty, light brown eyes. She had an Afro filled with dark brown ringlets. Her personality was infectious and could turn anyone's mood around. Scarlett often relied on her on their bad days to make them both smile when they needed it most. Olive glanced over at her roommate and laughed. "You must be really working hard over there, hmm?"

Scarlett sighed and put her phone down, then looked at Olive, who was checking her makeup and hair in the nearby vanity mirror. "Honestly, I haven't done anything since you came in," Scarlett mumbled.

"Something on your mind?" Olive asked, frowning in concern. She began to massage product into her hair as she watched Scarlett closely.

"I don't know," Scarlett groaned, rolling over onto her back. She began to count the little marks of dust on the ceiling. She'd memorized every one by this point. "I feel… cooped up, I suppose. Sad," she then said simply, her arms sprawled on the small mattress.

"Sad?" Olive repeated, turning her head to look at her roommate. "What happened? Was someone mean to you again? I'm telling you, just ignore them. These people are drunk and expecting to be waited on hand and foot. You're better off just forcing a smile until they walk away. You probably won't ever see them again. Maybe they'll fall off the boat."

Scarlett did laugh quietly at that. "If only," she murmured. "I met this girl," she then admitted. Olive stayed quiet, so she took that as a sign to continue. "She is very kind. We clicked immediately. She came to the first art show the day we left port."

"Is she that blonde girl you kept going over to talk to who was sitting in the back yesterday?"

Scarlett blushed. Had she been so obvious? "Yes," she answered. "She was going to come to the gallery last night, but... she said she got caught up. She has a boyfriend and..." she trailed off, unsure if she should be spreading Lucy's business like this. She wasn't sure how to vent about it *without* doing that.

"And...?" Olive pressed.

"And he's just not nice to her."

"How on earth do you know that if you only just met her?"

"I just know," Scarlett said curtly. "There are ways to tell. I met him today and she completely crawled back into her shell the second he was on the scene."

"Well..." Olive started. Scarlett wondered if she was *thinking* her answer through. Olive often did that when she was about to say something Scarlett didn't want to hear. "You don't really know her. I know you're concerned but... at the end of the day, we just work here. When Sunday rolls around, they'll be off the boat and you're never going to see them again. That's her problem to work out. Not yours."

Scarlett knew something like that was coming. She wished she could take that advice and listen to her *own* inner monologue, but she felt like she'd regret it forever if she did. "Yeah," she eventually said. "You're probably right."

"I'm sorry you're feeling sad. But we get to enjoy a port day later this week! Let's go get our nails done. You've worked so hard this week. My treat."

Scarlett smiled and held her hands up, wiggling her fingers above her. "I *do* need a fresh set. Desperately."

"Exactly. It's a date," Olive laughed, walking to Scarlett. She sunk onto the edge of her mattress then looked down at her. "We're confined on this boat most of the time. It's okay to go a little stir crazy once in a while. That's why you have a *wonderful* best friend like me to pull you out of those moments."

Scarlett smiled and pushed herself to sit up. She locked one elbow to keep her upright, then used her other arm to hug Olive around the shoulders. "Thanks for always listening to me."

"Of course," Olive murmured, squeezing her back. "Have you done your paperwork to renew your contract? It's due next week."

Scarlett's smile faded momentarily. That whole process made her grind her teeth. She wasn't sure she wanted to continue working on ships, but she really didn't know what else she'd *do*. She wanted to go back home to London to see her family and friends, but she worried deeply that *he* would come looking for her. She didn't feel strong enough to go back, to fend him off, to return to normal. She had been dragging her feet when it came to re-signing her contract for another two years. It felt more like signing her life away, despite finding a fierce and loyal friend in Olive.

"Yeah," Scarlett lied. "I just need to give it to Gavin. Thanks for the reminder."

"Always. Now, I need to run before I'm late and Gavin has a conniption. *You* need to figure out what color you want for Wednesday. I think I may go with a lavender," she said, standing up and looking down at her unpainted nails.

"That'll be pretty," Scarlett nodded, watching her disappear into the hallway. She looked down at her hands again and couldn't help but wonder what was Lucy's favorite color. She wished *they* could go get a manicure in the Bahamas together. Life would be much easier.

A fter what was an excruciating few hours with Chris consisting of the EDM trivia he'd lost and claimed was 'rigged,' a lunch filled with him going on about how much he *did* know about the music genre and playing multiple songs at the fullest, most obnoxious volume possible, and more complaints than she could keep up with about how he would rather do anything but go to the art auction, three o'clock finally rolled around. Lucy strode into the club-turned-gallery she'd grown to know, Chris trudging behind her, his head hung as he stared down at his phone. She looked around, not seeing Scarlett anywhere. She was probably busy doing something, but she'd be there.

Lucy hadn't been able to shake Chris and immediately felt bad for wanting to. It was unfair of her to beg for reparations in their relationship and then shoo him away when she wanted to… what? What *did* she want to do?

There were plenty of people in the room so it wasn't going to be as easy as Lucy had hoped to find Scarlett. Nearly everyone had a glass in hand, whether it be champagne from the auction or some other cocktail they'd gotten from one of the bars on the boat. A handful of people were wandering around the room, looking at the different art on display, and another handful were taking their seats near the front. Some people were just standing around talking to each other.

Lucy slowed her step and Chris collided with her back, dropping his phone. He swore under his breath and leaned down to get it, causing Lucy to turn around. "What'd you do?"

"*You* stopped walking," Chris mumbled, inspecting his phone screen. "I think it's cracked."

"I thought you had a screen protector. I bought you one for Christmas after we got your phone fixed last time."

"Screen protectors are for the weak."

Lucy made a face. "What does that even *mean*?"

"It *means* if you hadn't stopped in the middle of the floor like a crazy person, I wouldn't have dropped my phone. Can you call the fix-it place when we get back home and get it replaced?"

"Let me see it," Lucy said, taking the phone from him. She tilted it under the light of the room, not seeing anything dramatic. There was one small scuff near the corner, probably where it made impact with the ground. "I don't think we need to pay to get it fixed," she said, clicking the button on the side to unlock it. "I can see everything just fine. It's barely noticeable."

"But…" Chris began with a whining tone, his shoulders slumping. "You're not gonna fix it?"

"No," Lucy said, shaking her head. She held back any other comment she wanted to make. "Let's go find our seat."

Chris stopped her when she started walking toward the back half of the room. "Aren't we gonna sit down there with everyone else?"

Lucy looked at the lowered part of the floor with all the chairs. She frowned and decided against arguing with him. "Yeah. Okay." They walked down and took their seats at the end of the third row. Lucy couldn't help but glance around the room every few seconds, wondering when Scarlett was going to come out.

"Over here," Chris said, the sudden high volume in Lucy's ear making her jump next to him. She looked over and he was waving down — or rather, snapping his fingers at — a Chroma worker. A dark-skinned woman dressed in all black came to them with a smile that could've stopped rain.

"Yes?"

"What're you serving people in those glasses?" Chris asked, pointing to some other passengers.

"Champagne. Would you like some?"

"Ew, no," Chris grimaced immediately, recoiling back from her. "You got any whiskey?"

The woman — Olive, according to her name tag — smiled tightly and shook her head. "No, I'm sorry. We only have champagne. But I could make a mimosa for you if you'd like?"

"That's a girl drink," Chris scoffed. "You want one?" he asked, looking over at Lucy.

Lucy's eyes were wide and she was trying to communicate a silent apology to Olive without her boyfriend catching on. When his attention was on her again, the blonde shook her head. "No. I'm fine. Thank you. We can get you a drink after this."

Chris grunted and folded his arms, slinking down in the chair, his legs spread wide and taking up every inch of space around him. "Fine."

Olive was gone quicker than she'd come. Lucy couldn't blame her. Honestly, she *could* have used some alcohol right then, if only to stomach Chris's behavior in a public setting, but her stomach was dancing too much for her to keep anything down.

It wasn't like she was getting ready to take an exam she didn't study for. It was *just* a person she'd made friends with. It was bothering her that this was *bothering* her.

Time passed and Lucy began losing hope Scarlett would be there. Was this payback for Lucy standing her up? Was it all some sort of elaborate trick? Did Scarlett secretly hate her and this was a cruel prank on her part to give her a taste of her own medicine? Lucy's leg bounced and she began picking at the skin on the edges of her neatly French-tipped nails.

"Hey, quit it," Chris hissed, firmly planting a hand on her knee to stop the movement. "It's annoying."

Lucy muttered an apology and forced her eyes to stay forward and *not* look around the room for another Chroma worker. So far, she'd only seen the eccentric man running the show — Gavin, maybe? — and Olive.

No Scarlett Sinclair. At all.

"Well, *that* was a waste of time," Chris announced as they stood up once Gavin concluded the auction and encouraged them to come to their gallery on the third deck tonight.

For once, Lucy agreed with Chris. She sighed and didn't respond verbally. Standing with him, she gathered her purse and the flyer they'd passed out highlighting a few artists that would be on display in the gallery that night. Before they left, Lucy saw Olive walking around, swiping up empty glasses from the floor and tables. "Chris," Lucy said, turning to her partner, "could you just... I want to talk to her real quick."

"Who?"

"Olive."

"Who's Olive?"

"The worker who didn't have whiskey," Lucy said, trying with everything in her to keep her tone light and not annoyed.

"Oh. Why?"

God. Lucy inhaled deeply and slowly, blinked languidly, then spoke, "I wanted to ask her the details on the voucher I won from that raffle yesterday."

"Why?" Chris repeated with a slight laugh. "It's not like you're going to buy anything."

Lucy shifted on her feet. He went from never talking to never shutting up in a matter of seconds and it was *always* at the most inconvenient time. "Yeah, but... what if there's an art piece for a hundred dollars and I have the voucher? Maybe we'd get it for free with the discount."

"Hmm," Chris said, raising his eyebrows. "Yeah, that makes sense. It's crowded in here though, I'm going to wait for you outside."

"Okay, I'll be right there," she said. *Finally.* Lucy turned from him and walked over to Olive, grabbing the last few straggling glasses for her. "Hey," she greeted, putting the glasses on the tray Olive was compiling them on.

"Hi, how can I help you?" Olive asked in a professional tone, that gigawatt smile on her light red, painted lips.

"Um… Where is Scarlett?" Lucy asked, not knowing another way to phrase her question. She didn't have much time.

Olive tilted her head slightly. "She's off this afternoon."

"Oh…" Lucy said, furrowing her brows. Why would she tell her…?

"It's a recent change," Olive then quickly tacked on. "She was supposed to work the auction today but Gavin let her off."

"Oh," Lucy repeated in a different tone this time. "Okay. Thanks."

Olive smiled and looked as if she was going to say something, but instead turned to the glasses to transport them. Lucy watched her walk away and she tilted her head back for a moment, groaning under her breath. She felt like she was going crazy.

Lucy exited the room and couldn't find Chris. Her eyes darted to the whizzing lights and bells coming from the casino on the other side of the hallway. Surely not…

Her sandals might as well have been stuck to the linoleum floor. She slowly started to walk to the other side, but a tap on her shoulder stopped her.

"Where ya goin'?" Chris laughed when she turned around. "I told you I'd wait for you right out here."

"Sorry," Lucy said. Her shoulders relaxed. "I didn't see you when I came out here. I was going to go look for you."

"Here I am," Chris said. "Now check this out." He pulled

up the boat's daily itinerary on the app and scrolled. "Okay, here's the art auction we just went to... I was thinking we could go to this," he said, hovering his thumb over one of the scheduled events.

"'This or That?' What is that?"

"Look," Chris said, tapping the event. A new screen came up with a description. "'Come join us as we get to know each other. Pairs will join up and our host will ask various questions to see how well you can guess your partner's preferences. Do they like this? Or do they like that?'" Chris read, before looking at her. "It's on the third floor by the main bar. Do you want to do it?"

"Sure," Lucy shrugged. Might as well, right?

Lucy had half-hoped they'd see Scarlett on their way down.

They didn't.

Instead, it was a very uneventful walk down to the third floor where a group of people were dispersing from the previous game, and a different group of people were waiting for the next game to start. There was a large, busy bar on the left side of the room and a small stage to the right. In the middle was a big space and a few tables surrounding for people to sit. Lucy and Chris joined the new group of people and she glanced down at her phone. Almost four.

"Alright, everyone," the host, a tan-skinned man with long, braided brown hair, a blue DreamWave shirt, and a pair of khaki shorts said in a wireless microphone from the atop stage, "we're about to start 'This or That?' If you've never played this before, my name's Jaylin and I'll be your host. This is how it works: you'll partner up with someone you *don't know* and line up with your backs to each other. I will hand everyone a small card and pencil for your answers. When everyone has a card, I'll start a ten-second timer and begin calling out 'This or That?' questions. For example, I'd ask if your partner would prefer fruits or vegetables, then you'd write down what you think your partner would choose, then when the ten seconds are up, you'll turn to face your partner and I'll go down the line to see if you got your answers right. Sound good?" A hum of affirmative answers sounded and the host grinned. "Okay, go partner up!"

Lucy looked around to try and find a suitable partner. This sounded fun and she was glad Chris had suggested it. She hadn't spent enough time playing games.

"Okay, come on," Chris said, tugging her arm. "Let's go line up."

"What? No, we know each other. That's against the rules. He said we have to find someone we don't know."

"Oh, who cares? Do you want to win or not?"

Lucy frowned. "Chris. That's cheating."

"It's just a game, come on. Quit being a pussy."

Lucy's jaw went slack and her cheeks burned. "Excuse me—"

"Okay, is everyone partnered up?" Jaylin called out, his voice echoing around the room from the speakers.

"Come on," Chris said as he tugged Lucy into line and they turned away from each other.

Lucy was shaking. Her entire body was warm and she was

on the verge of making a scene. *Calm down, calm down, calm down.*

"Here are your cards," Jaylin said as he walked around and handed little pieces of paper with 'DreamWave' on the top and a tiny blue wave logo. They were numbered to 10. Lucy clutched her pencil so hard she worried it would splinter.

"Alright, first question, here we go, get ready, we're starting off easy," Jaylin said energetically as he paced in front of the stage. "Winter or summer?"

Lucy barely heard the question. She re-focused when Chris leaned his head back to whisper 'summer' in her ear. That boiled her all over again. "Stop it," she hissed back, glancing over her shoulder. "I am *not* comfortable with this!"

"Just write it down!"

Lucy huffed and wrote down the answer. She already *knew* he loved summer. It wasn't like she needed help. They were already cheating, what was the point of it if you needed help with the answers?

"Alright, time's up, let's get our answers," Jaylin announced, going down the line. He held the microphone to each person, asking their answers. The other person would either shake their head or nod excitedly and Jaylin would hype everyone up. He got down to Lucy and Chris and held the microphone up to Lucy first. "Alright, miss, what does your partner prefer? Winter or summer?"

Lucy squeaked out, "Summer."

Chris nodded and grinned, making Jaylin burst into his happy theatrics. "One point for you! Okay, now sir, what does your partner prefer?"

"Summer," Chris answered confidently.

Lucy's eyes widened and she twisted to look at him. "Winter!"

"Ooo, better luck next round," Jaylin said. "Don't worry, don't worry, you'll have more chances!"

Jaylin moved on to the next couples and Lucy was still half-turned toward Chris. "I can't believe you got that wrong. Are you kidding me? You know I *hate* the heat. I love the cold."

"Who the hell loves the cold?" Chris scoffed. "No way, you like summer. You lied because you're mad at me."

"I did not *lie*, and don't tell me what season I like! If you *must* know, I really prefer fall, because the leaves change colors and I can get a pumpkin spice latte."

"Oh, *God*," Chris groaned. "Don't start with the pumpkin spice latte—"

"Hey, you two, it's just a game, we're all having fun," a woman said cheerily next to them. She was facing the same direction Lucy was, her back to Chris.

"Stay out of it, lady," Chris snapped. The woman frowned and immediately turned her attention away from them.

"Chris," Lucy snarled, jerking her head back to look at him. "Apologize!"

"Okay! Next question," Jaylin said into the microphone. "Does your partner prefer coffee or tea?"

"You better get this right," Lucy muttered as she wrote down the answer.

Jaylin came back to them and held the microphone up to Chris. "Does the lady prefer coffee or tea?"

"Tea," Chris said.

Lucy bit the inside of her cheek. She shook her head solemnly at Jaylin and ground out, "Tea," when it was her turn to speak. Chris nodded and Jaylin cheered and moved on.

They still had eight more damn questions. Surely he'd get *one* right.

"Pineapple on pizza or pepperoni?" Jaylin asked.

"Pepperoni," Lucy answered and Chris nodded.

"Pineapple?" Chris answered, raising the tail-end of the word in an unsure tone. Lucy shook her head.

Seven more.

"Cats or dogs?"

Lucy exhaled. He'd get this one right. He would. Everyone knew how much she *loved* dogs.

"Cats!"

Lucy exhaled deeply and closed her eyes. No way he wasn't doing this on purpose now. "Dogs," she answered despondently, both in correction to Chris's answer and also as her answer for what he preferred.

Six more.

Birthday cake or ice cream? She loved ice cream. By extension, she loved ice cream cakes. Chris answered 'birthday cake,' which she had to convince herself wasn't technically wrong since ice cream cakes were still cakes.

Board games or video games? That was an easy one for her. Chris loved video games. She much preferred board games. He knew that, he *knew* that.

Yet, he still answered 'video games.'

Passenger or driver? No brainer. Passenger all the way. She hated driving.

Chris got that one right. Finally. Thank Christ.

Croissant or doughnut? Okay, these were getting easier. She loved doughnuts, especially glazed ones. He knew that because he loved doughnuts, too.

And… he said 'croissant.'

Lucy was sure steam was about to blow out of her ears. Two more questions. Two. More.

Zombies or vampires? This *had* to be a given for Chris. He preferred zombies, she knew that for a fact, but he knew how big her vampire phase was in college. She had been *obsessed*.

She crumpled her tiny paper in one hand when she heard 'zombies' from behind her.

One more. Then they were done. Then she could jump off the side of the boat and die a less painful death than experiencing this.

"Okay, everyone, last question. Would your partner rather call or text?" Jaylin said. "Write down those answers, hurry!"

Lucy didn't write anything down. She just stood there with her fists clenched. Her chest was heaving in shallow bursts and the lights were suddenly *very* bright in the room.

The next thing she knew, Jaylin was beside them. "Okay, what about you, sir? Does she prefer calling or texting?"

"Texting," Chris said.

Lucy just… couldn't do it anymore. "Yep," she lied, nodding like her head weighed a thousand tons. "He likes texting," she said, making Chris nod in response.

Jaylin moved on and when he finished, he went to the front and told everyone to tally their scores to see who won.

Lucy couldn't have cared less. She threw the piece of paper

and small pencil into the closest trash can she could find, then parked at the bar.

"Hey, what the hell, Lucy?" Chris said as he came to stand next to her. "I thought we were going to try to win?"

"We *were* until you apparently didn't know anything about me!" Lucy said, rounding on Chris. "Were you just trying to piss me off?"

"No!" Chris said, shaking his head. "Why didn't you just whisper the answers like I was doing? You wouldn't have gotten all those right if I hadn't done that."

"Yes I would have," Lucy said, her eyes glistening with pain. "I know you love summer because you used to go on beach trips with your family as a kid and you hated going back to school. You love tea — *sweet* tea — because your grandma made it for you every time you visited and you *only* liked her version. You love dogs because *everyone* loves dogs and you always point at one if we see it in public. You love going out for ice cream after we get dinner and trying the craziest flavor you can. You play video games nonstop and you drive us everywhere. Your favorite doughnut is one with strawberry frosting and rainbow sprinkles because it 'just looks like a doughnut.' Zombies over vampires because of your shooting game where you get to kill them with your online friends. And you always prefer texting because you can answer when you want without pressure."

Chris just stared at her. Lucy's eyes welled up and she furiously wiped them clear. "See? I paid attention a *little bit* in six years, Chris. Glad to see you didn't *at all*."

"Lucy…" Chris started, his neck and chest red and splotchy. "Baby, I… I'm an idiot."

"Finally, a correct answer," Lucy laughed sadly, crossing her arms.

"Look, let's just… go get something to eat and we'll do whatever activity you want. I promise. You get to pick for the rest of the night."

Lucy sniffled and cut her glossy, bloodshot eyes to him. "They're doing a belly flop competition at six."

A smile twitched onto her lips, and eventually Chris's. "Then we will *go* to that and watch all the belly flops you want. Let's go get dinner, which you *love* more than *anything* in the world, along with some coffee, doughnuts, dogs—"

"Okay, okay," Lucy said, laughing tiredly. "Come on, Chris. Let's just go."

S carlett looked up as Olive practically fell through their stateroom door. "Are you alright?!" Scarlett exclaimed, standing up from the bed. She was already dressed down in some black sweatpants and a black spaghetti-strap tank top.

"Yeah, but you're about to not be," Olive said breathily, kicking her shoes off.

"Why? What happened?" Scarlett asked, color draining from her face. Had something happened to Lucy? What went down at the art auction today?!

"Nothing bad," Olive reassured quickly, shaking her head. Her curls flopped with the movement. "The opposite, really. Your blonde girlfriend came in—"

"She's not my girlfriend."

"Uh-huh. What's her name?"

"Lucy Price."

"Okay, well, *Lucy Price* came in with her neanderthal boyfriend, who, by the way, is a real piece of work," Olive said while making a face. She was talking while putting her things away for the night. Scarlett made a noise at that last assessment. "Anyway, Lucy managed to shoo her boyfriend away after the show and she approached me, asking about you."

"What about me?" Scarlett asked. Was she breathing anymore?

"She just asked where you were. She looked pretty put out. I told her you were off and you should've seen the way her face just *dropped*. Like you told her her pet died."

"The fact that you're saying this with a shit-eating grin is kind of freaking me out."

"Sorry," Olive said with a laugh, but her face didn't disappear. "I'm not happy she was sad. Well, I am a little, because it means she was sad about you not being there."

"Well... did you tell her I didn't *mean* to be absent? I wanted to work and see her but I couldn't just tell Gavin I *didn't* want the time off. It would've looked suspicious and he probably never would have let me off the hook again. He'd think I'm some kind of workaholic."

"You *are* a workaholic. But that's not the point. I reassured her, don't worry, and she seemed to relax a little bit."

"And then what happened?!"

"She left!"

"Wait, that's it? Nothing else?" Scarlett asked, shaking her head.

"I thought about saying something about how *smitten* you are with her, but decided against it. I figured you could tell her that. The headline of the story is that she *wants* you."

"Olive, her asking about me when I told her to come to the auction and I wasn't there and her *wanting me* are two *very* different things."

"Not really. She was mortified being there with that ape."

Scarlett giggled at the descriptor. "What happened with him? I've only been around him once, and it wasn't like it was a very long conversation."

"He just… ugh," Olive groaned, tilting her head back. "He called me over like I was some kind of servant. I mean, I know I was getting people mimosas and shit, but he literally *clicked* his fingers at me, like this," she said, snapping her fingers a few times for emphasis. "He wanted whiskey but I told him we didn't have that and he couldn't *possibly* be seen with such a *girly* drink as champagne or mimosa."

Scarlett fake gagged.

"I thought Lucy's eyes were going to pop out with how hard she was staring at me. I don't know what she sees in him. I know you said she's not happy right now but *Jesus*, he had to have been a catch years ago or something to have grabbed her. She seems like a delight."

"She is," Scarlett said, smiling bashfully. She was over the moon that Lucy had asked about her — not so much that she'd been disappointed. Maybe she could have just shown up as a regular person and not a worker, but Gavin still would have questioned her. That arguably would have drawn even *more* attention, and if Chris was there, it probably would have been a complete disaster. Sometimes Scarlett didn't know when to shut her mouth, and the moment Chris said *anything* rude to Lucy, she was going to speak up and defend her. *That* certainly wouldn't go over well.

Or would it?

Scarlett sighed deeply and laid back down on the bed. "What am I supposed to do, Olive? This is so messy. And unlike me."

"You're living, so what? Worst case, it doesn't work out and she disappears on Sunday. You deserve to have a little fun. She does too, honestly. I doubt he even gets her off."

"Ugh, I don't want to think about that, Olive. Don't be so crass."

"Don't be so posh," Olive shot back with a laugh. "So what are you gonna do now?"

"I don't know," Scarlett sighed, turning over on her side so she could face Olive completely. "What do you think I should do?"

"Ask her out? Or maybe on your next off night try to plan something with her. When do you think the next time you'll see her will be?"

"Well, it's port day tomorrow, but she usually comes by the table at least once. She has been the last few days, anyway. Maybe when she comes by next I should… say something? I'm working a double tomorrow."

"Shit, that's right," Olive sighed. "Look, I love you, but I don't love you *that* much to take your double. What about our port day Wednesday? You want to invite her to nails?"

"No," Scarlett sighed. "I mean, yes, but… she probably has excursions planned. I could never ask someone on their holiday to forego the beach and get a manicure. She can do that at home."

"True," Olive agreed. "Okay, so port day is out. What about the next day?"

"I don't know," Scarlett groaned. She felt shy, embarrassed. She didn't even know what she would *say* to Lucy if it came to that. What on earth would they do together? Talk? Walk around? Something more? Scarlett absolutely could *not* bring her back to her stateroom, and it wasn't like she could traipse off to Lucy's cabin either, could she? Not with Chris lurking around, and that was even *if* Lucy liked women!

"Why don't you sleep on it," Olive said, eyeing her closely. "I'm here to help in any way you need."

"Thanks, Ol," Scarlett said pitifully.

"You all done with the shower and everything?" Olive asked, pointing to the bathroom. "Gonna go get my shave on in case Gavin wants to have a *meeting*."

"Gross," Scarlett laughed, waving her hand. "All yours, lovely."

Olive thanked her and disappeared into the small bathroom, leaving Scarlett by herself once more.

So many things had happened in such a short amount of time. She was becoming borderline obsessed with this woman. It was a little frightening, given she hadn't had any interest in hardly *anyone* since she left Raphael. Now she was wanting to drop everything to spend a second of time with Lucy.

Scarlett wondered if this was what all the stories talked about.

ucy leaned against the railing of one of the upper floors, the wind whipping through her blonde waves as workers scurried below to ready the ship for debarkation. Sunglasses, a pair of big white frames, rested on her face and she was… for once, feeling excited about something on the trip. The sun was shining and the weather looked gorgeous. She had foregone a sundress for the day and instead opted for a pair of dark blue, jean shorts, a cute, coral blouse that flowed down her torso, and a pair of white canvas sneakers. Nothing too crazy.

"Gonna be a great day," Chris sighed from beside her. He was wearing a sleeveless shirt with one of his favorite video game titles plastered on the front, some khaki shorts that stopped just above the knee, and a pair of brown flip-flops. His sunglasses were square-shaped and black, all very… normal. The man looked over at her and draped an arm over her shoulder, making her crouch *just* a little. He wasn't exactly tall enough to do it comfortably.

"Want to go down to the bottom so we can leave? I don't

want to be late to our excursion," Lucy said, leaning into his side.

"Yeah, sounds great," Chris agreed, taking her hand to lead her downstairs. The blonde watched him as he walked in front of her. Things had gotten better after dinner the night before and she had calmed down. Dwelling on their fights would only make things worse. She had wished the day would have at least included more Scarlett, but it wasn't like the woman was her personal distraction. She was entitled to a day off. She didn't have to spend every waking second with Lucy.

Ugh. She was a mess.

They got to the first floor of the ship, joining a crowd of people clad in floral button-ups, flowy dresses with different patterns, shorts, tank tops, sunglasses, hats, and definitely *not* enough sunscreen. Kids were dressed in their little swimsuits, carrying their favorite toys with them. Briefly, Lucy hoped they didn't lose any of them. She had been younger, on a small road trip with her parents, and had accidentally left her favorite stuffed animal — a small duck named 'Duckie' — at one of the gas stations when she'd been using the bathroom with her mom. She hadn't realized it at the time until they were a couple states away. When they'd gone back, after she cried and begged her dad to turn around, Duckie was gone. She had been devastated for a long time and had never really played with any kind of real toys at all after that.

She had only been six.

Likely, it had been the catalyst that sprung her into a life of burying her nose in books and writing short stories. She would rather escape into fictional worlds than live in the real ones where monsters stole a six-year-old's lost duck.

"Attention passengers," a man's voice sounded over an intercom above them, "gather on the first floor and have your ship cards and passports ready to show when you debark. If you booked an excursion through our cruise line, you'll find your guides across the long walkway gathered near the cluster of stores at the beginning of the port. Remember, the cutoff time to return is four this afternoon. If you are late, you *will* be left at port and forced to find your own way home. Be safe and have fun!"

Chris raised his eyebrows and exhaled as he looked down at Lucy. "Better be on time for once then, hmm?" he teased, nudging her in the side.

Lucy forced a laugh. Chris was late to everything. Every. Thing. It was one of the biggest pet peeves of her life. She took punctuality so seriously, and when people disrespected her time, she got very upset. Chris knew this and still rarely made an effort to get to anything on time, let alone early.

She walked with Chris through the tunnel leading out to the world outside. Sunlight exploded as they walked through and flashed their identification to the workers. She squinted, even behind her sunglasses, and began on the trek to find their guide for the day.

Water glistened against the sun as Lucy laid out on a long chair, a frozen drink nestled safely in the sand beside her. She watched as Chris snorkeled with some new friends he'd made on their excursion.

They had opted to go to a private beach with an open bar and buffet. It had been an easy choice. They had two other port days to go through, and would focus on more strenuous activities like riding ATVs, learning about history, and petting exotic animals on their other days around the coasts. This had been simple to just... ease them into Caribbean life.

When they'd found their tour guide, they all piled into a van to take a short ride to the beach. Chris was surprisingly social the entire time while Lucy just stared out the window. Her thoughts, again, drifted back to Scarlett. What was she doing? Was the boat quiet or were there still obnoxious passengers lingering? There had to be *some* people left on the boat, after all: those who had a little too much fun the night before, those completely disinterested in the beach or outdoor life, or maybe even parents whose children had gotten too sunburnt the day before at the pool. There were parts of Lucy that wanted to stay on the boat too, even if just to avoid Chris.

The day had been pretty normal so far and she felt a *little* bad that she wasn't giving her boyfriend the benefit of the doubt. It was hard to do it over and over when he showed no signs of changing or improving.

When they arrived at the beach, Lucy had gone swimming with Chris for a little bit, but there was only so much splashing she could take. It had never been her favorite sport or activity. She was glad he was occupied with others now. It was a nice break and she wasn't getting saltwater in her eyes.

Usually, she wore glasses, but she had been using contact lenses the last few days. With how much she'd been wearing sunglasses, it was just easier that way. Chris had made fun of her for bringing a dozen different frames, all of varying colors and shapes, but she wanted to make sure she had options for *every* outfit. Even though she was off work, she *always* wanted to be put together.

Perhaps she cared too much about what other people thought about her, but when her job was surrounded by what other people dictated as looking good, it was hard to not let that seep into her personal life, too. She had never had great self-esteem when she'd been growing up, having never been stick-thin or the *prettiest* girl in school. But what she wore was easily controlled, unlike a kid losing weight or the way she was born to look, so... she became obsessed with clothing.

She had grown into herself after puberty and in college, finding her niche when it came to taming her curls and doing her makeup, but there were still days when she felt inadequate. Chris had complimented her to a nauseating degree when they had first started dating, and had done thoughtful things for her like bought her favorite chips and drink to surprise her after a bad day of classes, or taking her to a bookshop and letting her pick whatever she wanted out, no matter how long it took her to look around. He just... wasn't like that anymore. He didn't *do* those things anymore. It was almost like he was bored with her, like she'd *always* be there, so why bother trying anymore?

She was sure she had her own faults in the relationship, but every time she practically begged Chris to communicate to her, to tell her what she could do differently to make him love her the way he used to, he always either stayed silent, or shrugged and said she wasn't doing anything wrong.

Eventually, she'd had no choice but to take his word for it, despite feeling like her heart was poisoning her from the inside out. She felt like she was rotting away half the time and there was no cure.

Lucy picked up her drink — a strawberry piña colada — and took a few generous sips that cooled her off immediately. She had shed her shorts and blouse, now clad in a high-waisted bikini with red bottoms and a black and white polka-dotted top.

Chris jogged up to where she was, kicking sand with every step. Lucy grunted unhappily to herself and stared down at her now ruined cocktail. She swallowed her complaint down and told herself she could just go get another one and it wasn't worth the fight.

"You coming back in or what?" Chris asked, waving one of the beach attendants over.

"I'm enjoying tanning right now. I already swam," Lucy said.

"Yeah, but you only swam for, like, fifteen minutes. Basically just for me to take pictures of you. Come *actually* have some fun. There are a lot of cool fish. My friends want to meet you."

Lucy barely stopped herself from making a face. There was nothing she wanted *less* than to meet a bunch of strange men who deemed her boyfriend good company. "I'm worried about my contacts getting messed up if the water gets into the goggles," Lucy explained. For the millionth time. This was exactly why she *didn't* like to go swimming. "It's not worth it to me if I'm risking not being able to see for the rest of the day."

"Oh, come *on*," Chris groaned, tilting his head back.

"Señor?"

Chris lifted his head again and made eye contact with the beach attendant he'd waved down. "Yes, finally. Get me an old-fashioned, will you?"

Lucy inwardly cringed. She *hated* going out anywhere with him where there was servers, because he was just so... condescending. He had always told her it was their job to do what he said and their tip depended on it. She had never seen him tip above 15 percent.

"Can I please also get another strawberry colada?" Lucy spoke up with a smile. As the man nodded, she sighed a quick breath of relief. Despite being a journalist, social anxiety consumed her sometimes. "Thank you so much," she gushed as he walked away, and she and Chris were alone again.

"Will you come swim with me again, please?" Chris asked, folding his arms. "Just for a little bit. You don't even have to go underwater. I just didn't think you'd spend the whole trip *sitting around—*"

"Okay, *fine*," Lucy snapped, getting up. She walked past him to the water and waded in. It was so *clear*. They had beaches back home, but they were not like this. They were still beautiful, but... this was just different. She assumed everyone probably thought the same thing about seeing some new landmark that was different than what their hometown had to offer. Beaches didn't usually wow her, but she'd been around them her entire life. She was lucky.

Chris followed her and wrapped his arms around her from behind, making her squeal in surprise. Thankfully, his new friends seemed to have taken the hint and left them on their own. Chris began kissing her cheek, then her neck, making her squirm and laugh. Lucy held onto his arms around her middle and gave into his affections.

This was what she missed. When they were *happy*. Now this was a mere snapshot in the album of their relationship. A pipe dream. A figment of her imagination.

It wasn't all bad. Nothing was ever *all* bad. But it was bad a lot of the time. It was so bad that it had started to overshadow the good, to the point where it was hard for Lucy to actually recall the happy times. She had thought they didn't exist anymore, until now.

She was going to cling onto it as long as she could. It would be easier than facing the music, facing that *this* was… slipping through her fingers. Her forever she had always dreamed of was cracking and crumbling, and all she could do was stand back and watch it disappear.

Or rather, take the kisses in the ocean when she could and bury everything else for the time being.

U pon returning to the ship, Lucy felt relief.

It had been a fun day with Chris and they hadn't gotten into any major fights, and things were just… easy. Almost normal. Not quite though.

Guilt crept in at her lack of confidence in him, but she wasn't going to focus on that. They had had a good time on their excursion and in the water, and most importantly, had made it back by the deadline and were on the ship as it pulled away. She had to admit there had been a *small* fear inside that something Chris did would make them miss it and *really* ruin their trip, and now contrition flooded her for assuming the worst.

It was hard for her to keep the same feelings about *everything* going on between them. One day she was sad things were strained, another day she was counting down the seconds to the day she never had to see him again, and another she was as happy as she'd been in the beginning and reminded *why* she fell in love with him in the first place.

It gave her headaches often.

Lucy held Chris's hand, their fingers laced together, as they walked back to their room to get showered and changed for the remainder of the evening.

"We'll have to look at the schedule, but I bet there are some cool things planned for tonight. Maybe we could do karaoke," Chris said, leading her down the hall to their cabin.

"Karaoke? Since when do you like to do that?" Lucy laughed, looking over at him.

"We don't have to *sing*, but it'll be good people-watching," he laughed. "Or we could just go and sit by the pool. Or at one of the bars."

Lucy nodded. "Let's just take a look at the schedule."

In all honesty, she wouldn't have minded a shower and a *nap*. Her thoughts roamed back to Scarlett, once again. Was she still working, preparing for another show, or off and relaxing? Did she get to enjoy the port day? Did she even *like* going out to the beach anymore? Lucy empathized with her if not, understanding when locals chose to do *anything* else but get out on the sand. She had grown tired of it over the years, but when she went away, and came back to visit, she was reminded how privileged she was to live where she lived.

But it didn't stop her from wanting to see other parts of the world.

As they entered the cabin, Lucy made a beeline for the bathroom while Chris set down a few souvenirs they'd bought and picked up his phone to check the itinerary for the day on the cruise's app.

Lucy stepped into the shower and sighed to herself as the

hot water hit her back. She could *feel* the sand and salt dripping away from her, and she knew she'd be in a better mood after this. She squirted some shampoo into her hands, then lathered it into her hair. A moment of solitude—

"Okay, so karaoke isn't until late tonight, at like, eight," Chris said from the doorway, making Lucy jump. He continued anyway. "Oh, I have an idea," he said.

"I'm listening," Lucy called out, rinsing out the shampoo. She moved for the conditioner next.

"How about we have a day at the spa?"

Lucy opened her eyes in surprise, then winced as they immediately burned from the hair products. She dipped her head back under the water and rubbed her face, then opened her eyes again. "The spa? Really?"

"Yeah, why not? We've been running around all day, I thought it could be nice. It's not like we have anything else to do until karaoke or dinner."

Lucy smiled slightly to herself and turned off the water, then wrung her hair out. She pulled the curtain aside and smiled as Chris handed her a towel. "Thanks," she murmured, drying off. When he didn't leave the room, she looked at him again and blushed at the expression on his face. "Okay, you can't have a spa day *and* sex, Chris. And I'm not giving you the choice because I know what you'll pick," she laughed, nudging him aside so she could throw on a dress. "I think I'm *long* overdue for a massage."

"Ditto," Chris said, moving to perch on the bed as she got dressed and ready.

"Aren't you going to shower?" Lucy asked as she pulled a

brush through her wet waves.

"Nah," Chris shrugged. "I mean, we're going to get massages done anyway. No real point in showering and all that. I can just do it later, or tomorrow."

"You sure?" Lucy pressed, frowning a little. "I mean, you can do whatever you want, but… like you said, we've been running around all day, and it's pretty hot out. We were in the water, too. You might feel better."

"There you go, you just answered your question," Chris said, holding out his hand. "We were in the water, therefore I'm clean."

"Okay…" Lucy said, turning away from him so she could find the hairdryer. There wasn't a part of her that was about to tell a grown man how to groom himself, and for the most part, he was a very clean guy, but… he had a *talent* for souring nice moments together. She just hoped the poor spa workers didn't hate them *too* much.

Hands kneaded into Lucy's back as she lay facedown on the massage table, her eyes closed. Chris was talking nonstop next to her and she had yet to respond to hardly any of it. At this point, she didn't even know *what* he was talking about. She had tuned him out after he ventured into minute four of explaining whatever video game he was playing at the moment.

"Isn't that crazy?" Chris asked from the table next to her.

"Mhm," Lucy grunted.

Historically, she hadn't been so dismissive. But there were only so many years a girl could take of listening to everything her boyfriend was interested in, yet when she tried to gush about something she enjoyed, he blew her off or told her he really didn't care. She was enjoying the spa time with him, but part of her knew she would have enjoyed it whether he was there or not. It wasn't the fact that she was there *with him*. A few years ago, it would have been.

Chris began barreling into another spiel about a trading card game he was into lately, and Lucy just continued to tune it out. She *tried* to like the things he did, but the quirks that had been cute and adorable at the beginning had turned into things that grated on her *last* nerve. She hadn't even questioned how he was paying for this expensive treatment, because she *knew* how. Perhaps it was wrong of her to exploit whatever money he won from the casino, but she was past the point of wanting to fight him. She felt a little hypocritical, but damn, for once it was nice not to have to shell out whatever money she had left in her bank account to treat herself, because Chris certainly wasn't going to do it. She wasn't sure if he would ever change, and she was coming to the realization that it wasn't her *job* to change him. Unless *he* wanted it, he would stay the same forever.

"What do you think?"

"What?" Lucy asked, coming back to the present.

"Have you been listening to anything I said?" Chris asked, lifting his head from the table. "Lucy."

"Yes, yes, you don't know which deck to choose from," Lucy said, hoping that would suffice. "Which one is your gut leaning toward?"

"I think the magic-based one… I need to watch more videos

about it online to make a decision," he mumbled, reaching for his phone.

Lucy heard the movement and opened her eyes, catching the tips of his fingers grazing a small table near them that held all their belongings. She pushed herself to prop up just a bit so she could fully see him. "You're not going to do that now, right?"

"What?" Chris shrugged, unlocking his phone. "You got the Wi-Fi, right? Let me get on it for a little while. It's not like you use it for what it's for anyway," he said, opening his browser to connect to the network and boot her phone off it.

Lucy cringed as a narrator's voice began *blaring* from the speakers on his phone. "Can you at least turn it down if you're going to watch? Put subtitles on," she suggested.

"No way," Chris laughed. "I hate subtitles. I want to be able to look at the video, not read the entire time."

"Please, Chris," Lucy begged.

"What's the big deal? I'm not bothering anybody," he said, twisting to look back at the masseuse. "Am I bothering you?"

The worker was silent and eventually shook his head.

"See? Quit freaking out," Chris said as he looked over at Lucy, then rested down to stare at his phone while the masseuse began working his muscles again.

Lucy shot both his masseuse and her own apologetic looks, then slowly relaxed back into the table. She took some deep breaths and closed her eyes again, the volume of the video screaming next to her all but setting *every* molecule of her body on fire. Chris had zero spatial awareness and never cared about others around him, which bothered Lucy to her core. She was acutely aware of everything she did and how it affected those near her, and *tried* to stay out of people's way. There were times, especially in her career, where she *had* to make an intrusion to be seen, but that was different. Chris would stand in the middle of the grocery store aisle with his cart sideways, blocking the entire thing while he stared down at his phone, reading some new conspiracy theory on a chat board. She would always have to usher him to move or just leave him alone in the aisle while she took the cart and finished their shopping. Then, of course, they'd get into another fight later about her not picking up 'everything he needed' despite asking him, and him being too glued to his phone to say anything else.

The massage turned painful, purely because Lucy was tensed and unable to relax. She powered through the rest of the hour they had, and when they were finished, she dressed silently. Chris was still filtering through videos as they got ready to leave.

It took everything in her not to say something to him or chuck his phone overboard.

Lucy had calmed down a little bit after the massage and dinner. Food had done wonders for her. It was time for karaoke.

As they walked through the ship's decks, they neared the area where the casino was… and where Scarlett was usually set up. A jolt shot through Lucy's body as they got closer and closer to the bright lights and hallway after. Was it because of Chris being near slot machines or because she might see Scarlett? For a moment, Lucy almost felt *embarrassed* to be seen with Chris.

It wasn't a foreign feeling, but she had never felt that way due to another woman. Or anyone other than her close friends and family who knew how bad things were.

The couple passed the casino without incident. Chris hadn't even looked toward it. He was engrossed in a conversation with Lucy, though he was the only one talking. Lucy soldiered on, nodding and humming in agreement when his voice left her ringing ears. They entered the hallway just past the casino and there was Scarlett's table...

Empty.

Lucy managed to keep a neutral face, but disappointment overtook her. She blinked a few times, then gave up on the possibility of seeing her new friend. Turning her head toward her boyfriend, she looped her arm through his and squeezed him close. She forced a smile and nodded again, tuning into what he was saying.

"I just really think the, like, *way* the movie is filmed is so cool. I know you hate it, but..."

"*Hate* isn't the word I'd use for *Pulp Fiction*, it's just... not my favorite. That's all. But I'm glad you like it," Lucy said. She didn't even have to guess to know which movie he was droning on about. She'd rather poke her eyes out with dull scissors than ever sit through that monstrosity again.

"You just need to watch it again. They show movies on the ship, maybe I can put in a request."

"I'm sure all the movies for the week have been scheduled," Lucy muttered. So help her God if they weren't...

Lucy and Chris walked into the designated room for karaoke. There was already someone on stage singing their heart out to a Lynard Skynard song. She smiled and tried not to cringe at how bad the person was, but it was all in good fun. She looked around and nudged Chris when she found a couple of open seats at a table near the back. She pointed and they made their way over, sliding into the corner. A server came by to take their drink orders and Lucy politely declined while Chris ordered a beer. She wasn't a fan of his drinking, but… it wasn't as bad as his gambling problem, she supposed. They were on vacation and she knew asking him to cut back on drinking was a one-way ticket to another fight. She was trying to *enjoy* the rest of the evening and the cruise, if possible.

Singers came and went, some good, some… not so good. It was entertaining and she was glad Chris had suggested it. There were a few songs she knew and sang along to.

"You wanna go up there and do one together?" Chris asked, squeezing her thigh.

There was a time where his touch excited her to no end. Now it just made her tense. "Oh… I'm enjoying just watching. I'm no singer."

"Well, me neither. That's not the point of karaoke. We should go," Chris said with a smile. "Come *onnn*."

Lucy shook her head and blushed. "No, I really don't want to. You can go up there and do it if you want. I'll take a video."

"Seriously?" Chris scoffed, removing his hand from her leg. "You won't go do it with me?"

Lucy frowned and straightened up her sitting position. "I don't think it's a big deal that I don't want to do it. Why are you getting angry?"

"I'm not angry," Chris said pointedly. She could see his jaw clench. "I just wish you would actually act like you give a shit about me. Like you *want* to be seen with me."

Lucy felt her eyes burn. She swallowed down any tears and steeled herself. Her chest felt heavy. "I give more of a shit about you than anyone else in the world does, Christopher. I'm the only one who hasn't given up on you," she hissed.

"Really?" Chris laughed. "Any time I ask you to do something, it's like I just told you to swallow a bunch of rocks and glass. I just want things to be happy again."

"So do I," Lucy said, her frown deepening. "Look," she sighed, her heart rate increasing, "if you really want to do karaoke, I'll go up there with you and—"

"No, I don't want to anymore," Chris muttered, waving his hand dismissively. Lucy *hated* when he did that. "We can just go back to the room since you're not having fun."

"I never said I—"

"Come on," Chris interrupted, utterly uninterested in anything she had to say. Lucy heaved a sigh and moved around the table so they could leave.

So much for a nice night. With any luck, she'd be able to fall right asleep and get to the next day.

Chris stared up at the pitch black ceiling as Lucy breathed evenly beside him. He felt manic.

He had been tossing and turning in his sleep, unable to truly drift off with how fast his mind had been whirring. He thought about Lucy and how obviously unhappy she was. He knew it and had known it for years, but nothing he did seemed to be good enough for her. Any extra money he had, he spent on gifts for her, he spent on *trips* like this for her. Why didn't she want to *be around him* anymore? Why wasn't it *fixing* everything?

Reaching over, he grabbed his phone and woke it up.

1:12.

He grunted to himself and turned on his side, trying to ignore the sway of the boat as he closed his eyes again. His mind wandered to the day in Grand Turk and how much fun they'd had, as well as the spa. He had been relaxed beyond belief, but had gotten the sense that Lucy was still in a bad mood afterward. He assumed she was just still angry about his time at the casino, but that *wasn't* his fault. He was in recovery and was faced with temptation. It wasn't like he murdered someone, he had just played a few games, won some money, and had a good time. He didn't have a problem, and he wasn't planning on running back to the casinos as soon as they got home and getting bad again. They were on vacation and a lot of other people were doing it, so why couldn't he? There were even *kids* in the arcade using their parents' money to get toys and tickets and prizes — how was *that* not a problem?

Karaoke had ruined everything. He felt like an idiot for suggesting it. Maybe if he hadn't, they wouldn't have gotten into their fight. He didn't know why he reacted that way and blew everything up. He *knew* Lucy had severe social anxiety and wouldn't want to do anything like get up in front of strangers and sing some random song out of key. Why was he like this? Why were *they* like this?

He blinked open his eyes and exhaled. Sleep just wasn't going to come. Slowly, he grabbed his phone and tucked it into his sweatpants pocket, then carefully slid from the bed. Glancing back down at Lucy, he could tell she was still asleep. Good. He grabbed the hoodie he'd draped over the back of the chair by the vanity earlier in the day and pulled it over his head. Swiping his glasses from the nightstand, he threw them on and slipped out of the room silently.

Chris curled his fingers around a fresh old-fashioned and lifted it for a generous sip.

He was camping out at one of the many bars aboard, trying

to pass the time and clear his head.

His leg bounced as he took another gulp, then motioned for the bartender to give him another. He had gone to guest services the first day they'd been on board — after his fight with Lucy — and had put a separate card on file for his keycard, not wanting Lucy to see his transactions. She didn't need to know how much he was drinking or what he was spending money on. All she would do is *freak out* again.

Things hadn't been horrible like this the entire time they'd been together. They had been *happy* for all of their relationship, and all of a sudden Lucy just picked a fight about everything. He couldn't put his shoes on right, he couldn't get the right milk at the store, he had the T.V. up too loud, he played video games too late instead of coming to bed with her. She didn't even want to sleep with him anymore. Any time he tried to come to bed like she asked and initiate contact, she would shrug him off and say she was too tired. Wasn't that the whole *point* of a relationship?

Chris had done nothing but give to her. When they started dating, he spoiled her with lavish gifts and trips away during their breaks from college; after college, he had picked out this gorgeous apartment with a view of the entire downtown cityscape in Orlando for them to share. He had been making good money with his dad, had let Lucy go out with all her little friends while he did the same, and they were *happy*. She wasn't bitching at him for doing things he liked or 'not spending time with her.'

This was honestly all his dad's fault. If he hadn't gone crazy and cut him off just for being late a *few* times and oversleeping *once* — okay, *twice*, maybe three times — then Lucy wouldn't look down on him. He knew she was probably just embarrassed to be seen with him. After all, he had been in charge of the relationship at the beginning and made all the money, which is obviously why she started dating him in the first place. It hadn't made him upset by any means, that was how the world worked. He was sure that's how his father got his mother to marry him and start a family. Money talked, and woman *loved* men with money.

They had gone from riches to rags. From a penthouse apartment in the heart of the city to a studio in the slums.

Chris glanced behind him at the whirring lights and sounds from the casino just a few yards away. He pressed his lips together firmly and shook his head to himself, then turned back toward the bar. All he had to do was win big *once* and he'd be back on his feet. Lucy wouldn't have to work so much to afford their *terribly* tiny apartment, and he could go back to being the man in the relationship. Lucy just had to *trust him.*

Chris finished his drink and ordered another one, without the soda this time. Taking the glass of whiskey with him, he wandered over to the casino, where more than a few people were getting reps in at the machines and tables. He didn't see *their* girlfriends or wives or husbands or boyfriends jumping down their throats. Maybe he just wasn't with the right person.

He could play *one* game.

Chris walked over to the poker table and slid into a seat next to a few other older people, all with drinks or cigarettes in hand. He took out his wallet and slid a hundred-dollar bill to the dealer, getting a stack of chips in return. He stared at the table and cards, his stomach twisting. The people around him began chattering and cards were flying between hands, sliding around the red velvet lining.

This was his happy place. When he was here, all the bad thoughts went away. He could just *exist*. There was no judgment, only winning or losing. And when he lost, he was always encouraged to try again. Lucy didn't *do* that. When he was down, she just made him stay there. She never told him to get back up and keep going. She always told him to *quit*. He wanted to be around *his people*.

A few hours passed and the group he was with trickled out one by one until he was the only person left at the table. He looked down at the chips he had and counted them up. He had about a thousand dollars. Chris grinned and gathered his chips, then took them to the concierge to be cashed.

See? He didn't have a problem. He was quitting while he was ahead. He had only spent a few hundred dollars on the games, and had come back in the green. The math was obvious.

Chris took out his phone once he stuffed his new cash into his wallet and felt hopeful. It was barely 4 a.m., Lucy likely wouldn't be awake and he could get a few hours of shut-eye before they had to be up for the next port day. She wouldn't even know he was gone.

He walked back to the cabin and crept in as quietly as he could. Sliding into bed next to her, he wrapped her in his arms and pulled her close.

"Where'd you go?" Lucy asked sleepily.

"What?" Chris whispered, his heart lurching.

"You just came back to bed... Bathroom?"

"Yeah," Chris answered quietly, snuggling close to her. "Boat rocking upset my stomach."

"Hope you feel better, there are antacids in my bag if you need them," she murmured, burying her head against his chest. Her breathing evened out after a few more seconds.

Chris let out a quiet breath and closed his eyes. Too close.

"**C**ome *on*, Chris," Lucy groaned as she pulled on his hand. They were very slowly making their way off the boat and to the port the ship had docked at overnight. "I know you're tired, but you'll perk up once we get going. We're riding those ATVs you like so much," she gushed, glancing back at him.

He looked *exhausted*, even behind those sunglasses. He was just in a light blue t-shirt, a pair of black swim shorts, and some black tennis shoes. She was in a short, simple, green sundress that served as a cover-up for her bikini underneath and some white sandals. Her hair was twisted up in a curly bun, a few tendrils hanging around her face, and she had a pair of green-framed sunglasses to match her ensemble. She felt *good*.

Chris definitely wasn't as lively as he'd been the day before, but he had told her he hadn't slept very well. He also had a headache. She hated it for him. She had slept like a baby.

"I wish we could switch the excursions and things we did yesterday to today," Chris grunted, following his girlfriend.

"What if I fall asleep on the ATV?"

"I'll drive," Lucy said with a smirk. "You're so dramatic sometimes," she teased. They arrived at the hub where passengers were filtering through to find their tour guides. She wondered if it was always this busy or just when ships came to the island. Lucy glanced down at the paper they'd been given the night before and went to their designated area. The weather was beautiful again, which she was so thankful for. Living in central Florida, you never knew *what* the weather was going to be like, and she knew these port workers took the forecast — rain especially — *very* seriously.

The area was gorgeous. It still took her breath away, despite being used to pretty beaches back home. The water was so blue, so unpolluted, so *clear*. She looked around as they walked with their tour guide through Amber Cove to the warehouse where the dune buggies were kept. Different shops scattered the area, as well as tall, green trees and yellow sand. As excited as she was about all their fun activities today, she could have happily spent the day exploring the town instead. It was radiant. She could *feel* the salt from the water seeping into her pores, and she was certain it was healing every wound inside her.

When they arrived to the warehouse, they sat down for a safety demonstration of the vehicles. Everything seemed pretty normal: wear your protective gear, don't go too fast, don't pass up the tour guides, follow the rules of the road, keep your hands and feet inside, and don't crash into anything or get anybody killed. Easy.

Chris hopped into the passenger seat while Lucy took control in the driver's seat. She had mercy on Chris and left the radio off, not wanting to upset his headache with any loud music. Their group rode through the roads of Puerta Plata, Lucy taking in the scenery as much as she could while paying attention to the road. Colorful buildings, trees, and people lined the paved road, matching what they'd seen on their walk earlier. She glanced over at Chris, who was leaned over against the side of the buggy, not moving. A sad look crossed her features and she reached over to squeeze his leg affectionately. Despite all their disagreements over the first half of the week, she didn't want him to be *sick* during their time at the ports. He had paid good money for all of this.

Roads were soon forgotten as they went off the beaten path and began trekking the ATVs through the woods. Lucy laughed to herself with every bump, having the time of her life. She *wished* Chris was awake so he could take some pictures or videos of them both, but she supposed living in the moment wasn't that bad either.

A hushed noise grew louder and louder the further they drove through the forest, and soon they were met with a *huge* waterfall that took Lucy's breath away. There was a bright blue-green pool at the base of the waterfall, rippling with all the activity. Their guide instructed them to park the ATVs, and Lucy took off her protective helmet.

"Wow," she whispered, then looked over at Chris, who was still asleep. "Chris, wake up. We're here."

"Unnnh," Chris groaned.

"Chris!" Lucy snapped, jiggling him a little harder. This did the trick. "Look."

Chris slowly sat up and took off his helmet, then looked

around. "Wow," he said quietly. "This is awesome."

"See?" Lucy laughed, opening the door so she could get out. She grabbed her bag from the back and walked around the ATV to get a closer look at the water. Chris joined her and they followed their group on the footpath around the waterfalls. Brown and green stone stood as tall as she could see, lining the area underneath the falls. There was greenery *just* over the top of the rock where she couldn't quite see all of it.

"Alright, my friends," the tour guide called out, getting everyone's attention. "We have two hours here, then we'll be off to our next location. Feel free to go for a swim and enjoy yourselves."

Lucy grinned and took Chris's hand. "Come on, let's go."

She was thankful Chris's nap on the way there seemed to have cured whatever he was feeling when he woke up. They picked a spot to set the bag down, then Lucy began shedding her dress to reveal her swimsuit. Her bikini this time was all black with no patterns. She carefully folded her dress and kicked off her sandals, letting them join their bag on the ground. Chris was already shirtless and pulling off his shoes. She didn't know *why* he wore sneakers to their excursion, but it wasn't her who would be dealing with wet socks.

She jumped in the water, then laughed as Chris did the same. This was fun. This was fine. Everything was going to be okay. It wouldn't do either of them any good if she just moped the whole time about how sad she was. And there was no better way to forget how upset you were about how your life was going than to swim in a Dominican spring.

"What's this place called?" Chris asked as they treaded

water next to each other.

"Uh…" Lucy started, thinking for a moment. "Damajagua. But the whole area we're stopped in is Puerta Plata, and technically Amber Cove, I guess."

"How do you remember all this?"

"Do you not remember the nauseating amount of research I did on these excursions before we booked them?" Lucy laughed, moving closer to him. She wrapped her arms around his neck and stayed in his embrace. "I'm glad you're feeling better. You usually don't have any problem sleeping. I didn't even notice the boat was rocky."

"Yeah…" Chris sighed, shrugging. "Just a weird night for me, I guess. Those massages didn't do their jobs to relax me enough," he laughed.

"Sorry," Lucy said, poking out her lower lip. "But we're gonna have a great day. After this we get to go play with monkeys."

"Actual monkeys?"

"Yeah," Lucy said. "Chris, this was the excursion *you* picked out. I'm surprised you don't remember at least *some* of the details."

"It's been a while since we booked this trip," he said, shrugging. "But now I remember. Do we have a port day tomorrow, too?"

"No. It's a day at sea, then one more port day in Nassau, then another day at sea, then we're back in Orlando."

"Cool," Chris nodded. He waded through more of the water and simply relaxed. "I like how clear the water is."

"Me, too," Lucy said, looking down at their kicking feet

rippling below the surface. "Thanks for doing this for us, Chris. I don't know if I really ever *said it*, but I'm having a good time and I'm glad we're here."

At this, Chris smiled. He leaned forward and gave her a kiss. "You're welcome, babe."

Lucy squealed happily when the tiny squirrel monkeys made themselves at home atop her shoulders.

This was her version of a *perfect* day.

"Chris, Chris! Look!" Lucy laughed as one monkey moved atop her head and held onto her hair. "Take a picture, quick!" Chris did as he was told and pulled out one of their phones, snapping a few photos and a short video. Lucy continued giggling and the monkey climbed down to rest back on her shoulder. The monkey on her other shoulder hopped off and wandered over to Chris.

"No, thank you," Chris said, shaking his head as he took a step back from the primate. "Seriously. Back off."

"Chris, it's harmless, look," Lucy said, now cradling the monkey she had left. "They're so small and cute. I'll get your picture!"

"I said I don't want to," Chris snapped, a deep frown on his face.

"Okay, okay, it's alright," Lucy reassured, shaking her head. The monkey darted off as Chris stamped his foot at it and Lucy tutted. "Did you *really* have to scare it?"

"It worked, didn't it?" Chris huffed.

"Why did you pick this excursion if you don't want to be

around monkeys?"

"You *love* monkeys," Chris muttered.

Lucy's heart did a somersault at those three simple words. Monkeys were her *favorite* animal and she was always so happy the few times they visited the zoo. She could spend hours just watching them, *any* kind of monkey. She loved spidermonkeys, gorillas, orangutans, baboons, squirrel monkeys, *anything* that was related to a monkey.

Except maybe some *people*.

"Well, thank you for your brave sacrifice," she said with a smile, reaching out for his hand. When he took it, the monkey in her other arm jumped onto Chris now that he was so close. Chris yelped and tried his best to wiggle the monkey off, but it was holding on for the ride. Had it been Lucy, she would have been giggling up a storm, but she knew he was genuinely terrified, so she quickly called for the tour guide to help them.

A few seconds of chaos passed and Chris was eventually free of his furry attacker. Lucy was immediately by his side, checking him for any scratches or wounds. Luckily, he was unharmed. "Are you okay, love?"

Chris felt all over his body and eventually calmed his breathing down. "Yeah… Yeah, I think I'm fine. I was just scared," he admitted, moving to grab her hand. "Thanks for getting it off me."

"Of course," Lucy murmured, squeezing his fingers comfortingly. "Thank you for picking this for me. I really appreciate the thought."

"I just want you to be happy," Chris said quietly. "That's all I've ever wanted."

Lucy's heart lurched again. She snaked her arms around Chris and closed her eyes. Why couldn't he be like this *all* the time? What was it about her that brought out the worst in him?

Playing with the monkeys was some of the most fun Lucy had ever had — minus the debacle with Chris. She knew the pictures they took from that morning would be her favorites for *years* to come. But none of this surprised her. It wasn't like anyone could really have a bad time on a beautiful island with tiny, cute monkeys crawling all over them.

Well. Maybe that wouldn't be *everyone's* idea of fun — as she had realized — but it was definitely hers.

She and Chris hadn't fought at all that day, even *with* the monkey incident, and it made her feel like maybe they could *be okay*. There was still a long journey between giggling and kissing under a waterfall and repairing a relationship that had been fractured for several years, but she wasn't going to think about that. She was just going to focus on the moment, on *having fun*, and making memories from this cruise that would stay with her whether *she* stayed with Chris.

Scarlett looked down at the red polish the nail technician was painting on her fingertips. She had decided to go for a classic look. Usually, she liked to do designs and whimsical ideas, but her heart hadn't been in it.

She and Olive were sitting together in their favorite salon in Amber Cove, one they went to *all* the time when they stopped at this particular port. A perk of going to the same handful of destinations over and over was getting to frequent local shops and make friends with the residents. Olive had worked for DreamWave Cruises longer than Scarlett had, so she had turned her on to doing things like mani-pedis near the beaches rather than snorkeling with tourists.

"Oooh," Olive cooed as she leaned over for a peek, her hands being carefully worked on by another technician. "That red looks so good on you."

"Thank you, darling," Scarlett said with a smile. She eyed her friend's hands, then turned her attention back up to her. "Shows how spoiled we are that we go to the beach and get our nails done instead."

Olive laughed quietly. "Listen, you got sunburnt *way* too many times. We did it. It's the same beach over and over. And dressing cute and getting my nails done is the only thing that keeps me going in that soul-sucking ship," she teased, looking down at her hands. Olive and Scarlett both were in bikinis with thin cover-ups wrapped around their waists. Olive's swimsuit was a pastel blue and Scarlett's was black, their wraps matching their respective bikinis. "Besides, I think we needed a little bitch sesh," Olive laughed.

"Definitely," Scarlett sighed. "What's going on? Are you and Gavin still…?"

"*Ugh*, don't get me started on that dumbass," Olive groaned, rolling her eyes. "He's being too professional right now. Ever since he got promoted to art director, he's just been… different. I know he's technically my boss now, but… it's not like anything has changed between us. He's still the same Gavin and I'm still the same Olive."

"So no more 'olive you' jokes that make me want to vomit? I'm crushed…"

"*Bitch*," Olive laughed again, nudging her shoulder with her own. "That's cute and you know it. Anyway… I don't know. I'm not talking to him at the moment. Outside of work anyway."

"I'm sorry," Scarlett said with a frown. "I know he makes you happy. It makes me sad when you're fighting."

"I think it's just because we're around each other all the time. It's hard to go out on dates and do anything other than…" she trailed off, shooting her a sideways glance that left *nothing* to the imagination. "Sometimes I feel like it's never going to be anything deeper than the physical side of things. Is there a future for us beyond this ship?"

"Of course there is," Scarlett automatically answered, frowning at her. "How could you even doubt that?"

"You are *such* a hopeless romantic," Olive said lightly. "We'll see. But enough about me, let's talk about *you*."

"I'm not seeing anyone, you know that."

"Are you not? What about… what's her name? The blonde girl."

"Lucy," Scarlett said. "What about her?"

"What's going on with that? Have you thought about what you're going to say to her next time you see her?"

Scarlett hesitated, then shook her head. "I don't know. We haven't seen each other in a day and she's probably having fun with her boyfriend. I'm not a home wrecker. I've never even…"

"Never even what?"

"I've only ever *dated* Raphael. I've fooled around with old girl friends before, but it was never anything serious. I was always tipsy or high those times, too, it was never…"

"Meaningful," Olive finished. "But… you have feelings for her?"

"I just like talking to her. We haven't spent enough time around each other for me to know whether I have feelings. And she's *in* a relationship with a *man*. And she's going to disappear in a few days. There's really no point in doing anything, or even *thinking* about doing anything."

"I don't know," Olive sighed. "With modern technology, phones, social media, it's pretty easy to stay in touch with someone."

"Who's the hopeless romantic now?"

"I'm serious," Olive laughed. "Where is she from? Do you know?"

"She's from Orlando."

"There you go," Olive said, beaming at her. "We stop there all the time. When it's your turn next to go out on the town, get in touch with her and have lunch or something."

The three of them — Scarlett, Olive, and Gavin — rotated on who got to leave the ship on starting port days each week. She hadn't cared much about the schedule until now. Before, it wasn't like she'd ever had time to do anything like go to theme parks or go shopping, but if she was going to spend time with Lucy, she didn't *need* all day to grab a drink or bite with her. Hell, they could go on a walk by the port for all she cared.

"I just don't know. She's probably just being nice," Scarlett sighed.

"Or she likes you back," Olive countered, examining her nails as the technician gave her hands back. "Look, how about this…" she continued, swiveling in her chair to face her best friend. "Do you want to switch shifts with me tomorrow? I have tabling duty in the morning, but I was off at night. You can table in the morning and have your night. Maybe Lucy runs into you while you're manning the table, then… you two can plan to spend some time together when you're off the clock."

"Olive, that's… I don't *know*," Scarlett groaned, putting her head in her hands. The technician hissed and quickly pulled Scarlett's fresh hands away from her, and Scarlett shot the woman a sheepish and apologetic look.

"You can do what you want," Olive said, reaching for her

purse so she could get some money out. "But we're switching either way. It'll give me a chance to sleep in," she said, handing the money over to the technicians. The women stood from their chairs and exited the nail salon. "You hungry?"

"Starved," Scarlett responded, following her to a nearby shack that sold the best seafood and had the *best* drinks.

She was so thankful for this sweet, loyal woman in her life. She would have definitely gone mad on that boat without her.

16

L ucy sat across from Chris in one of the port's restaurants near the cruise ships. It looked like a beach shack, but was pretty packed with people. There was sand surrounding the outdoor area and tables, making a faux beach, and all the umbrellas and fake palm trees really completed the look.

They had been on their way back from the excursion and Chris had suggested they pop in for a little while, considering they had about two hours left until the ship was supposed to leave. Or at least, until they were supposed to be back on it. They were sitting inside at a high-top table, servers and customers bustling around them. Everyone probably had the same idea they had. The restaurant was lined with wooden tables and a bar near the back. There were two bartenders shaking their hearts out and pouring drinks. They were probably getting *loaded* with tips. She was happy for them.

Their food had come out quickly though, which eased her anxiety marginally. Even with a full day exploring Amber Cove, Lucy wasn't very hungry, and would have been fine going back to the ship just to *make sure* they made it back in time, but she was trying to bottle the good day they'd had together and didn't want to do anything to ruin it.

"What do you wanna do tonight?" Chris asked as he powered through one of his fish tacos. She had just gotten a burrito. She really just wanted to go back to the cabin, shower, and take a *long* nap.

"I'll have to look at the schedule. But maybe I can show you this artwork I really like," Lucy said with a smile. "It's really pretty. It's this scene of two people—"

"I don't want to go to an art gallery again," Chris groaned, tilting his head back. "We already *did* that. We didn't even win anything. All that art is stupid and boring."

"It's not stupid or boring," Lucy retorted, frowning deeply. Her dark eyebrows stitched together and she stared at him. "Just because it doesn't make noise or move around and tell you what to kill on a T.V. doesn't mean it's boring. I think it would look nice in the apartment."

"Our apartment is fine," Chris said, taking another bite of his food. "Besides," he said in a muffled tone, chewing his way through the taco, "we already have plenty of decorations up. All of my movie posters. And if I'm going to become a professional streamer one day, I'll need to keep them up to have a cool backdrop. Nobody's gonna wanna see some painting behind me."

"Since when do you want to become a 'professional streamer?'" Lucy asked.

"Since now. Figured since Dad is still being a dick about everything, I'll take matters into my own hands. I'm getting pretty good at all my first-person shooter games. I could definitely go pro. Then you won't have to complain so much," he said, wiping some sauce off the corner of his mouth with the back of his hand. "Win-win."

"How do you even get into that job? Don't you need a camera set-up and a microphone and editing software? I didn't know you knew how to do that."

"Well, I don't, but that's why I have my badass creative girlfriend to help me," he said, sipping his drink, a smug smirk on his face. "You know how to do all that stuff."

"I don't know the first thing about online streamers."

"Yeah, but you know how to work a camera, how to edit videos, what good audio sounds like. You can film me and then edit it, then I can upload it online. It's called teamwork."

Lucy began bouncing her leg. She stared at her boyfriend, then blinked a few times.

"What?" Chris asked, setting his cocktail down. "What's that look for?"

"You want me to do *all* of the work for your *streaming* career, on top of my *own* career? The one where I actually make money."

"See, there you go again," Chris scoffed, leaning back in his chair.

"There I *what* again? *What*?" Lucy snapped. She was at the end of her rope.

"You never believe in me!" Chris countered, throwing his hands up. He had attracted a few nearby tables' attention, but he didn't care. He never fucking cared about anything that wasn't *himself.*

"I *do* believe in you," Lucy hissed, her cheeks hot with embarrassment. "You just expect me to do everything for you. When we started dating, when we *moved in* together, I didn't think I'd be the one responsible for *everything*. I don't make that much money, Chris. I live paycheck to paycheck and pick up extra hours when I can. I've even thought about getting a second job when we get back home just so I'm not stressing about finances so much."

"But… if you got a second job, how would you have time to edit my videos?" Chris asked, tilting his head.

Lucy stared at him, wide-eyed. For the first time in her existence, she *truly* contemplated whether life in prison would be *that* bad.

Without another word, Lucy grabbed her bag and stood, the tall chair she was sitting in scraping against the wooden paneling on the floor. She stormed away from the restaurant and Chris, ignoring him calling out and questioning her. She didn't care, she didn't care, she didn't *care*.

Lucy eventually hid away behind one of the touristy shops across the port entrance. She rested back against the cement wall of the building and put her head in her hands. She felt like screaming. Tears burned behind her eyes and it was taking everything in her not to sink down to the floor and just sob.

"Lucy?"

The blonde's head snapped up and she met the sweet, concerned eyes of… Scarlett.

Lucy sniffled and tried to blink back tears, but she failed. They rolled down her cheeks and only then did she noticed Scarlett wasn't alone. Lucy gently dabbed under her eyes, careful of her contacts, and cleared her throat. "Hi… sorry."

"Don't be sorry," Scarlett said softly. "Lucy, you remember Olive."

"Nice to meet you. Officially," Olive said with a sad smile.

"Wish it was under better circumstances," Lucy said to Olive, her eyes glassy but *tired*. "I'm not usually like this."

"What's going on?" Scarlett asked. "Are you *okay*?"

Lucy stared into her eyes, that last question hanging between them. The longer she looked at this woman, the more upset she got. Lucy brought her hands up to her face again and just burst into tears.

"Come on," Scarlett said, closing the distance between them. She wrapped an arm around her, Olive following suit on the other side of Lucy, then they carefully walked her back to the ship.

carlett swiped the keycard to her and Olive's room and ushered Lucy inside. They had to be sneaky getting her there, considering passengers weren't allowed in workers' cabins. Not that Scarlett cared too much, but she didn't want to get fired.

Lucy had stopped crying, for the most part, but Scarlett wasn't going to let her be alone.

She sat Lucy down on the bed and went to get a bottle of water for her. Unscrewing it, she handed it to the blonde and urged her to drink.

"Thank you," Lucy sighed after she downed a quarter of the bottle. "Sorry again… I'm so embarrassed."

"Girl, don't be," Olive said, waving her hand dismissively. "Happens to the best of us. We got you," she reassured. She pulled up a chair and sat down across from Lucy, then shot Scarlett a look that had gone unnoticed by Lucy.

Scarlett took her cue and sat down on the bed next to Lucy. Not too close, but a comforting distance.

"What *happened*?" Scarlett asked, turning her body toward the woman next to her.

Lucy sighed deeply and absently fiddled with the water bottle as she spoke. "Chris happened. The last six years of my *life* happened. He's just… We can be having the best day and he just finds a way to ruin it," she blurted out, then blushed. "I shouldn't even be saying any of this. You barely even know me."

"Nah, you can say it," Olive chimed in. "Fuck that guy. What'd he do?"

"What *didn't* he do," Lucy muttered whilst rolling her eyes. "Chris comes from a very wealthy, successful family and was supposed to follow in his father's footsteps at the tech company he runs. He was going to be this big fancy software engineer and have his life set up forever. That's not why I started dating him, of course, but it was nice to know we'd be taken care of while I got started in journalism," she said quietly. "Chris started to slack off more and more as we got closer to graduation and the months after, and then… his dad gave him a wake-up call. Chris wasn't allowed to sleep the day away and just expect Rob to bail him out," she explained. "Rob… his dad, cut him off completely financially, until he could get his shit together. Chris spiraled and started going to casinos and gambling to get some money back. This was about a year after graduation. Two years ago. He won pretty big on his first visit, while I was away visiting my parents at home, and when I came back, he was just… different. All he could talk about was how these card games worked or how the casinos rig slot machines. He was always telling me some new cheat he found to make the machines spit out money. He gambled his entire savings away and claimed he didn't need to get a job because he could make all the money he wanted at the blackjack table," she muttered, shaking her head. "It got to where we had to move to a smaller apartment because we couldn't afford it. Now I pay for everything."

"Does he have a job now?" Scarlett asked.

"No," Lucy laughed tiredly. "No, he doesn't. He sits at home. He went to rehab about six months ago and I thought he was better, but the second we got on this boat, he went straight to the tables and slots," she said, her eyes welling up again. "I feel like I've just been *wasting* my life away on someone who doesn't give a shit about me."

"What happened today that made you so upset?" Olive asked. "You said you were having a good day and he ruined it."

"Yeah," Lucy said shakily. Scarlett reached over for a tissue off the box on the nightstand and handed it to her. Lucy quietly thanked her and continued. "We were having fun on our excursion, swimming, loving on each other… He was being nice. He even picked the excursion *specifically* because it had monkeys. He hates animals, I *love* animals, monkeys especially. Then we went to eat at that little beach-shacky restaurant by the port entrance… Anyway, we were talking, and he told me he was going to become a professional streamer."

"A what?" Scarlett asked. "What the hell is that?"

"I guess it's someone who streams their video games online," Lucy explained. "He plays video games *all* the time. He said he's going to start making money doing it."

"Well… I mean, would he?" Olive asked.

"No," Lucy scoffed. "At least not right away. I don't think

he has what it takes to do that. Maybe that's bad of me to say, but… he told me I'd be the one doing all the filming and editing. He'd just be playing the games and talking to the camera."

"Wait, what?" Scarlett asked. "Isn't the filming and editing like… *all* the work?"

"You see why I was crying," Lucy sighed, raising her eyebrows and shrugging her shoulders weakly. "I told him I wouldn't have time to do that with my career and everything else. I told him I was even thinking about getting a second job to make ends meet and all he was worried about was that I wouldn't have time to make his videos for him."

"Yeah. Fuck that guy," Olive repeated, shaking her head. "You should drop him. All he's doing is bringing you down."

"I can't just drop him," Lucy said, her voice small. "We have a life built together. It's not that easy."

Scarlett's heart twisted and she felt like she was looking into a mirror. She had said almost *verbatim* the same thing when she had been venting to her friends back home about Raphael. It had taken her so long to realize what a piece of shit he was and that she was losing herself, but she had been so scared to start fresh. Signing up for a life at sea was one of the most terrifying things she'd ever done in her life.

But in that moment, she had never felt more glad that she had.

"At the end of the day, *you* have to be the one to make those hard choices," Scarlett said, gently placing her hand on Lucy's shoulder. "We can tell you all day long you deserve better, but until *you* believe it, nothing will change. But we'll be here to support you in whatever you need. I know you just met us, but… we're here for you."

"Thank you," Lucy said with a pitiful sniffle. She sighed and hung her head. "I'm just so tired of the fighting. It's *constant*."

"I know. You should be having fun, not worrying about what's going to set him off next," Scarlett said. "Do you know where he is now?"

"No," Lucy said, shaking her head. "I left him at the restaurant. He probably doesn't even care where I am or if I even made it back onto the boat."

"I'm sure that's not true," Olive said, leaning forward to squeeze her knee. "He's lucky to have someone in his life who obviously cares *so* much about him and his future. If you didn't, you wouldn't be upset right now and you wouldn't be fighting so hard."

"I just… wish someone felt that way about *me*," Lucy admitted quietly.

"The right person will," Olive reassured, glancing at Scarlett. Her friend was looking at this woman as if this entire situation was shredding her on the inside. Olive tore her gaze from Scarlett, then looked at Lucy, who still had her head hung. "This is a big ship. There's plenty to do. You don't have to see him."

"I do when I go back to the room to change and sleep and shower," Lucy mumbled.

"Hopefully he won't be there then," Scarlett jumped in, rubbing her back. She was trying not to be overly touchy, but she couldn't help it when the poor woman was sobbing next to her and begging for someone to love her. It completely ripped her in half.

"You guys are so nice," Lucy said, moving her head so she was looking toward the ceiling, her eyes red-rimmed from crying. "God, I can't wait for the day I'm *done* crying over him."

"Maybe that can be today," Olive smiled, standing up. "You should go do something fun."

Scarlett stood and Lucy mirrored them. "Yeah," Scarlett said. "There's a lot of stuff planned for today," she said, swiping the day's itinerary from her vanity. She unfolded the brochure and ran her finger down one of the pages. "The mini-golf course is open right now. And Olive and I don't have to do any work until…" she trailed off, reaching to tap her phone screen. "Seven. That gives us about two hours to goof off."

"Are you sure?" Lucy asked, looking between them. "I don't want you to have to babysit me during your only time off."

"Please," Olive laughed, grabbing her sunglasses. "Let me and Scarlett change and then we'll grab ice cream on the way."

Lucy smiled and nodded. Scarlett felt her heart skip a beat at seeing Lucy's face light up again. Thank goodness they'd rescued her.

18

"You are... *really* bad at this."

Lucy glanced over at Scarlett and tried to glare, but couldn't hide the smile bursting from her. "Listen, I write for a living. I don't often go on the green and... whatever it is they do," she laughed, before turning her attention back down to the ball by her feet. She carefully lined up her putter and tapped the ball forward. The little, bright blue sphere rolled across the green carpet and along a few small hills, then went *right* into its hole.

Lucy turned her attention quickly to Scarlett and stuck her tongue out. Scarlett merely laughed and put her hands up in defeat.

Surprisingly, Lucy was having a really good time. Olive and Scarlett made it easy to forget about Chris, who she assumed had actually made it back on the boat. She supposed she would find out tonight when she went back to the room to go to sleep... or maybe at dinner. The thought of sitting down for another meal with him made her stomach turn though.

The blonde stepped aside so Scarlett and Olive could have their turns. *This* was what the fun in a cruise was supposed to be. Not her crying behind a building on a port in the Caribbean. She looked over toward the water surrounding the ship, seeing the island growing smaller and smaller in the distance. The wind flew through her hair, which was now half-tied up in a bun, half-down. She was still in her outfit from the excursion, but she didn't care.

Scarlett had changed from her earlier bikini ensemble to a pair of black chino shorts and a plain, fitted white t-shirt. Olive was in a pair of light denim shorts, a bikini top, and a loose cover-up that was open in the front. Scarlett's dark brown hair was down and flowing, ending just past her shoulders. Olive's was curly and bouncy as usual. They both definitely embodied what Lucy imagined a permanent cruiser would look like.

Lucy couldn't help but stare at Scarlett as she putted. She was *covered* in tattoos, something she hadn't really registered until they were in her room and she had finally stopped crying. She had no clue, what with Scarlett always being buttoned up to the neck in some professional outfit.

The tattoos weren't exactly cohesive, they were just random items that obviously each had a story. Up her arms were various designs: birds, flowers, insects, abstract things Lucy couldn't quite make out. They were bursting with every color on the rainbow and Lucy's eyes were feasting on them. Her legs were also covered in similar designs, the patchwork tattoos going all the way up her calves, her thighs, and disappearing under the shorts she had on.

Why did Lucy think it was *hot*?

She was trying to pretend not to notice how those delicious black shorts fit Scarlett's long legs and how her t-shirt, something so simple, hugged her in all the right ways. She could see faint outlines of more tattoos under the thin, light material of the shirt and it made her clench her thighs together. She wanted to see and ask her about every single inch of ink—

"You're up again, Luce," Scarlett called out, holding out her little blue golf ball for her.

Lucy blushed and snapped out of her treacherous inner monologue. She walked over to her, taking the ball. "Thanks, *Scar.*"

The other woman laughed and rolled her own bright red ball between her fingers. "We're friends, right? We can't have nicknames?"

"We can," Lucy reassured. She walked to the next hole with them and set her ball down.

She had some friends like this back home, but most of them were coworkers. They all got paid so little that they couldn't do a whole lot with each other on their off days at the weekend, and she was usually occupied with whatever Chris wanted to do anyway. Even though these women worked on the ship and would be busy most of the time, she was thankful they decided to spend their free time making her feel better.

And playing mini-golf in the middle of the Caribbean wasn't the *worst* way to pass the time.

"So what's your schedule like tonight? After you do your work at seven," Lucy asked as she lined up her shot, then hit it. The ball went flying very far away and not at all near the hole.

Olive laughed and sighed. "I'll go get it," she said, jogging across the course to find the ball.

Scarlett stepped up and put her ball on the ground. "We don't have to do anything with the galleries tonight, Gavin is handling it. But we need to catch up on our social calendar and make sure we meet our engagement quota with our digital marketing plans," she said, gently hitting her ball. A flash of red rolled across the greenery and landed about halfway to the hole. Scarlett stood up straight and looked at Lucy. "So after this we'll have to disappear again. But tomorrow morning I'll be tabling."

"Same spot?"

"Always."

Lucy nodded and thanked Olive for retrieving her ball when the woman came back to them. As Olive took her turn, Scarlett and Lucy kept talking.

"But after I'm finished tabling, I'll be off for the night. So…" Scarlett trailed off.

"So…?" Lucy prompted, tilting her head. It seemed like Scarlett wasn't sure of something. She almost looked… nervous?

"So she wants to know if you two can hang out," Olive finished without looking back, tapping her ball toward the hole. It bumped into Scarlett's and knocked hers way off course. Olive laughed naughtily to herself and walked across the pathway, the other two women following her.

"Only if you want to," Scarlett said quickly, looking at Lucy. "I don't want to intrude on any plans you might have."

"Pfft," Lucy scoffed, shaking her head. "Trust me, a night with you would be welcome if it means I can stay away from

Chris and all his stupidity. What time do you get off?"

"Three."

"It's a date then," Lucy smirked, nudging her gently with her club. "What do you want to do?"

"I'll have to look at the schedule. Maybe we can get something to eat and just… lay by the pool."

"Boring," Olive groaned.

Lucy laughed quietly and let them get their balls in the holes, then they moved on to another course. "We can just play it by ear if you want. We don't have to plan anything. I can come get you at three and we can go from there. Unless you want to change or something afterward?"

"Uh… yes, actually. Could we maybe meet at the piano bar on the fifth deck?" Scarlett asked.

Lucy put her ball down again and carefully butted her club against it. "Sure. What time?"

"Half-four?"

"Half-four," Lucy laughed, shaking her head.

"*What*?"

"You're just *so* British," Lucy teased, hitting her ball. Thankfully, it didn't go haywire this time. But it still didn't get into the hole. Or… even remotely close.

"Technically I'm *English*, thank you. And you are horrendously American," Scarlett snapped back playfully, nudging her aside with her hip as she set her shot up. "Fine, four-*thirty*," she cooed in her best American accent, which made both Olive and Lucy giggle. Olive wasn't even American either, Lucy had asked her about her accent on their way to the golf course, and she had informed her she was South African. Her family lived in Cape Town and she had wanted to get out and travel the world, and this had been the easiest way for her to do it affordably.

"Four-thirty it is," Lucy said with a smile, her eyes roaming over Scarlett as she laughed with Olive. She was gently nudging Olive's yellow ball over and over, making Olive threaten to beat her with her golf club.

"How long have you two known each other?" Lucy asked.

"Two years," Scarlett answered. "When I came aboard the ship."

"Has it been two years already?" Olive smiled, glancing at her best friend. "I remember it like it was yesterday. Scarlett looked like she had seen a ghost. Her eyes were so wide and she was shy."

"*You* were shy?" Lucy asked, her attention on Scarlett.

"'Shy' might not be the right word," Scarlett smiled. "I was more nervous than anything. I'd never left home before. Not like that anyway. I really had just traveled around Europe, but that's easy. You can just hop on a train and go anywhere. But I was starting this brand new life and didn't know where to… look, I suppose."

"Well, *I'm* glad you showed up. You made things much easier here. Not only with work, considering I didn't have to be the only one preparing and breaking down galleries anymore, but you took some of the focus off me from Gavin. I love that boy but… he can be *a lot* sometimes," Olive sighed.

"So what's the story with you and Gavin?" Lucy asked with a smirk.

"What do you mean?" Olive asked, her smile slowly creeping out. "Is it *that* obvious?"

"No, not to normal people. But with how you just talked about him, I had a hunch," Lucy reassured. "Has that been going on a long time?"

"Eh, on and off," Olive shrugged, their golf game momentarily forgotten. "Honestly, it started not long after Scarlett came. I had only been here about a year before that. When she came and some of the workload was lifted, I had more time off, as did Gavin, and we just… got drinks one night after putting together a show and hit it off. He wasn't director then, but that's what he always worked toward. We had another director, Sayir, who didn't do much of anything," she sighed, propping a hand on her hip. "He was quick to tell you what you were doing wrong but not what you were doing right. And would never offer to help. We were so happy when he finally left," she laughed. "Then Gavin slid into his position and it's been the three of us ever since. But we try to keep things light. This place is too cramped for us to be around each other more than we already are. And…" she lowered her voice, "we're not exactly *supposed* to be hooking up. So don't tell anyone."

"Your secret's safe with me," Lucy reassured, zipping her lips closed.

"Cool," Olive said. She pulled her phone out and raised her eyebrows, then turned it around for Scarlett to see. "We better get going if we both want to shower and get ready in time."

"Yeah," Scarlett sighed, then she looked at Lucy. "I'll see you tomorrow, okay?"

Lucy smiled and walked with her to put their clubs and golf balls up. "I promise. For real, this time. No boys will stand in my way."

Scarlett laughed and held the door open for her and Olive as they left the mini-golf area. "Perfect."

"**G**ood morning!"

Scarlett looked up and turned her head to the side as a cup of green liquid was suddenly in her face. She stood up and set her pen down on the table covered in black cloth, then laughed at the bundle of happy blonde woman in front of her. "What's this?"

"Coffee, of course. Well, matcha," Lucy smiled, shaking the drink a little.

"How did you know my order?" Scarlett asked, taking the cup from her. She took a sip and sighed happily to herself. The morning had come far too early and she had been sluggish getting out of bed. She hadn't even had time to really dry or treat her hair. She had barely swiped on some mascara before she dashed out.

"You told me, remember? The other day," Lucy said. Scarlett could feel her gaze raking over her. Suddenly, Scarlett felt a little... self-conscious.

"Your hair is all wavy," Lucy continued, that radiant smile

still beaming. "Usually it's straight."

"I know," Scarlett sighed, setting the cup down. She lifted her hand to touch her hair and shook her head. "I overslept and didn't have time to straighten it. Or even dry it. It's still kind of wet. I'm sure it's going to frizz up later," she muttered, rolling her eyes.

"It looks great," Lucy reassured. "It's nice to switch it up every once in a while. Give your hair a break. But I get it," she said, touching her own hair, which was pulled back in two pretty French braids. "Sometimes my hair has a mind of its own. My friends call it my mane," she laughed. "It can be hard to manage, and brushing it is a nightmare. I let it do what it wants for the most time."

"I wish," Scarlett said with a smile, leaning back against the edge of her table. "If your hair is usually untamed, it looks brilliant. Mine just makes me look like a homeless person."

"Oh, *please*," Lucy scoffed. "I don't think you *could* look like a homeless person. You always give *very* Anne Hathaway."

"As opposed to a *little* Anne Hathaway?"

Lucy scrunched up her nose and Scarlett laughed again. She felt like she was always laughing around her. She took another sip of her drink and eyed her. "But *which* Anne Hathaway is the question? I hope not *Les Misérables*."

"Hmm… Maybe the beginning, but I was thinking more *Princess Diaries*. Or maybe *The Devil Wears Prada*."

"Ah… just not the fringe," Scarlett smirked. "I liked both of those films."

"They're good," Lucy said. "What's your favorite movie?"

"Good question," Scarlett said with a sigh, tilting her gaze up toward the ceiling. "Probably *Titanic*." She looked at Lucy, the blushed as she merely *stared* at her. "What?!"

"*Titanic*? Really? That's a little on the nose, don't you think?"

"Just because I work on a ship doesn't mean it isn't a great film."

Lucy smirked and shook her head. "I guess… I've never actually seen that, you know."

"*What*?"

"Yeah, yeah," Lucy said, waving her hand. "I almost *don't* want to see it because I get that reaction every time."

"It's so good!"

"So I've heard," she said. "Just not my thing. I like romance movies, just… I don't know. Not really my cup of tea lately."

Scarlett understood. She didn't want to push it, so she shifted the conversation. "What's your favorite film then?"

"Probably *Halloween*."

"*Halloween*? Like, Michael Myers?" Scarlett asked, moving her free hand in the air in a stabbing motion.

"That's the one," Lucy laughed. "Not what you expected?"

"Honestly? No. I figured you would have said something like… *Clueless*."

"I *do* like *Clueless*, but… I'm not *that* much of a girly-girl," she said, then smiled as Scarlett slowly raised her eyebrow in accusation. "Okay, *fine*, I am a girly-girl, but I love horror too. They're fun to watch. And *Halloween* is a classic," she shrugged. "Have you ever seen it?"

"Once, I think," Scarlett smiled. "I don't have much time for films anymore. It's not like I can go to the cinema, and I'm never off at the same time as when they're showing films on the ship. Nor do I ever really have a reason to do most of the activities here. Once you do them, they get kind of boring," she said with a sigh. "Thank you for the matcha, by the way. I don't think I actually said that out loud."

"You're welcome," Lucy said. She looked over, seeing people filtering in slowly down the halls. "Guess everyone's starting to wake up now."

"Yeah," Scarlett sighed. "Will probably have to go back to the land of begging people to come see more art, even though I know they're not going to buy any. It's always easier to sell things when people are drunk. It's too early for that, and the day after port is always tough because people are tired or hungover... or both."

"I wish you luck," Lucy said with a smile. "We still good for *half-four*?"

Scarlett grinned and tried to fight her warming cheeks. "We are. Piano bar," she reminded, tilting her plastic cup toward her. "Don't stand me up this time."

"I didn't *mean* to," Lucy groaned, tilting her head back. "You can thank my *lovely* partner for that. I'd never stand you up willingly. I was in an existential crisis. They're becoming more and more frequent, sadly enough for me."

Scarlett gave her an empathetic look. "Were things okay last night when you went back to your cabin? Did he bother you?"

"Things were... tense. We didn't talk much," Lucy admitted quietly. Scarlett watched her shoulders draw in just a bit, and she was shifting from foot to foot. "All he said was he was glad I made it back onto the boat. We didn't address what happened or where either of us had been between getting back on board and going to sleep. I didn't really care, honestly. I probably didn't want to know the answer."

Scarlett's lip curled and she reached out, gently touching her upper arm. "I'm sorry, Lucy."

Lucy shook her head, clearing her throat. "It's fine," she said, her voice a little shaky. Scarlett met her eyes when she looked up and her heart shattered seeing the glassiness there. She just wanted to wrap her in her arms and never let go.

She also half-wondered how she could push Chris overboard and make it look like an accident.

Willing murderous thoughts away, the dark-haired woman squeezed Lucy's arm, then dropped her hand. "Try to have some fun between now and this afternoon. Then we can have some drinks and hide away from the world."

Lucy smiled and wiped at her cheeks with the back of her hand. "That's exactly what I need. You're the best."

"I try. But I do actually have to attempt to get some work done now. If Gavin comes by and sees I've been talking to the same person for fifteen minutes, he'll gut me."

"Gavin," Lucy scoffed, shaking her head. "What does Olive see in him anyway?" she asked, a teasing smile on her lips.

Scarlett mimicked her. "Far too much."

Lucy laughed, the sound spreading through Scarlett's veins, warming every icy corner she'd tried to abandon over the years. "Alright, I'll leave you to it," Lucy said. "By the way… are you allowed to exchange personal information with passengers?"

"No," Scarlett said, shaking her head.

Lucy sighed. "Let me rephrase. *Will you?*"

"Are you asking for my number?"

Lucy raised her eyebrow. "*Maybe*. But a social media page will work too," she said.

Scarlett smiled and gestured for her to take out her phone. Lucy opened up Instagram and went to the search bar, her thumbs hovering over the screen expectantly. "It's just my name," Scarlett said.

"Lame," Lucy muttered, typing it in. An account popped up and she flipped the phone screen around to face Scarlett. "This you?"

"That's me."

Lucy tapped on it and hit the blue 'follow' button, then tucked her phone away. "I expect a follow back at your earliest convenience, ma'am."

"How very posh of you," Scarlett teased. "When I'm off, I'll try to get on the Wi-Fi. It can be slow sometimes," she said.

Lucy smiled and lifted her cup in farewell to the woman. "See you soon. Have a good shift."

"Thanks," Scarlett responded. She watched her leave for a little *too* long.

Ugh. She was a bloody mess.

20

Carefully, Lucy folded up one of the white towels in front of her, then folded it again, and again, until it... *sort of* resembled an elephant.

She had taken the day for herself, or at least, she'd tried to. After she left Scarlett to focus on her work that morning, she had gone for a walk on the top deck of the ship and took photos of the pretty, glistening water surrounding them. They had another port day the next day, then they'd have one more day at sea, then they'd be back at home. She was a little sad the trip was already half-over, but she was thrilled she'd made a new friend. Or two, if she counted Olive.

She had bought the Wi-Fi package on the second day of the cruise, thinking if she wasn't going to be spending time with Chris the whole trip that she'd at least be able to keep herself busy. Or get in touch with him if she needed to find him. She doubted he'd ever want to find her.

She had been trying to take any route to avoid passing the casino when she could, purely because she wasn't sure she could handle *another* fight. She was at the point where she just didn't care if he wanted to go against her wishes and gamble all his money away.

Lucy looked down at her little elephant, then smiled to herself. This had been exactly what she needed. She had been at a loss at what to do other than eat or lay by the pool, but the second she saw 'Animal Towel-Folding Class' on the itinerary, she all but ran to the fifth floor where it was being held. One of her favorite parts about the trip, and something that eased her nerves a bit every time she returned to the stateroom, was the little towel animal perched perfectly in the middle of the bed. Perhaps being at the class was juvenile, given she was surrounded by kids and parents, but it was a nice respite from all the drama surrounding that boat. She pulled out her phone and took a few pictures from different angles.

Sadness began creeping into her body and try as she might, she wasn't quite able to shake it. Not even cute towel animals were enough to distract her from the inevitable implosion of her relationship. Though Chris annoyed her, she felt like she was mourning a death in the family. She wouldn't say she wasted *all* her time with him, because there had been multiple years of goodness, but… it was hard not to focus on all the bad that had been happening lately. Little things she overlooked once were piling up and driving her insane. It became more obvious with each day that he didn't *really* care about her, which broke her heart.

At the same time, she felt guilty. She knew, deep down, it wasn't her fault that Chris had no drive to better himself as a person. She knew it wasn't her fault that his parents had cut him off. She loved him and cared about him, and operated under the logic that it was her job to take care of her partner when things got difficult. But he was making no effort to make them easier. She wasn't sure if the roles were reversed that she could be complacent in her partner working themselves to the bone because she was too lazy to get a job or even *apologize* to her parents.

Her friends hardly even gave her advice anymore, and usually shut her down when she would text any group chat to complain. She knew it didn't come from a malicious place, and if she had someone complaining constantly about the same thing without doing something to fix it (like Chris) then she'd get fed up, too. Her friends loved her, and she knew that in her heart, but she wasn't quite ready to do the excruciating part of letting that man go.

When the class ended, Lucy gathered her little towel elephant and wandered back down to the lower deck where her cabin was. She ventured through the long hallway, sidestepping passing families who were either just waking up or changing into their swimsuits. Swiping her keycard, she opened the door and was surprised to see Chris in there still.

"Hey," Lucy said stiffly, letting the door swing shut behind her. "Didn't want to go check out the medieval trivia?"

"They had medieval trivia?" Chris whined as he looked up from his phone. "Damn it."

"Sorry to be the bearer of bad news," Lucy said with a laugh laced with no humor. "Just taking the day off, I guess?"

"Eh… Sort of. I didn't want to leave in case you came back."

"Why?" Lucy asked, setting her elephant down on the bed.

"Because— Is that an elephant made of towels?" Chris asked, pointing to the little bundle at the foot of the bed.

"Yeah," Lucy said, her smile growing. "I think I'll name her Ellie."

"Ellie the Elephant," Chris said, pushing himself to sit up completely. He reached out to pick it up, but it completely unraveled when he did so. His eyes widened and he looked at Lucy. "Uh…"

Lucy forced a smile and shook her head. "It's fine. I can fix her later. Why were you waiting around for me?"

She would not get upset. She would not get upset. She would not get upset.

"Well, we haven't really talked since you stormed off yesterday at that restaurant. Are you mad at me?"

Lucy blinked and took great effort in controlling her breathing. She swallowed any sarcastic response she *desperately* wanted to say, and instead went with, "I'm not currently *mad* at you, but I was upset yesterday. I feel under-appreciated. You know that. I've told you this a million times."

"I know," Chris said, his shoulders slumping. "I'm sorry."

She felt her chest constrict and a balloon swelled in her throat. He didn't apologize very much, but when he did, it was her weakness. She didn't know why, it wasn't like he ever *meant it*. He would apologize, be *really* perfect for two or three weeks, then slip back into whatever bad habits he had apologized for and swore to break. It was like clockwork. Every time she told him the next time they had that conversation, she would leave. But she always fucking stayed.

Why?

"What are you sorry for?" Lucy asked slowly, staring at him.

Chris stood up and walked over to her, taking her face in his hands. "I'm... sorry for not treating you like I should."

Lucy tried to fight the tears. "I need more than that."

Chris frowned, then wiped some tears from under her eyelids. "I'm sorry I asked you to edit my videos for me."

A shuddered breath came out of Lucy's parted lips and she gently shrugged out of his hold. "Okay."

"What?" Chris asked, dropping his arms by his sides. "Tell me what to do to fix this and I *will*."

"I don't want to *tell you*. I want you to just *know*," Lucy said, her voice quivering. "You always need me to *tell you* what to do. I have to tell you you need to clean something up, or that the trash piles up and *I* have to ask you to do it because you won't take it out on your own, or I have to remind you when my birthday is, or—"

"Okay, I get it," Chris snapped. "I'm not perfect, okay? *Sorry*. Why is it *me* that has to do all of the chores? Why do you have to ask me to take out the trash if it's piled up? You see it's piled up, *you* take it out."

"I *always* take it out!" Lucy shot back viciously, backing up from him. "I *see* it needs to be done so I do it. *You* see it piling up. You see laundry overflowing. You see the dryer full of clothes. You *see* everything, but you just go about your day because you know I'll be the one to take care of it. I'll *always* be there to save the day."

"I do a lot for you," Chris scoffed.

"I'm not *saying* you don't do anything for me."

"You're just saying it's not enough," he said, nodding. "I see."

"Christopher," Lucy sighed in defeat, bringing her fingertips up to press against her temples. "Why can't you just *love me*?"

"What?" Chris spluttered. "How could you say that? I *do* love you."

"You don't act like it," Lucy said, her voice small, weak. "I don't feel important to you. I always feel like an afterthought."

"You're *everything* to me. I don't know what I'd do without you," Chris said, stepping forward to pull her into his embrace. He hugged her close and kissed the top of her head. "I love you so much, Lucille."

Lucy laughed tearfully into his chest. She remembered when he'd found out what her full name was after he visited her parents' home the first time, and had always saved it for special occasions. She closed her eyes and hugged him tightly to her, trying to keep her sobbing at bay. "I'm so *sad*, Chris."

"I know," Chris said quietly. "I'm sorry."

Hearing him apologize again broke her heart even more, because it didn't give her the same relief it had in years past.

It just made her realize that she couldn't tell him she loved him, too.

"Let's go do something together. You and me," Chris said, rubbing her back. "Let's look at the itinerary and pick something you want."

Lucy pulled back and wiped her rosy cheeks. She had cried more on this cruise than she had in weeks. "Um... I actually have plans."

"What?" Chris asked. "What do you mean? With *who*?"

"With... Scarlett."

"Who's Scarlett?"

Lucy suddenly felt less... *bad* about everything. Here we go again.

"She's the art person I introduced you to the other day. Black hair, tall..."

"Oh," he said. "The rude one."

"She's not *rude*."

"She was *so* rude when I met her. She looked at me like she hated me."

"She doesn't hate you, she just..." Lucy trailed off, but it was too late.

"She just *what*?"

Lucy folded her arms and retained eye contact with Chris. "I was sad one of the times I saw her and she asked what was wrong. I told her I got into a fight with my boyfriend. Then she must have remembered that when she met you. It's just a girl looking out for me, that's all."

"Do you regularly tell strangers our business? What else does she know?"

"Calm *down*," Lucy said with a frown. "She doesn't know *anything*. I just confided in her. It wasn't even bad. I'm sorry—"

"And now you're going off to do *what* with her, exactly?"

"I think we're just going to have a few drinks, I haven't really..."

"So you're going to talk about me some more."

"*No*," Lucy lied. "Chris, listen, I just..." she trailed off again. She was *not* about to invite him along, despite feeling pressured to do so. He wouldn't intrude on that time with her. She was *allowed* to have other friends, especially when he was being so damn cruel to her.

"You complain constantly about me not treating you like you matter, and when I try to do something nice, you blow me off for some person you met a few days ago," Chris said, his tone rising angrily.

Lucy finally sighed and sunk down onto the bed. Her eyes were burning from the tears and her contacts. "I'm tired, Chris," she finally said, almost too soft to hear.

"What?" Chris asked, his arms folded. He leaned down and craned his neck toward her. "Speak up."

"I *said*, I'm tired," Lucy hissed, snapping her head up at him. "I'm tired of *this*. Of *us*."

Chris's face fell and he stood up straight. "What are you saying then?"

"I don't know," Lucy said, shaking her head. The words were *right there* on the tip of her tongue, but she couldn't bring herself to swing that axe down on their relationship and sever the tie forever. Not when they had to stay in the same room for a few more days.

"Do you want to break up?"

"No," Lucy answered automatically. Then she regretted it. "I don't know. I just know I'm *tired* of all the fighting. I want some space."

Chris nodded and looked at her for several painstaking seconds, then he snatched his wallet off the nearby table. "You got it."

Lucy winced as the door slammed behind him and she was left alone in the cabin again. Several minutes passed of her just... sitting on the bed, feeling numb. She wanted to cry, but no tears were coming out.

When she stood, she began pulling one edge of the bed. There was no goddamn way she was sleeping next to that *monster* tonight. She never wanted to sleep next to him ever again. It made her stomach turn with disgust.

When her half of the bed was in the furthest corner she could squeeze it into, she looked around. Now they really were just like roommates, completing the mental vision she'd had in her head of their relationship for months, *years* now.

Ding!

Lucy's attention turned to her phone, which was on the vanity, the screen lit up. Walking over, she picked it up and let out a relieved, tearful laugh.

SCARLETTSINCLAIR IS NOW FOLLOWING YOU.

She swiped on the notification and as she did so, a message came through on the app.

SCARLETTSINCLAIR

Hey! I just got off. Hopping in the shower then I'll be ready. See you soon, Lucy Goosey.

Lucy laughed again and wiped some tears that managed to fight their way from her eyes. Nobody had called her that name since elementary school. Leave it to Scarlett Fucking Sinclair to make her laugh when she felt like she wanted to die.

She stared down at the message, then sniffled. She wasn't

going to let *anything else* bring her down on what was supposed to be a *vacation*. She double-tapped Scarlett's sweet message, then locked her phone.

Looking toward the bathroom, she stared at it in thought, then she looked back at the open wardrobe next to the vanity. She began rifling through the hanging clothes, then pulled out a dress she'd been saving for one of the formal dinners. It was a black dress that hugged her curves and was low-cut. It stopped mid-thigh and she had a pair of black heels to go with it. She smiled to herself as she tilted it back and forth in her hands, the slight sparkles in the material glimmering in the dim cabin light.

Scarlett was someone who had made her *feel* important since they'd first started talking, and she deserved to get effort from her. Lucy wanted to get dressed up and look good, *feel* good, because that's what this was all about.

She hung the dress back up, then disappeared into the bathroom.

She was *excited*.

S carlett stared at herself in the vanity mirror, a tube of lipstick between her fingers. She had done her eye makeup dark and her hair was pin straight. It gleamed down her back, brushing against her exposed shoulders. She was wearing a sleeveless, black bodysuit and some high-waisted, light blue, ripped skinny jeans. She had some black combat boots on and a black belt around her hips.

Tattoos littered her skin, blossoming every inch with bright colors and designs. She kept herself covered up at work, per the policy, but took any chance she could *outside* of office hours to show them off. She had paid a great deal for them, she wanted people to see them. That was the whole point.

She had two sides to her: Professional Scarlett and Real Scarlett. Her professional side was on show most of the time — big smiles, handshakes, and hard work. But when she got a chance to let her hair down, she was bubbly, goofy, and loved to talk and dance *all* night.

Scarlett carefully swiped her dark red lipstick across her

mouth and rubbed her lips together, then pursed them at the mirror. Capping the lipstick, she stood up and looked at herself completely. Rotating on her toes, she glanced behind her, happy to see everything was sitting *just* right.

Sometimes she didn't feel very pretty. She used to not have that problem growing up, getting attention from all the boys, but after Raphael, she had had a hard time seeing *that* Scarlett anymore. She felt changed, jaded almost. Now she just leaned into her buttoned-up persona, but… it was nice to see that old version of her peeking out and beckoning her to have some fun.

She was 31 now and hoped she didn't *look it*. Deep down, she knew it wasn't *that* old, but without having a clue how old Lucy was, she felt self-conscious. She knew she couldn't be *that* much older than her, given she spoke about graduating from college recently, but… still.

Scarlett grabbed her phone and swore under her breath at the time. She would be a little late. Shit.

In a plume of earthy perfume, she was out the door and rushing down the hall.

Scarlett wandered into the piano bar, looking around. Spotting a mane of honeyed curls *just* over the heads of some people standing in the middle of the room, Scarlett waded through them. She didn't even have a chance to register what Lucy was wearing by the time she'd tapped her shoulder and the woman turned around.

A small breath hitched in Scarlett's throat as Lucy swiveled on her chair with a red, frozen drink in hand and a smile that silenced *every* demon in her head.

She was *resplendent*.

Her blonde waves were loose and tumbling over her shoulders, her eyelashes were longer than Scarlett had ever seen — or maybe noticed — and she was so close that Scarlett could count every freckle on those pretty, rosy cheeks. Her eyes roamed downward, noting how pretty the silver snake pendant against her neck was.

"Hey, you made it," Lucy said, interrupting her inspection. The woman laughed, a sound that made chills pucker beneath Scarlett's skin. Suddenly, Scarlett felt arms encircle her and pull her close. She let out a quiet huff and hugged Lucy back. She had no choice but to hyper-focus on the way her body felt against her, the way this little black dress clung to every *mouthwatering* curve of her body.

"Wow, you smell good," Lucy breathed into her neck, slowly pulling back.

Scarlett's hands gently trailed down Lucy's middle as they pulled back enough to look at each other. *Say something!* her mind pleaded with her, snapping her back to reality.

"You look amazing," Scarlett finally settled with.

Lucy grinned and nudged her. "No, *you*. I didn't say it yesterday, but your tattoos are *awesome*. You'll have to give me a tour before the night is done," she said, gently taking one of her arms to turn over each direction. "I don't have any tattoos. I'm scared it'll hurt."

"They *do* hurt," Scarlett laughed, feeling a little more relaxed. She had *not* been ready for this.

"See!" Lucy said, then she glanced back at the bar. "We

don't have to sit up here. I was just getting a drink while I waited."

"I'm sorry I was late. I hope you weren't here long."

"Nah," Lucy said, waving her hand. "You were only, like, a minute and a half late. Not that I was counting," she grinned. "Can I get you a drink? Please."

Scarlett nodded. "Yeah," she said, her voice catching just a bit. She was *really* out of practice. Damn.

"What do you want?"

"Uh…" she said, blinking a few times. She had to *tear* her gaze away from Lucy, the fog in her mind immediately dissipating once she did so. "Just a dry martini. Please."

"Do you want extra olives?" Lucy asked, turning her body fully to the bar. At Scarlett's silence, she looked over her shoulder. "Scar?"

"How did you know I like extra olives?" Scarlett asked. She could *not* handle this. This was a bad idea. She probably looked a *fool*.

Lucy merely smiled and shrugged. "Lucky guess."

When Lucy turned back to the bartender, Scarlett ran a shaky hand through her hair. Her heart was racing and she was suddenly overwhelmed. It wasn't like she often went out with passengers or *anyone*. She hadn't even slept with someone since… almost a year ago. She hadn't even really *dated* in even longer, since before Raphael. Nothing had been like Raphael.

She then stopped that line of thinking. This *wasn't* a date. They were just two women getting a drink. Two women getting a drink and ignoring the fact that one of them had a shitty boyfriend that the other one loathed.

Scarlett sighed almost silently and looked up as Lucy handed her a *very* full drink. "Thanks," she said. Scanning the room, she saw a small, corner booth across the room. "Want to go sit over there?"

Lucy turned and followed her line of sight. "Perfect."

The women walked to the opposite side of the room and sank onto the dark brown cushioned seat together. Their thighs were pressed against each other in the close confines, but neither woman made a move to put any distance between them. Scarlett sipped her drink, *very* much needing some help with her courage. She had *never* felt so nervous for something that *wasn't* a date before.

"I love your outfit," Lucy complimented, holding her straw between two fingers as she took another big sip of her daiquiri. "Do you sing in a rock band, too?"

Scarlett laughed, her shoulders widening just a bit. She leaned back against the hard wood of the booth and shook her head. "I wish. But thank you. That dress is stunning," she said.

"Thanks," Lucy said. If the lighting weren't so poor, Scarlett would have sworn she blushed. She put it down to her imagination. Wishful thinking.

"Did you have a good day? What did you do?" Scarlett asked. Lucy told her all about walking along the deck, taking photos, her towel class, then... she hesitated. The dark-haired woman frowned and leaned a little closer. "What's going on? Was it him?"

"Yeah," Lucy said, her voice wavering and her eyes watering.

Scarlett frowned and set her drink down, then scooted closer to her. She hugged her against her. She could *feel* the tension in Lucy's body. "You don't have to hold it in," she murmured into her hair. "It's okay to cry. It's necessary."

"I just *hate* crying over him," Lucy said sadly. "I'm so sick of it."

Scarlett nodded. "I know the feeling."

"You do?" Lucy asked, moving so she could look at Scarlett.

"I do," Scarlett smiled sadly, bringing her hand up to brush a few tears away from Lucy's face. "My ex-boyfriend made me cry all the time. So much that I ran away from home and started a life at sea."

"Really? *That's* why you took this job?"

"Yep," she said, picking up her drink. This story could not be told sober. "He was my first serious boyfriend. I'd had some flings here and there, but nobody I could ever say I *loved*. Then Raph — Raphael — came into work and hired me to design the inside of this new home he was building. We hit it off and once the job was done, we started dating. But… he changed," she said, her eyes distant. "We dated for five years. We lived together, he supported me financially, despite my job being good. Thank *God* I was clever and put money into my savings during that time. I shouldn't have let myself become so dependent on him, because he used it against me when things got tough. He just became… irritable, cruel," she said, a deep frown etching her features. "He would start putting me down every time I wanted to go out with my friends. He'd call me a slag, tell me I'd cheat on him so why bother trying anymore; just vile stuff," she said, shaking her head.

"My final straw was when things became physical," she said. Lucy placed a hand over hers on her thigh, and she squeezed it instinctively. It wasn't enough to bring her back to the present. She was *right* back in London.

"He…" she started again, then swallowed thickly.

"You don't have to talk about it," Lucy reassured.

"It's alright," Scarlett said, shaking her head ever so slightly. "Wow, I realize now I've never actually… said this to anyone out loud before."

"Scarlett…" Lucy said sadly, squeezing her hand even tighter. "You're safe now. He can't hurt you anymore."

Scarlett's chestnut eyes brimmed with tears and she shifted her gaze to Lucy, who was also on the verge of crying. Scarlett's lower lip quivered and she closed her eyes, droplets falling onto their joined hands. It was Lucy's turn to pull Scarlett into her arms and hold her while she cried.

After several long seconds, Scarlett's breathing evened out, and she just… sat there in Lucy's embrace. The only sounds humming through the room were people talking, drinks shaking behind the bar, and the pianist calling out on the microphone to different people for requests.

"When are we going to get through one meeting without one of us crying over a boy?" Lucy then asked, causing Scarlett to burst out laughing. Lucy stroked a hand down the back of Scarlett's head, then retreated so they could still be close, but see each other. "I know we only just met, but… I think we were *supposed* to meet."

"Me, too," Scarlett breathed. She was so *close*.

"Hey! You two girls have any requests?"

Scarlett jumped so bad at the loud voice coming from the speaker system that she actually bumped heads with Lucy. She and Lucy mutually groaned and put their hands up to their foreheads.

"Sorry about that! Didn't mean to spook you!" the pianist called out. "I'll play whatever you want, on the house."

"Ugh…" Scarlett groaned, rubbing her head. "Any ideas?"

Lucy brought her hand back down and sucked down the rest of her strawberry drink. "Come on. I know the perfect song." She dragged Scarlett to her feet and kept hold of her hand as they walked to the other side of the bar where the piano was. Lucy let go of Scarlett's hand momentarily and leaned over to the pianist, murmuring something in his ear. When she came back, she stepped close to Scarlett, close enough where she could smell her shampoo.

"What'd you pick?" Scarlett asked.

"You'll see," Lucy said, smiling as the keys started up.

It took Scarlett less than two seconds to recognize the tune. Her eyes widened and she looked at Lucy. They were eye-level now thanks to Lucy's heels and Scarlett's *lack* of heels. "'Home Sweet Home?' I *love* Mötley Crüe."

"Do you?" Lucy asked with a grin. "I'm just making lucky guesses left and right tonight, aren't I? Do you want to dance?"

"Yes," Scarlett answered immediately. They melded into each other's arms and began stepping, a few wolf-whistles and whoops coming from some people around them.

They danced together like there was nobody else in the room. The two women fell into step, blending together so perfectly, Scarlett wasn't sure where she stopped and Lucy began. Her heart raced as they spun each other around and dissolved into fits of giggles against each other.

Scarlett felt so *happy*.

ucy laughed with Scarlett as she held her close. Their song had come to a close, but the musician next to them seemed to support their little... *whatever* this was, and kept the slower vibes going with 'Purple Rain' by Prince. Soon enough, she and Scarlett were swaying together, singing the chorus at the top of their lungs.

Lucy had done her homework before showing up to the bar. As she'd been getting ready, she had all but stalked Scarlett's social media profile, which could have been seen as creepy, but she was just trying to score some cool points with her. She had seen pictures of her at concerts, with drinks containing multiple olives in hand, with friends, at different ports. She seemed so *amazing*, and she had wanted to impress her.

It seemed to have worked, at least.

Scarlett had just... taken Lucy's breath away the second she made eye contact with her. She had gotten up to hug her simply because she couldn't contain herself. She looked so effortlessly cool, and Lucy was jealous of *all* sides of her, both personal and professional. She was put together all the time, which had shocked her to find out she had such a turbulent past. Her packing her bags and fleeing London made all the sense in the world now, and she didn't even know the finer details. She could make fair guesses, but forcing Scarlett to relive that trauma wasn't doing anybody any favors. All she needed to know was it had been *bad*.

"I like your glasses," Scarlett said over the music as they continued lazily swaying together.

"Oh, thanks," Lucy said with a smile, adjusting them against the bridge of her nose at the compliment. She was wearing simple big, square, black frames. "My contacts were hurting my eyes. Too much crying, I guess," she teased, rolling her eyes skyward.

"That'll do it," Scarlett laughed. "You look beautiful either way."

"You're full of compliments," Lucy smiled, then narrowed her eyes. "Are *you* just trying to get more olives out of me?"

"Am I that transparent?"

Lucy laughed and shook her head, then sighed deeply. Being close to Scarlett was stirring up feelings within her she hadn't felt since… high school.

She had been on the soccer team for her school as a ninth grader, but had played for a few years in a city league growing up before that. It had been her first time on her *school's* team. She had felt so cool, and had been so excited for the season to start up. She had been the goalie and things were *fine* up until their first game.

Before that, during practice, she hadn't changed with the

other girls. Her mom or dad had always been there to pick her up after practice (which they watched every time) and she had showered and changed at home. However, after her first game, the coach had wanted them all in the locker room to congratulate them on their win. All the other girls started changing, so she had too. It wasn't like it was a big deal, right?

Wrong. So fucking wrong.

There were some older girls on the team and they started changing, and Lucy had felt awkward about just being in her bra and panties around her teammates, despite them all being her friends. A group of older girls had stripped down to use the showers.

Shame flooded Lucy's body when she realized she had been *staring* at them. Thankfully, nobody had been paying attention to her and she had quickly thrown on a change of clothes and dashed out of the locker room.

She also quit the soccer team the next day.

After that, she had tried to just focus on boys, like a *normal* girl. She hadn't wanted to be called any names or be bullied. She had finally started to grow into herself, and had blossomed from an ugly duckling into a beautiful young woman. She started doing her hair, her makeup, focusing on her outfits, and garnered attention from boys she hadn't had before.

It helped her forget, but *every* now and then she would think about those girls and how she had felt warm all over.

It was that same feeling now with Scarlett.

Lucy came back to Earth and looked at the woman plastered against her body. "Guess what."

"What?" Scarlett asked.

"They're showing a movie on the pool deck tonight. Maybe we could go watch it."

Scarlett smiled. "Which film?"

"No idea. But I can almost guarantee it's not *Titanic*," she laughed, Scarlett chuckling with her.

"Sounds fun. Let's go. Do you want to grab a drink to take with us?"

"Yeah, I can get it," Lucy offered, going back to the bar. She felt so giddy, it was electrifying.

Lucy walked up to the pool deck with Scarlett, drinks in hand. The stars were so *beautiful* that night; the pollution was so heavy back at home that she never got to see them like this. They were endlessly lighting up the sky.

"There are two chairs up there," Scarlett pointed to another deck up. In a small, secluded area there were two lone chairs on a platform.

"Perfect," Lucy said. They wouldn't be disturbed.

They climbed the steps together and settled in the chairs, their drinks on the table between them. Lucy looked at the screen, which just had a generic picture of the cruise line's logo: a simple design with three, squiggly blue lines to represent waves, and a few glistening stars around them. It wasn't *quite* time for the movie, but it didn't matter, Lucy would happily find a way to fill the waiting period.

"Do you think you'll do this forever? Cruising?" Lucy asked, folding her hands over her stomach. She had grabbed a towel on her way up and had it draped over her legs — the wind was a *little* chilly without the sun to warm her up in that dress.

"I don't think so," Scarlett said, shrugging. She turned on her side and propped her head up on the heel of her hand. "Honestly, I'm kind of scared to go back. I don't know what I'd do. I don't think I could go back to interior design."

"What about art?" Lucy asked. "Surely you could be a curator or something at a big museum?"

"Maybe," Scarlett responded. "But... I worry *he* will find me."

"You're *really* scared of him, aren't you?" Lucy frowned, turning over to face her. She pulled the towel up more on her hips so she didn't flash anything. "I'm so sorry someone makes you feel that way. It's evil. Do you think he knows you work on a cruise ship?"

"Probably," Scarlett said. "But there are so many different ships for this company. I move to different ones almost every time. It's not often I stay on the same boat twice in a row. So it would be somewhat difficult for him to figure out which one I'm on. I have a restraining order against him. But I don't think he'd care about following that. His parents could make any charge just... disappear."

"I hate people like that," Lucy said, shaking her head. "Ones that think they can just do whatever they want in life because they have money. What is your family like?"

Scarlett smiled. "My mum is a kind woman. She had me when she was a bit older, and it's just me. No siblings. She's called Ava. My dad's a stocky bloke, but kind. He looks a little scary but he's really just a big teddy bear. He's called Thomas."

"They sound nice. They have to be if they made you," Lucy complimented. "And they live in London?"

"Nearby, yeah. What about your family?"

"My family doesn't live in London."

"*Lucy.*"

The blonde grinned, sticking her tongue between her teeth, then she spoke, "My mom and dad live in Daytona Beach. It's about an hour outside of Orlando. I have one sister, she's younger. My mom's name is Claire, my dad's name is Sam, and my sister's name is Laura."

"Lucy and Laura," Scarlett teased in a sing-song voice.

"That's us," Lucy laughed.

"Do you get along with your family?"

"Oh yeah," Lucy said, nodding adamantly. "I mean, not always with my sister, but that's a given. But my mom's my best friend. I tell her everything."

"What does she think about the whole Chris situation?"

Lucy sighed deeply and turned on her back, staring up at the night sky. The movie hummed to life in front of them, but she couldn't be bothered to pay attention. "She… doesn't approve. She liked him at first, we *all* did, but she doesn't like how unhappy I am. She tells me I deserve better."

"Clever woman."

Lucy smiled sadly and continued looking at the stars, the moon. "Yeah… I don't know. It's hard. I've given six years of my life to this man. I feel like I'm giving up on a chunk of myself if I leave."

"He does *not* equal *you*," Scarlett said firmly. "You have *so much* more life to live. How old are you?"

"Twenty-five."

"Oh, God," Scarlett laughed. "You've got *plenty* of time! Honestly, if you're not dumping your long-term shitty boyfriend in your mid-twenties, you're doing it wrong."

Lucy laughed quietly and shook her head. "How did you know when it was time to leave?"

It was Scarlett's turn to roll on her back and look at the sky. "Well… aside from the black eyes…" she trailed off, waving away the apologetic noise that came from the woman next to her, "I just got tired of feeling like shit. I found a way out. I got accepted into this job and ran away without looking back. I felt trapped up until then. My friends told me I was hollow compared to *before* Raphael. I suppose that door opening to *freedom* was what gave me the courage to take a leap of faith," she murmured.

Lucy listened to her intently, her heart lurching. She swallowed, soaking in every word she said. "Were you scared?" she asked quietly.

"Of *course* I was scared. I'm still scared," Scarlett laughed softly. She laced her fingers on her stomach like Lucy did. "Not only scared of whether he'll find me, but scared of life in general. I'm in my thirties now and I don't have anyone to settle down with. I don't have a plan. This *isn't* what I thought my life would be ten years ago, even *five* years ago. I love traveling and I love finding myself, but… I miss having someone to do it all with. I don't know if that makes me sound clingy or needy, but…"

"It doesn't. I get it," Lucy said. "That's exactly how I feel. Chris and I have been attached at the hip for over half a decade, and now it's becoming real that one day… we probably won't be anymore. And that terrifies me, just because I don't remember what life was like before him, without him. Obviously I know I would be okay, but… it's difficult to imagine something you've never really experienced before."

"I understand," Scarlett said. "But you're right. You *will* be okay. Take it from someone whose life was practically destroyed in front of her, you *will* recover. You just have to be brave enough to get yourself out. Because he's never going to change. They *never* change, Lucy."

"That's what I'm most afraid of," the blonde said. "He promises to be better but… he never is. Not permanently, anyway."

"Raph said the same thing. He wouldn't hurt me anymore, he didn't mean it, he loved me," she said, then fake gagged. "Makes me sick to even think about it now. I was such a fool. I look back on all the shit I put up with and don't even *recognize* that poor girl. I'd never put up with it today."

"Yeah," Lucy said. "I have always tried to be strong, independent, and I guess in some ways, I *am*. I pay for my apartment, the utilities, the groceries, I have my career, I'm *good* at it… the only part that's lacking is my relationship. I just want to be the girl that has everything figured out."

"It's *okay* to not be though," Scarlett said, lolling her head to the side to look at her. Lucy met her gaze and smiled weakly. "I promise you, you aren't worth any less just because you don't know what next year holds, or next month, or even tomorrow," Scarlett said.

"Thanks," Lucy said softly. "I'm thankful for you, Scarlett."

Scarlett smiled back at her. "I'm thankful for you, too, Lucy."

Lucy's heart soared at those words. This date-that-wasn't-a-date was the most *perfect* outing she'd ever had with anyone. Chris had been sweet on their first date and had taken them to a nice Italian restaurant, then a movie she'd been talking about wanting to see. It hadn't been anything overly flashy or complicated, but it was enough for her when she was nineteen.

Lucy was busy trying to memorize every inch of Scarlett's face when she broke the short silence. "We've missed most of the film. I don't even know what it was," Scarlett laughed, nodding to the big screen that had some action going on.

Lucy turned to look at the screen and shrugged her shoulders. "I literally have no clue. Doesn't seem like something I'd be interest—"

A loud *boom!* cut Lucy off and made her yelp. An explosion happened within the film and startled her. She breathed deeply and looked down, her hand somehow laced with Scarlett's. "Sorry," she panted. "I hate loud noises, I didn't expect that. Number one reason why I'm *not interested* in action movies."

"I'll protect you from the loud noises, don't worry," Scarlett said, cupping one of Lucy's ears with her free hand. The women dissolved into giggles and leaned against each other, their chairs touching.

They never dropped hands.

23

"You know, I think the arcade is still open," Lucy said. They had since moved from sitting in the chairs to walking around the top deck. It had grown a little too chilly and they wanted to get some blood flowing.

Scarlett looked over at the woman and smirked. "You gonna try and win me something, Lucy Price?"

"*Maybe*, Scarlett Sinclair," Lucy giggled. "If you play your cards right."

Scarlett's smirk morphed into a big smile and she squeezed Lucy's hand, which was still nestled firmly against hers. "Let's go."

Painstakingly, they had to drop each other's hands when they got down to the lower decks. Scarlett mourned the loss of contact, but knew it was the safest option. They had no clue if they'd run into Chris, and the *last* thing Lucy needed was fuel for the fire her boyfriend stoked every day. Scarlett was happy to settle in close beside Lucy as they walked, though, and it only took a few minutes for them to get down to the fifth deck where the arcade was.

"You know, I always want to stop in here every time I come see you at your little table," Lucy confessed while walking through the lit up doorway that led to a bunch of brightly colored and loud gaming machines.

"Why don't you?" Scarlett asked, following her. She was trying to remain a perfect lady and *not* check Lucy out from behind as they walked, but she was failing spectacularly.

"Eh, I don't know," Lucy shrugged. "Not as much fun when you're by yourself, I guess."

"Well, you have me now," Scarlett said, moving to take her hand again.

Lucy smiled and glanced at her, her freckled cheeks rosy yet again. Scarlett found she *loved* making her blush. They shared a few precious moments looking at each other, as if the other would blow away in an instant.

"Which one do you want to play?" Scarlett finally asked, tearing her gaze from Lucy's to look around. "Lots to choose from."

"Oh, I don't know," Lucy sighed deeply, turning on her heel to take a full survey of the room. There were a few claw machines filled with different toys: stuffed animals, mini basketballs, rubber ducks, wads of tickets, even some folds of cash. Scattered throughout were different skill games that had prizes like cell phones, drones, underwater cameras, gaming consoles, headphones, and pretty much anything else that would normally cost half a grand. Filling the leftover space were normal arcade games like racing, ball throwing, spin-the-wheels, shooting, and dancing.

"Can I tell you something… embarrassing?" Scarlett asked as they walked through the small room so Lucy could pick.

"Of course," Lucy said, squeezing her hand with both words.

"I've always had this stupid fantasy of, like… someone winning a stuffed animal for me. Isn't that just so childish? I grew up watching a lot of American films and seeing the guy win a little bear for the girl after throwing a ball at some milk bottles always made me smile. I thought real life would be like that, that *dating* would be like that, all happy and filled with surprise stuffed animals but… obviously I was wrong."

Lucy stopped their pacing and she turned to face Scarlett. Scarlett's heart was in her throat. The other woman spoke. "That's not embarrassing at all. I actually had a similar fantasy growing up. I *did* go to those fairs you see in the movies and I'd see the older kids winning stuff for their boyfriends or girlfriends. I couldn't *wait* to grow up and have that be me. Not exactly how it worked out, but," Lucy laughed softly, "I still had a good time. Chris has never done anything like that for me before. I mean, he's bought me things, of course, and I love a stuffed animal as much as the next girl, but we've never even been to the fair or carnival together."

"Why not? They just not come to town or something?"

"No, Orlando has a pretty big one. There are also games like this at the theme parks. Guess he just never really was into that sort of thing. We did other fun stuff, but… now that I think about it, it would've been nice to do something like that."

Butterflies swarmed Scarlett's stomach. She let go of Lucy's hand and tried not to feel too hopeful at the disappointed look on the blonde's face. The way her fringe fell against her pretty, dark eyebrows just above her eyelashes was driving her crazy with desire. She was determined to run her hand through those locks and bring her head exactly where she wanted it.

"Let's fulfill a couple fantasies right now then," Scarlett said.

Lucy jerked her head over to Scarlett. "What?" she spluttered.

Scarlett barely had time to remind herself *not* to look smug. "Win each other something."

"Oh," Lucy breathed, that blush creeping up on her face again. "Yeah, that sounds perfect. Fun. Yes. Great."

Scarlett laughed under her breath at Lucy all of a sudden being flustered. Good. That's how she wanted her to be. "I'm pretty good at the claw machine."

"Bet you I'm better."

"Is that a challenge, blondie?"

Lucy grinned and scrunched her nose. Oh, Scarlett loved that, too. Very much. "Yep. Sure is, brunettie. Let's go. I'll tell you which one I want."

They walked to the machine filled with small, stuff animals: dogs, cats, cows, pandas, pigs, monkeys, and more Scarlett couldn't quite make out near the bottom.

"I want the monkey," Lucy announced, poking her finger against the glass of the game.

"You like monkeys?" Scarlett asked. She would have pegged her as... well, as an anything-else-girl.

"Yep, ever since I was little. They're my favorite land animal."

"What's your favorite non-land animal then?"

"Hammerhead shark. Obviously."

"Obviously," Scarlett laughed, rolling her eyes.

"What about you?"

"I've never really thought about my favorites. Land or otherwise."

"So think about it now. Everyone has a favorite animal. What do you like when you go to the zoo?"

"Never been to the zoo."

"*What?!*"

"Yeah, yeah," Scarlett said, waving her hand dismissively. "Spare me."

"There aren't zoos in England?!"

"We have zoos in England, of course, I just never went to one as a child or as an adult. I wanted to, but it never worked out, I suppose."

"We need to change that immediately," Lucy scoffed. "Okay, back to the issue at hand: favorite animal?"

"Hmm," Scarlett hummed, tapping her chin with her index finger. "I'd have to say… a giraffe."

Lucy twinkled. "A giraffe!"

"Should I pick again?"

"No! Giraffes are perfect, just like you."

Now it was Scarlett's turn to blush. She cleared her throat and got them back on track. "As far as non-land animal… the Loch Ness Monster."

"That doesn't *count*," Lucy moaned.

"Does too. You can't prove it's not an animal."

"You can't prove it *at all*."

"Touché," Scarlett smirked. "Okay, fine. Fine. An alligator."

"That's *technically* still a land animal."

"No way. They swim in water. That counts."

"Okay, fine, it counts," Lucy conceded. She looked into the claw machine and grinned, jabbing her finger against the glass once more. "Ah, look. There's an alligator. I'm gonna win it for you."

"Not a chance," Scarlett huffed. "It's wedged between all those other ones."

"Just watch and learn, Sinclair," Lucy teased, reaching into her little black clutch purse. She pulled out her cruise card and swiped it against the machine's reader. The game whirred to life, music and all, and a countdown began below the joystick. Lucy quickly took hold of the red knob atop the small stick and moved the claw across the machine until it hovered above the general area the alligator was stuck in. Scarlett shook her head as Lucy moved around the entire machine to get every angle she could.

"Time's almost up," Scarlett reminded.

"Shh, in the zone," Lucy muttered, before coming back to the front of the machine. She tapped the joystick to the left a *hair*, then pressed the big red button beside it. The claw descended and fit *perfectly* between the other animals, its arms sliding down and under the alligator. The claw closed around the alligator and excavated it from its stuffing-filled tomb. Scarlett watched in awe as the soft, little green reptile rose into the air, moved a short distance across the machine, and down into the square-shaped chute to its new home. Lucy leaned down and pulled it out, holding it up triumphantly at her. "Aha! See! Fantasy granted."

Scarlett didn't even know what to say. Not only were Lucy's claw machine skills impressive, it was also such a *nice* effort. She hadn't a clue what possessed her to confide in this woman about that silly dream she forgot she had, but she made her feel safe. She brought out the best sides of her, the sides Scarlett had nearly abandoned.

For the first time in years, Scarlett felt like she could be free again.

"Thank you," Scarlett gushed, taking the little gator from her. "He's so cute."

"It's a boy?"

"Mmm, you're right. No boys allowed. What shall we call *her*?"

"You pick. She's *your* alligator," Lucy grinned.

Scarlett laughed softly and looked down at her. "Lucy."

"I do *not* look like an alligator."

"I don't know, in this light…" Scarlett started, arching a brow and giving her a once over. Lucy nudged her and they both dissolved into giggles. "Seriously. Is that lame?"

"Not lame. Lucy Junior. I like it," Lucy said, giving her a thumbs-up.

"Now you'll be with me wherever I go," Scarlett smiled. Lucy blinked a few times, those pretty, long eyelashes fluttering. She was a vision. "Okay," Scarlett sighed, looking around the stuffed animals inside the machine, "time to win your monkey."

"Good luck," Lucy said with a laugh, looking into the machine as well. "That one seems easy enough." She pointed to a blue monkey perched near the top by itself. "Or is that too difficult for your mad skills?"

"I'll show you mad skills," Scarlett muttered, taking her small, black wallet from the back pocket of her jeans. She pulled out a five-dollar bill and fed it into the machine.

"You don't get a cruise card? I didn't even know we could pay for stuff with cash," Lucy said.

"Nah." Scarlett focused on moving the claw where she wanted once the timer started. "Our wages are low but we get room and board and most meals covered. We don't get to go gorge ourselves on free champagne or anything, but we can go to the buffets or restaurants on the upper deck and get meals. I put on a stone when I first started working here. The gym became my best friend." She surveyed the perimeter of the machine like Lucy had done and when she was confident with her location, she pressed the button and down went the claw. It picked up the monkey, but the little animal fell through the arms when it was halfway to the top. Scarlett groaned and waited for the claw to reset itself so she could go again.

"You have some more tries, it's okay," Lucy reassured. "How much is a stone?"

"Eh… six kilos?"

"Okay…"

"You are *painfully* American," Scarlett laughed. "I dunno, like… fifteen pounds or something close to that. I'm fit again now though."

"Very fit."

Scarlett gave Lucy a *look* that was interrupted by the claw going down toward the animals in the middle. Scarlett swore under her breath at the waste of a try, then she nudged Lucy with her elbow. "No more distracting me! I'm trying to be a perfect gentleman and win you your damn monkey."

Lucy rested her chin on Scarlett's shoulder and purred in her ear, "What if I don't want a perfect gentleman?"

Scarlett exhaled shakily and felt her vision go for *just* a second. She shrugged Lucy off her and forced herself to focus on the game. "You will be the death of me, Lucy Goosey."

Lucy's warm laugh coated Scarlett's bones as the other woman pulled back and kept a safe distance of half a foot from her. "Okay, okay, sorry. No more distractions. Show me whatcha got."

Scarlett exhaled again and made another go at winning the monkey. This time, when the claw dropped, it hugged around the monkey and brought the blue, toy primate up, up, up, and finally around to the square chute. The toy dropped down and Scarlett immediately bent over to snatch it out. With a triumphant noise, she presented it to Lucy. "Your monkey, my lady."

"Why, thank you, perfect gentleman," Lucy teased, curtsying a little as she wrapped her hand around the monkey. "I suppose she'll be Scarlett Junior?"

"I mean, it *is* a great name," Scarlett said innocently.

"They make a cute pair," Lucy grinned, holding Scarlett Junior up to Lucy Junior. Real Scarlett smiled to herself and *almost* made the alligator give the monkey a little peck on the mouth, but decided against it. Despite the blatantly obvious flirting Lucy was torturing her with, Scarlett still felt nervous.

"Thanks for indulging me," Scarlett murmured as they left

the arcade.

"Of course," Lucy said. "You have to take Lucy Junior all over the world with you, no exceptions. Lucy Senior doesn't get to travel much so I'll have to live vicariously through her."

"Deal." Scarlett looked down at the little green alligator and felt overwhelmed with happiness.

"We should take a picture with them together. To document this," Lucy said with a smile, reaching into her little clutch for her phone. She pulled out the device and opened up the camera app, then handed it to Scarlett. "Your arms are longer."

Scarlett took the phone and stretched it out in front of them. Both women held up their new stuffed companions and smiled. Scarlett tapped the circle at the bottom of the screen a few times, then pulled a funny face that made Lucy dissolve into laughter. Scarlett kept taking as many pictures as possible, even when they were both just laughing and looking at each other rather than focusing on selfies. Slowly, Scarlett handed Lucy's phone back to her. "Send those to me?"

"Okay," Lucy said as she looked down and idly began scrolling through them. "I'll edit the good ones—"

"No," Scarlett said, placing a hand on her arm. "I want *all* of them. Please. Edited or no."

Lucy smiled and nodded, clicking her phone dark. "Okay. Whatever you want. Promise."

Scarlett and Lucy talked until *late* into the night after the arcade, just wandering various parts of the ship. It was nearly one in the morning by the time they decided to part ways.

They walked to the elevator together and both women stalled in the holding area between all the elevators instead of going in one.

"I'm glad we got to know each other more. This is the most fun I've had in a long time," Scarlett murmured as she looked into Lucy's cobalt eyes.

Lucy beamed. It was the kind of smile that made Scarlett's insides melt. "Me, too. Thanks for taking my mind off everything. I'm… sad that I'm leaving in a few days."

Scarlett's stomach lurched. Her face fell for a moment, then she swiftly recovered. "I know. But we have each other on socials. We dock in Orlando all the time. When you leave the ship at the end of the week, it won't be the last time we see each other. I promise."

"You better," Lucy grinned, reaching over to squeeze Scarlett's arm. "I should probably head back. Me and Scarlett Junior are tired."

"Yeah, it's late. Scarlett Junior needs her beauty sleep, and *you* have a port day filled with fun tomorrow."

"Maybe," Lucy sighed, rolling her eyes. "What are you doing tomorrow?"

"Nothing *remotely* fun," Scarlett muttered. "Until I find a way to see you again."

Lucy blushed. It made Scarlett want to squirm. "Goodnight, Scarlett."

"Goodnight, Lucy." Scarlett watched her step into the elevator, but she didn't follow. The doors closed on Lucy waving at her, then Scarlett stood there for just a few moments in a daze. She looked down at Lucy Junior and decided to go for another walk around the ship instead of returning to her room. She was far too wired to sleep and she wasn't quite ready to share how wonderful the night had been to Olive if she was still awake.

Scarlett went back up to the top deck, ignoring the bite of the wind. She pulled her hair around one side and leaned against the railing of the ship, the water pitch black beneath the boat. She had one hand *tight* on the little alligator, not wanting it to fly overboard. It was a beautifully clear night, the water was calm and the ship was steady. There were days when rough seas made it difficult for her to get comfortable in her room or even standing in the gallery, but conditions like this almost made her forget she was on a boat to begin with.

She wondered if she should have made a move on Lucy. Somehow, it didn't feel right. They were only *just* getting to know each other. She didn't want to move too fast, and there was the *little* problem of Chris Ford to deal with. Scarlett never wanted to pressure Lucy, despite all the flirting they'd done. It was driving her insane, thinking back over every little detail from the night. Maybe Lucy was just being a good friend. Maybe she was just a *good* person.

Scarlett felt no better than a man when she thought about that beautiful woman. Could she not be friends with someone without wanting to shag them?

Well, she was friends with Olive and had never once thought about shagging her. Maybe she was a *little* better than a man.

Right now, she knew Lucy needed a *friend* more than anything. And she was determined to be that for her. If someone had come leering after her following her break up with Raphael, she would have pushed them far away. She *never* wanted Lucy to push her away.

Scarlett thought about going home, back to London. It made her want to vomit, not because she hated where she came from, but because the risk of running into Raphael or any of his friends or family made her sick with worry. She missed *her* family though, *her* friends. She kept up with them almost exclusively through social media. Every time she saw a post of her girls at a bar they used to love, or doing another bottomless brunch, she mourned her former life. Her mum would send her pictures of their family dog doing something adorable, or her dad would tell her something funny her mum did, and it made Scarlett want to cry with loss. She *hated* that she let a man drive her to isolation. She liked to think she had healed for the most part, and maybe someday soon she'd be able to go back, but... it still freaked her out.

She still hadn't signed her contract renewal for DreamWave. Something was holding her back, and the closer she grew to Lucy, the more she wanted to get off the boat and resume her life as a normal person. A perpetual holiday was nice for a time, and had been exactly what she needed after leaving London, but her life was changing now. Her *needs* were changing.

The feelings she was developoing for Lucy were swallowing her.

It scared her.

As she had told Olive, she had never seriously been with a woman. She had hooked up with a few friends back in uni when she'd been under the influence, and it hadn't been much more than some drunken kisses and *maybe* some foreplay, but it had never been anything *meaningful* as Olive had commented. As the years went by after Raphael's departure from her life, she felt more comfortable sliding into her sexuality. Honestly, after Raphael, she had *no* interest being with a man beyond a one-night fling ever again. She had slept with one of the tour guides on an island DreamWave frequented *once* and had felt so disgusted with herself afterward. Not that there was anything wrong with one-night stands, she just… didn't feel like that was *her*. She craved a connection, a *relationship* with someone. She wanted a partner, not someone to warm her bed and leave the next morning.

There had been a few other people that caught her eye — usually another worker or maybe a passenger — but nothing ever stuck. It never went further than a passing fancy. Usually her mind was swiftly occupied with something to do with work immediately after. Scarlett was far too guarded to let anyone in. Yet, when Lucy came along, her walls crumbled down almost immediately. She felt *safe* with her. Perhaps it was a savior complex on Scarlett's part, wanting to save the poor girl from becoming trapped in a life Scarlett had barely clawed her way out of. Scarlett hadn't wanted to assume, but it was difficult to ignore Lucy's body language around her, and she wanted so desperately to believe Lucy felt the same way about her: *safe*.

As much as Scarlett wanted there to be *more* between her and Lucy, wanted them to not be trapped on a boat and able to do this *properly*, she couldn't risk wilting the budding flowers of friendship that were growing between them. This felt far too important and whatever Lucy needed from her, she would provide.

God, she just hoped the woman still wanted to talk to her when she was long gone from the ship and back home with Chris. She prayed to anything that would listen that she didn't forget about her the moment she stepped back onto Orlando soil.

ucy returned to the room after her night with Scarlett and thankfully, Chris hadn't been there. She didn't know *where* he'd been, but she had gone to sleep alone and woken up alone.

Relief flooded her.

She got ready for the final port day by throwing on a shorter, light green dress with yellow flowers on it. It stopped just above her knee, and she completed the look with a pair of white sandals and Cruise Lucy's signature floppy, white hat. Grabbing her sunglasses (green, of course) and small, brown clutch purse, she was out the door and ready to take on the beach.

They had excursions planned, but Lucy hadn't wanted to risk running into Chris. She couldn't take another fight. She couldn't take another *anything* with him.

The blonde debarked the ship and made the trek down the walkway to the port. She didn't feel safe exploring on her own, so she decided to just stay in the touristy areas nearby and not go too far. Not that Chris was any kind of bodyguard, and she couldn't even think of a time he had ever defended her from cat-calls or even just a rude guy at a bar, so it wasn't like this was a *huge* change. Even still, she didn't get messed with *as much* when she had him next to her compared to being alone.

She finally settled on a nearby beach, not far from the port's central hub, people milling about nearby. Most of the chairs were filled with families, but she found a somewhat secluded area nearby where she could try and relax. She set her bag and hat down on the chair beside her, then began stripping. Pulling the dress over her head and kicking her sandals off in the light sand, she was left in an all white bikini. She grabbed her hat and put it back on, then sunk into the other lounger next to her things. . The sun wasn't beating directly on her — thankfully, a few trees overhead shielded her from the rays and provided a bit of shade. Maybe she wouldn't go back looking *quite* like a lobster. Pulling out her phone, she took a few pictures of the scenery, then twisted in her chair to take a selfie with some of the water in the background. Despite her life falling apart, this wasn't the *worst* backdrop to have mental breakdowns in.

She looked down at the pictures and smiled sadly to herself. Most of the photos she took or posted lately didn't have anyone else in them. Honestly, she... didn't take photos much at all anymore. She didn't feel *pretty*. She didn't feel *good enough*. Any of her friends or family would always negate that and reassure her, but... it was hard to believe when the person you used to worship more than the sky didn't look twice at you anymore.

As she scrolled through the pictures, a small box popped up on her screen showing her a few public Wi-Fi networks available from the nearby bars, shops, and restaurants. She clicked on one and raised her eyebrows when it actually connected *and* put her through online. A few texts and notifications came through from the period between the last time she'd been on Wi-Fi on the ship. She went through the notifications one by one, clearing them out slowly. She came across a message from her mom, a simple '*I love you, hope you're having fun!*' and it made her heart ache.

Clicking on her mom's contact, the small icon for video-chatting lit up. She sighed and tapped it. As the phone screen changed and a few consecutive beeps rang out, her mom's face popped up after a few seconds.

"Well, hi! I didn't expect to hear from you until next week," her mom, Claire, said cheerily, her face beaming as she held the phone a little *too* close.

Lucy laughed under her breath. Her mom could fix *anything*. She had never stayed sad or mad for long when she got a chance to talk to her.

"Yeah, I just... wanted to call you, see how you were doing," Lucy said.

The older blonde woman smiled and shook her head. "I'm fine, but not as good as you, beach babe. Look at that view. Show me around!"

Lucy obliged and flipped the camera, panning around to give her a good scope of the beach she was at. She flipped it back on herself and leaned her head back against the chair. "Last port day. Then it's back on the boat and then home."

"You don't sound as happy as someone in the Bahamas should," her mom said. "What's going on, darling?"

All it took was that one question, in that *sweet* voice that soothed her soul like honey, to make Lucy break down into tears. A few heads turned her way, but she didn't notice or care. She brought her free hand up to her face and tried to keep her sobs at bay, but it was too much.

"Oh, *sweetheart*, don't cry. What happened?" her mom continued. "Where's Chris?"

Lucy sniffled, composing herself a little bit more. "He's… I don't know where he is. Honestly, I don't even *care*. Mom, I… I think I'm going to break up with him."

"That's big," Claire said, her eyebrows raised. "But I know you wouldn't even consider a decision as life-changing as this if you haven't *really* thought it through. I know it isn't easy. But you haven't been happy for a while."

"Yeah," Lucy said sadly. "And…"

"What is it? You can tell me. Has he put his hands on you?"

"No, Mom, no," Lucy said quickly, shaking her head. She wiped the stray tears from her rosy cheeks and sighed deeply. "Nothing like that. I'm… having feelings I haven't had in a long time."

"Talk to me, baby girl."

Lucy grit her teeth and her throat shrank. A few more tears spilled over onto her lap and she took a deep breath. "I… met someone here."

"In the Bahamas?"

"On the boat," she explained.

"Okay… Does he live in Orlando? Or…?"

"Um…" Lucy started, hesitating to continue.

"What?" her mom pressed gently. "You know you can

always tell me anything. If you're worried about liking someone else while still being with Chris, it's okay. You aren't a bad person. These things happen. You fall out of love and sometimes you're mentally checked out of the relationship before you are physically checked out. It's *life*, sweetheart. It happens to everyone."

"Not this," Lucy said, shaking her head.

"Did you… *you know*, with this new guy?"

"No, no, I…" Lucy said, failing again to get the words from the tip of her tongue out into the world. She took a deep breath and shook her head quickly. "It'snotaman."

"Come again?"

"Mom, I know you don't… I know it's *weird* and I've dated Chris this whole time, but—"

"Lucy, wait, you froze for a second. What did you say before? It's not, what?"

Lucy blinked a few times, realizing she had to *actually* say it again. "I said…" she started slowly. "The person I met is not a man. She's an art dealer who works on the ship."

Her mom stayed quiet for a second, then smiled. "Did you just officially come out to me? It's about time."

Lucy let out the breath she'd been holding almost *violently*. She furrowed her dark brows, then tilted her sunglasses down so she could *look* at her mom. "Excuse me?"

Her mom just laughed. "Lucy, you're my girl. I've known you your whole life. Do you think I didn't catch on *years* ago when you all of a sudden quit the soccer team in high school and refused to explain at all? And you also were weird about going out in a swimsuit with your friends for *months* after that?

And you were *serially* dating boys?"

Lucy's mouth gaped a bit and she forced it closed. Then she opened it again and squealed, "What?!"

That only made her mom laugh harder. "I didn't think you were *fully* gay, but… maybe halfway. Looks like I was right. Your dad owes me ten bucks."

"You bet money on my sexuality?!"

"Aw, you're not mad, are you? We love you just the same, sweetheart, nothing's changed. I promise."

"No, I'm not mad, I'm…" Lucy trailed off in shock, then she *burst* out laughing. She covered her mouth and tears flowed, this time for a different reason. "I can't believe this."

"That makes one of us," her mom teased. "So tell me about this art dealer! What does she look like? What's her name?"

"Her name is Scarlett Sinclair and she's… Mom, *gosh*," Lucy said, holding a hand to her chest. "I've never looked at someone this way. From the first moment we met and talked, she has just *consumed* me. I know it's wrong and—"

"Stop saying that."

"What?" Lucy spluttered, looking at her mom on the screen.

"Stop saying it's wrong. You're *okay*. Just focus on being happy. Now what does Scarlett Sinclair look like? Tall, short?"

"Tall. So tall. She's from London."

"Oooh," Claire gushed. "An *accent*."

"I know right," Lucy giggled. "She has dark brown hair and these beautiful brown eyes. They're like… chocolate. Smooth, milk chocolate. She's so smart, so funny. She's *covered* in tattoos," she said, her cheeks blushing again as she thought about her. "She's so *cool*, Mom. I know she probably doesn't think of me as anything more than a momentary friend, and I'm sure she does this a lot with the people she's constantly meeting, I just… Last night, we hung out for *hours*. We just talked, laughed, I didn't want the night to end. I want to be with her *all* the time."

Her mom smiled and tilted her head. "I've never heard you talk about Chris like this. Not even at the beginning."

"I'm sure I did," Lucy said, shifting in her seat. "Surely."

"Not to me," her mom said, shaking her head. "Lucy, *you* know what you have to do. You know what's right in your *heart*. You follow that and everything else will work itself out. Okay?"

Lucy took a deep breath and nodded. "Okay."

"And whatever decision you make, your dad and I will be there for you. We will help you move out if needed, or we will help move *him* out if that's what it takes. You can stay with us as long as you need, you know that. Maybe we're due for a family cruise, you could get Scarlett's work schedule…"

"*Mom*," Lucy laughed, scrunching her nose. "What am I supposed to do? Do I tell her? *How* would I even tell her?"

"I think you need to do things one at a time. This is a lot during a time when you're supposed to be relaxing and not stressing," the older woman said. "I do think you need to work out what you've got going on with Chris. You aren't going to be able to *truly* give yourself to *anything* if that isn't taken care of first. Do you have Scarlett's contact information?"

"Yes."

"There you go. You can get to know her more, and then if the moment arises, maybe you can talk to her about how you're feeling. If you had as dramatic as a connection as you talked about, I'm sure she'll hear you out no matter *how* she feels about what you say. And then you can go from there. If she doesn't like women, maybe you can remain long-distance friends. If she does, you can figure out if it's worth it to go through the hard work of a long-distance relationship."

"But… do you think it's too soon, Mom? Is it crazy that I feel like I…"

"Like she's the one?"

Lucy stayed quiet and simply looked at her mom, unsure of what to even *say*.

"Have I ever told you the story about how your dad and I met? How he proposed to me?"

"Maybe… Wasn't it on an airplane or something?"

"Yes, it was. I was sitting next to him and he was doing a crossword puzzle. I kept looking over to just watch what he was doing, his guesses, and because I finished my book and there were still four hours left in the flight. He noticed and just casually tore one of the papers out and handed it to me, and he even gave me his pen. He was so cute. We talked and talked and *talked* that entire flight and I just couldn't get enough of him. It was definitely love at first sight. We got off the plane and went to the baggage claim together, and thank *God* we had the same final destination. When the bags rolled around, we had the *same suitcase!*" she laughed, the phone screen shaking a little bit with her movement. "He asked me out to dinner that night. We went to a diner right by the airport because nothing else was open. Even though we were from different places, we just *knew*. He dropped everything to come to Florida with me.

We were married three months later."

"Wow," Lucy said. She had *never* heard that story in that much detail before. Her parents had been together almost three decades now. "So you don't think I'm crazy?"

"Not at all. You'd be crazy to pass this opportunity up. You're young, you have time to make mistakes. But you've also got a better head on your shoulders than most twenty-five-year-olds do. I know you'll make the right choice. I support you in *whatever* you decide to do."

"Thanks, Mom," Lucy said, feeling herself grow emotional again.

Her mom, of course, sensed it. "Enough with the waterworks! Hang up the phone and go enjoy your vacay. We'll talk *all* about it when you get back, okay? Take lots of pictures and videos. I love you more than you'll ever know, angel."

"I love you, too, Mom. Talk to you later," Lucy said, then the phone beeped and returned back to her mother's contact card. She sighed and locked the phone, then held it close to her chest.

She felt like she was drowning and on top of a mountain at the same time.

"Have you seen Lucy?"

Scarlett looked up from her tablet and blinked a few times upon recognizing Lucy's boyfriend standing in front of her, looking distressed. "Excuse me?"

"Have you seen Lucy?" Chris repeated. "She wasn't in the room when I came back today."

"It's port day. She's probably enjoying the destination she spent time traveling to," Scarlett said, looking back down at her device. She hoped that her disinterest would be hint enough for him to walk away, but obviously she expected *far* too much of him. Lucy was rubbing off on her. Heaving a great sigh, Scarlett locked her tablet and looked up at Chris. She supposed it wasn't his fault he'd stumbled upon her, she was sitting in a common area trying to get a little work done. She had felt cooped up in her room and hadn't wanted to go outside when everyone else was off the boat enjoying themselves.

"What do you want, Chris?" Scarlett asked finally.

"What's going on between you and Lucy?" Chris asked,

folding his arms. "What's your *deal*?"

"My *deal*?" Scarlett scoffed, standing up. She was taller than him by a few inches, so it was *very* satisfying when he cowered *just* enough. "What is that supposed to mean? There's nothing going on between Lucy and me. We're friends. Can she not have those now?"

"You don't even *know her*," Chris hissed. "Ever since we got on this boat, ever since she met *you*, she's been different. She talks about art now, she blows off hanging out with me to spend time with you, she's *mean*. What has she been telling you, hmm? Lies, I'm sure."

"She hasn't lied at all and what she's told me is none of your concern," Scarlett said angrily, her hackles rising. "I'm not going to stand here and let you belittle me like you do her. You don't deserve her *little finger*, let alone *her*. You are *lucky* she has stuck around this long. She's doing you a bloody favor. But give it time. I'm sure she'll come to her senses and find someone who actually shows her what she's worth rather than dragging her down with him. How much have you had to drink?"

Chris opened his mouth to snarl something back, no doubt, but quickly snapped it shut. His cheeks were red and Scarlett could have *sworn* his glasses were going to fog up with how steamed he was. She desperately wanted to ruffle that greasy hair, *just* to piss him off a little bit more.

"Leave me alone, Chris. I'm not trying to steal your girlfriend. That is between *you two*. I don't know where Lucy is and I'm not going to traipse around the ship looking for her with you when the logical explanation is *obviously* the beautiful island we're parked at."

"You're a bitch," Chris growled, before storming off.

Scarlett watched him and huffed under her breath, her eyes wide. What a *freak*. She didn't know how Lucy put up with him for so long. Well, she *could*, and now she understood how her friends felt when they were around all the awkward public fights she and Raphael had gotten in when she did something he hadn't liked. Once, she had held a fork wrong (apparently) and had completely set him off. She hadn't been able to see out of her right eye for two damn days. He had never done anything physical to her in public with witnesses, but more often than not he had scolded her quietly, but sternly in front of their friends, as if she were a toddler who was screaming the place down. She had always felt so *small* around him.

With Lucy, she felt like she was queen of the world. It was a little concerning that Chris had come to ambush her, but he wasn't in his right mind, and it *did* make sense that he turned to her when looking for Lucy, considering they spent basically all their free time together.

She smiled to herself, thinking about the night before. She had barely been able to *sleep* afterward. Olive *had* been awake when she finally returned near 3 a.m. and Scarlett hadn't been able to help herself. They had gone through every detail she could remember, even the tense moments she had *sworn* were something but eventually convinced herself she was overthinking them. Olive had reassured her that she wasn't overthinking and exclaimed she was *so* happy they'd had a great night together.

Scarlett had never felt this strongly, this fast for someone, not even Raphael. Even the minor flings she'd had weren't anything close to this. It was never more than a few hours of fun, a few hours to get her mind off whatever shitty memory plagued her thoughts. It was always someone who wouldn't bother her later, wouldn't make her life a living hell ever again. Someone she *wouldn't see* ever again.

She hoped with everything in her that Lucy wouldn't fall into that category.

It was difficult, because she wasn't a home wrecker. However now, given the few encounters she'd had with Chris *and* what Lucy told her over the last few days, she wasn't sure there was much of a home to wreck. As she had personally decided the night before, she was just going to be there for her in whatever capacity Lucy needed and let her set the pace. If she wanted things to stay platonic, perfect, and if she eventually wanted to explore something more, Scarlett would make sure she felt *worshiped*.

She sank back into the chair she'd been sitting in before Chris rudely interrupted her and she opened her tablet up once more, trying to get back in the groove of creating her marketing content for the month. She felt a *little* concerned that Chris couldn't find Lucy, purely because that meant Lucy was alone somewhere, but she tried to put those worries out of her head. She knew the blonde was probably just enjoying her time at the beach and having some moments to herself. She needed it.

Stepping back to admire her work so far, Scarlett looked around at all the pieces of art displayed around the room.

She was preparing for their final gallery on the last day at sea. They were running sales and promotions, purely because their numbers weren't as good as they should be at that point and they wanted to bump them up as much as they could.

They had to reach a certain quota of art sold each cruise cycle or else it reflected badly on them. Gavin took these metrics very seriously, and things were usually fine either way. It wasn't as if anyone had gotten fired over not selling enough art on the boat. But they were scolded and Scarlett *hated* it. She couldn't stand when a man tried to tell her what *she* did wrong, when he had just as much to do with the reports as she had. But Gavin was her boss and she knew she needed to respect that. It wasn't *his fault* he was a man.

"Need any help, Picasso?"

Scarlett whipped around at the sound of an angelic voice and grinned ear-to-ear upon seeing a sun-kissed Lucy Price standing near the door, looking like she'd just hopped off an island.

Well. She had.

Lucy mirrored her smile and closed the distance between them. Scarlett was thankful she was alone in the room and had been put in charge of doing this herself. That morning, she hadn't been happy about the amount of work she was thrown into, but... everything worked out how it was supposed to.

"Did you have fun today?" Scarlett asked, hesitating slightly. Did she hug her? In her country, it was customary to greet a friend with a peck to the cheek, but she was suddenly worried that would come across as too much. Too creepy, maybe?

She didn't have much time to fret internally though before

Lucy wrapped her arms around her and held her close for a *very* nice hello. Scarlett relaxed and enveloped her in her arms, smelling the salt water on her skin and hair.

"I had a lot of fun today," Lucy said softly as she pulled back, her hands slowly trailing away from Scarlett's body. "I called my mom."

"Yeah?" Scarlett responded, tilting her head. "How did that go?"

"Well. Really well. I talked to her about Chris, I needed advice. I just… couldn't think about it all by myself. She always knows what to say."

"I'm so glad," Scarlett said.

"Me too," Lucy nodded, then hesitated for a moment. "I talked to her for a long time about you," she added, her cheeks darkening *just* a little bit. Scarlett wondered if that was from the sun or… something else.

"Hopefully all good things," Scarlett laughed quietly.

"Of course," Lucy smiled. "She's glad I'm happy, despite everything else happening. She was worried all of this drama would ruin the trip for me."

"I'm glad it hasn't," Scarlett murmured. "And I'm glad I can make you happy."

Lucy stepped a bit closer, not a lot, but enough where Scarlett noticed. She could smell the sunscreen on her, the slight oily residue glistening against her skin. Her curls were wild and wavy, looking like they were about to burst from under her cute hat. She was glad she wasn't hiding those pretty blue eyes under her sunglasses. Scarlett let her eyes roam unashamedly over the woman, before dragging her gaze back to Lucy's face.

"I can let you get back to work," Lucy murmured, her voice breathy. Scarlett's toes curled inside her flats. "It looks great in here. I should probably go shower."

Scarlett deflated a *little*, but tried to keep it discreet. She *wanted* to beg her to stay, to keep her company, to shut the door and push her up against one of the canvases, but… she didn't do any of that. Instead, she stayed casual. "I have a lot to do tonight to prep for tomorrow, so I… don't think I'll be able to get any time away from work," she admitted. "But tomorrow I'll be at the auction here at noon. Then if you maybe want to get anything, I'll be at the main gallery at five. I'm off at night."

Lucy nodded and tucked some hair back behind her ear. "It's a date."

It was Scarlett's turn to blush now. She laughed under her breath and *tried* to think of something suave and cool to say, but words were escaping her. Instead, all she came up with was, "Enjoy your shower."

Lucy turned to leave the room and before Scarlett could even think, she was speaking, "Unless you wanted to sit in here and keep me company?"

The blonde woman stopped and turned back to face Scarlett. The smile on her face could light up *space*. "I'd love nothing more. Do I have to sit in one spot like a good girl or can I follow you around like a puppy?"

Scarlett ignored the twitch that scurried through her stomach and down between her legs at the first half of Lucy's statement. "Puppy's fine," she managed, her pale cheeks coloring.

Lucy grinned wider and slid up next to Scarlett, their

shoulders brushing. "You're going to have to explain everything you're doing, you know."

Scarlett let out a quiet, amused exhale and nodded. "Your wish is my command." She walked to the back of the room and into an open-doored room that had a few lingering canvases propped against each other. "I have a list here," she said, pointing to the piece of paper with artwork names printed in a list sitting on a table in the room. "I just go down the list and bring each piece out and set it up. I'm nearly finished, I just have a few more to go."

"Is there a certain spot you have to put every one?" Lucy asked, eyeing the list. "How do you remember what they're all called?"

"It's part of our training to learn the pieces. And to answer your first question... yes and no. We try to pair artists' work together. These three, for instance, 'Innocent Eyes,' 'Hide and Seek,' and 'Universal Stare' are all pieces by Stephen Fishwick. I'll display them in a row together in case someone wants to buy the set."

"Do you have to buy the set?"

"No. You can just buy one. For these, anyway. Sometimes we do sell pieces as sets, but we usually give so much of a discount, it's worth it rather than splitting up the art," Scarlett said, grabbing one of the three pieces she mentioned earlier. Lucy moved to grab one, but Scarlett shook her head and stopped. "No. I'm sorry, Lucy, I appreciate the help, but if anyone saw you handling the art, I'd get sacked."

"Oh," Lucy said, immediately putting her hands up. "Okay. Back to puppy status."

Scarlett smiled and walked out of the room with the piece of art. She had 'Innocent Eyes,' a wildlife-themed piece with a juvenile monkey's head as the subject. Its eyes were big and… well, innocent-looking. She set it up on an easel, then returned to the room for the other two pieces, Lucy on her heels with every step. 'Universal Stare' showcased a large tiger's head, looking somberly at whomever gazed upon it. She briefly thought about the bloke who had been interested in this piece the other day and tanked her sale numbers by not getting it. 'Hide and Seek' featured a small red panda's head nestled between long grass.

"I like that one," Lucy chimed as she hung up the final piece in the trio of art.

Scarlett looked at the collection, then the art Lucy was pointing to. She couldn't help but giggle. "The little red panda?"

"Yeah, it's cute," Lucy laughed.

"You would know," Scarlett teased, earning a blush from the other woman. *Success!* They walked back to the room and went down the list more. After about half an hour, the rest of the artwork was displayed and the room was filled in every corner.

"Looks great," Lucy complimented, hands on her hips as she swiveled slowly to take in the work.

"Thanks," Scarlett smiled. "Sorry I don't have more free time. I'm glad you stayed with me though."

"Me, too," Lucy gushed.

"You're in *such* a good mood," Scarlett said with a light laugh. "It's kind of freaking me out."

"Am I not allowed to be in a good mood? That stings,"

Lucy scoffed, putting a hand against her chest.

Scarlett's perfidious eyes stole a glance down at that wonderfully tantalizing piece of skin under her fingertips. She brought her gaze up to Lucy's face and smiled wider. "You're just always the poster child for depression when I see you."

"Ha, ha," Lucy said, rolling her eyes. "I told you, I had a great day. Now it's even better because I got to see you."

Scarlett's insides warmed. She debated telling Lucy about her run-in with Chris, but… that would probably only cause problems. She would *never* be the reason for Lucy's anguish. As much as she'd *love* to never see that man again and kiss Lucy until she forgot her own name *and* all the bad things her boyfriend brought into her world, she knew better. She didn't want to be selfish. Lucy was already going through enough, and Scarlett hadn't behaved in the most mature way when she'd encountered Chris.

But she'd still say all the things she had again until she was blue in the face.

Perhaps it was just better to play dumb.

"So, given you spoke to your mum about both Chris and me, I assume he wasn't with you at the port today?"

"Nope," Lucy said, shrugging. Her hair bounced with the movement. "I actually haven't seen him since before our date yesterday."

"Our date, hmm?" Scarlett teased.

Lucy blushed *deeply* and Scarlett wondered just how far that blush went. It was a good look for her, and she wanted to make her even more flushed while she—

"You know what I mean," Lucy said, waving her hand

dismissively. "We got into a fight before I came to the piano bar and he stormed out. I have no clue where he is."

"Probably thinking of ways to piss you off."

Lucy snorted a laugh. "With how often he does it, it wouldn't surprise me if he rehearsed and practiced while I'm not there."

"Ugh," Scarlett grimaced, "I'm sorry, Lucy. Truly."

Lucy sighed and shook her head. "It's alright. Not your fault. Anyway, look at the cute pictures I took today." Lucy put her happy face back on and pulled out her phone, opening up her photo app to show Scarlett the selfies she'd taken.

Scarlett hungrily looked at the pictures. Lucy was laying in her lounge chair on the beach, bikini showing off far more than Scarlett had ever seen of her. "You and that hat," Scarlett rasped, trying to *not* seem like she was unashamedly gawking at Lucy's body.

"My signature," Lucy sighed dreamily, then swiped again. Scarlett momentarily bristled when the selfies seemed to be over and now they were looking at pictures of a bright, sunny beach.

Lucy kept scrolling and it was just beach, beach, more beach, cocktail, beach... "No more pictures of you? Just the selfies?" Scarlett asked, glancing over at her. Did she sound innocent? Nonchalant? *Not* like she wanted to jump her bones and peel that bikini right off those mouth-watering curves of hers?

"Just the selfies," Lucy sighed, keeping her eyes on the phone. "I don't take a lot of pictures of myself anymore."

"Why not?" Scarlett asked. She had stalked Lucy's

Instagram profile when they followed each other and had noticed she hadn't updated it in a while. She just thought perhaps she wasn't overly active on social media.

"I don't know," Lucy said, her voice a bit despondent. "I guess I just don't think about it anymore. Maybe I've grown out of it. I used to take them all the time, and I have some I never post just when I'm wearing a cute outfit and want to document it, but… it's not like anyone but me sees them."

"May I see?"

Lucy looked over at Scarlett and the art dealer smiled. Hesitantly, the blonde turned back down to her phone and began scrolling up on pictures. Before she got far, Scarlett's hand rested over her wrist. "Wait," Scarlett started, "I'm not going to see any dick pics of Chris, am I?"

"*Jesus*, no," Lucy immediately said, making a noise in the back of her throat. "I don't have anything like that. I told him at the beginning of our relationship that I wasn't into nudes. Don't worry."

"Ah, so I won't see any of yours either then," Scarlett said.

Lucy lifted her head and flicked her eyes over to Scarlett. "No, I prefer to give in-person demonstrations."

The air in Scarlett's lungs evaporated. She quirked her head to meet Lucy's gaze. They were so close. Her lips were *right there*, full and pink, so perfect…

A high-pitched ringing sound broke the spell they were under. Scarlett and Lucy both jumped at the noise and Scarlett swore under her breath as she pulled her phone out of her blazer pocket. Her screen was lit up with a notification that read *AUCTION MEETING IN GALLERY!!!* Scarlett sighed deeply and clicked the button below the notification to silence the phone and clear the screen. "Sorry, I set alarms because I lose track of time. I have to go," Scarlett said.

Lucy clicked her phone dark and tucked it back into her purse. "That's okay. I don't want you to be late. I *really* need to take my shower anyway."

"I probably won't get to see you again today."

"I enjoyed the time I did get with you."

Scarlett smiled sadly. Why did this feel so *hard*? It wasn't like one of them was going off to war. She was just going two floors down for a meeting and Lucy was going to the other end of the ship for a shower. They were still stuck in the ocean together. Scarlett put her phone back into her jacket and resisted touching Lucy. "You'll come tomorrow though, won't you?"

"I told you I would," Lucy reassured. "Noon?"

"Sharp," Scarlett nodded with a smile. "Now go. You stink."

Lucy poked out her tongue and scrunched her nose, an expression that made Scarlett want to *scream* with frustration at how cute she was. Scarlett mirrored Lucy's wave and watched her walk out of the room, unable to keep her eyes off the way the woman's hips swayed with every step. That little green dress was working wonders for her. Only when Lucy was out of sight did Scarlett feel like she could breathe again.

ucy returned to her room and showered, then spent most of the rest of the evening resting in the room or sitting in a chair on one of the upper decks. She hadn't come across Chris yet, but she knew it was only a matter of time. She had seen a few messages come through on her phone when she reconnected to Wi-Fi from him, asking where she was, saying he was sorry, all the usual crap he would bombard her with right after a fight.

Usually, she was very communicative and always wanted to talk things out rather than prolong a fight, but... he could sweat for a little while. She didn't have the energy anymore to even be civil. She was thankful he took the hint and gave her some space.

It was their last day at sea before returning to Florida and she felt like a new person after speaking to her mom. Plus, the stolen minutes she spent sneaking off to Scarlett while she was setting up the day before had really just... driven everything home. Even just *hugging* her the other night made her feel like electricity was going through Lucy and her heart raced every time that beautiful woman so much as looked into her eyes. She wasn't exactly sure how to proceed, given Scarlett was working and Lucy was technically a customer, but… she wanted to try. She didn't want to leave that boat without saying *something*. Luckily she had another day and a half to do so.

She also had to work out what she was going to do about Chris. How did she even bring it up to him? She was always big on communication and immediately confronting issues when faced with them, but this frightened her. She was stalling, delaying the inevitable, and she didn't know *why*. Wouldn't it just be easier to cut her losses and move on to something that would make her happier? At this point, being alone would make her happier than being near him. There had been quirks of his that she'd enjoyed, like his joking sense of humor *all* the time, even in serious moments, the way he would just goof off and have fun, the way he dressed so casual, and a million other little things. As the years went on, she began to resent those things about him. She began to resent *everything* about him, and it broke her heart to think that. It wasn't ever something she thought would even be possible. This was the man she thought she'd marry and mother children with, but… there was *no way* in fresh hell that was ever going to happen.

And yet… there was still a part of her holding back. She wasn't sure if it was just the fear of the unknown, of leaving something she'd been so comfortable and familiar with for six years, or… lingering feelings she just couldn't quite shake.

She didn't wish anything *bad* on Chris. She wanted him to be happy because he deserved it, but he also deserved someone who loved him with *everything* in them. Lucy only loved him with a morsel of her entire being. The majority of her yearned for something else, some*one* else. It made her feel guilty to even think that, given she was against infidelity from past relationships, but her past relationships hadn't had real adult things involved like these complex feelings, an apartment, a *life*.

Thankfully, she felt support from every corner of her world. Her parents, her friends, even Scarlett were on her side and she knew that no matter what choice she made, she would have people to lift her up during the process.

When noon came, Lucy ventured to the fifth deck and waded through some people. She passed the casino and against her better judgment, glanced around as she walked. She didn't see Chris, but she couldn't see *all* of the casino either. For once, she hoped he was there, just because he'd be too occupied to come and bother her.

Spotting Scarlett at the door to the auction made a smile break across Lucy's lips. She quickened her pace just a bit and fell into line behind some other people trying to get in. They were talking to Scarlett and Lucy couldn't help but watch. This job was perfect for Scarlett. She was passionate and *so* knowledgeable about so many pieces of art and different artists. She had an aura about her that was just calming, *collected*.

When she finally caught Scarlett's eye, her smile widened and she could tell the other woman was trying to keep her own smile at bay in front of the other passengers ahead of Lucy in line occupying her attention. One by one they filtered in until Lucy was face-to-face with Scarlett. The blonde resisted reaching out for a hug, knowing it would be inappropriate in a moment like that. There were too many people around and they didn't need to be embracing in front of her coworkers or boss.

"You made it," Scarlett said, smiling *fully* now.

Lucy *swooned*.

The blonde nodded and held out her arms. "In the flesh. Where should I sit in there?"

"Anywhere you want, but if you sit in the back like last time, I can probably stand by you most of the auction," Scarlett smirked, winking at her.

Lucy half-worried her knees would buckle. She blushed and nodded, tucking a stray curl behind her ear. A pair of dark, high-waisted jeans hugged her thighs and hips and a cropped, white t-shirt with a skeleton surfing a wave in the middle sat perfectly on her torso, accentuating her breasts. She forewent contacts again to give her eyes a break, *not* because Scarlett had complimented her glasses the other night. Nope. Definitely not. Lucy's waves were twisted up into a half-bun, the other half of her hair down her shoulders and back.

"Cool shirt," Scarlett said, making a point to *slowly* look her over.

Lucy could have sworn she actually *felt* her panties dampen. That was… new. She swallowed and put on a brave face. "I like your outfit, too. Red's your color." She nodded to the deep red blouse Scarlett had on to go with her black suit. It matched her nails. Scarlett's hair was down and straight again. Lucy, however, needed to catch her breath before she fell out on the table, so she tilted her head toward the door. "I'll see you in there then," Lucy said, walking past her into the room.

It was packed.

Lucy took her seat in the back as instructed and looked around. There were people chattering and looking around at all the different art on display throughout the room. Without Scarlett in there to distract her, she really catalogued all the pieces there. The wildlife ones were right where they left them, but there were plenty of others she hadn't even *noticed* because she'd been too busy staring at Scarlett. Twisting in her seat, she saw her favorite that she'd found that first day propped up against the wall near the front. She frowned to herself and wondered why it was up there and not on display. Had someone bought it?

"What's wrong?"

Lucy turned to see Scarlett standing next to her, her eyebrows furrowed in concern. Lucy exhaled and shook her head. "Nothing. Why is 'Spring Night' propped up at the front like that and not on an easel?"

Scarlett followed her line of sight and nodded. "Oh, it's going to be displayed as a primary piece for the show today."

"So people can bid on it and buy it?"

"Right," Scarlett said.

"How much does it start at?"

The dark-haired woman pulled out her tablet and began typing against the keyboard, then turned it around to show Lucy. "You can buy it outright for twelve-hundred, but the auction will probably start at eight-hundred."

"So whoever wins the auction will get it and then that's it? It isn't available anymore?"

"That's our only one, yes," Scarlett nodded. "That's the one you really liked the first day, isn't it?"

"Yes," Lucy nodded. "But I don't know if I can do twelve-hundred… eight-hundred maybe but…"

"What can you do?"

"Eight-hundred would be the max."

"And you really want it?"

Lucy thought about that. She had wanted to buy a piece of art the entire cruise, but hadn't felt like she could, especially with Chris being so financially irresponsible. But why shouldn't she be able to splurge on herself? She had a little cushion saved up and no credit card debt. She could do it, couldn't she?

"I do," she finally said.

Scarlett nodded and gently trailed a hand down her back. "I'll just be a minute," she murmured, before walking over to the front where Gavin and Olive were prepping for the start of the auction. She said a few things to them, words Lucy couldn't make out from how far she was, and suddenly Gavin was putting a cloth over the artwork she loved so much and setting it aside. Lucy blushed and watched the scene unfold. Olive leaned closer to Scarlett as she spoke near her ear, then the woman turned to scan the room. When her eyes landed on Lucy, she smiled and gave a wave. Lucy returned Olive's greeting and shot Scarlett a look that said, *What did you do?!*

Scarlett came back to where Lucy was sitting and smiled. "Nobody else will have a chance to buy that one. You don't have to commit to anything, and if we get down to the end and you don't want to spend the money, it's okay. You aren't locked in," she said reassuringly. "But now nobody else can steal it from you if you really want to go through with it."

"Thank you. You didn't have to do all that," Lucy said. She was sure Chris would just shoot down any kind of art she wanted to buy, claiming it was a waste of money. As if he had any room to talk about what was considered wasting money. He didn't even *have* money.

"You're welcome," Scarlett said, remaining by her side as Gavin began animatedly speaking to the other passengers eager to bid on some artwork.

"Do you ever get annoyed with this whole… over-the-top act from him during these things?" Lucy whispered to Scarlett, their shoulders touching with how close they were to each other.

"It just makes me laugh. Maybe cringe a little," Scarlett whispered back with a smile. "It works wonders on these people though. See," she said, gesturing to a woman who was literally *jumping* out of her seat and waving her bid card around so enthusiastically, her mimosa was spilling over the edge of the champagne flute in her hand. "We get people like that all the time," Scarlett continued. "I know it sounds wrong but… the more people drink and get excited, feel like they *know* you, the more likely they are to buy. We have a quota to meet every cruise."

Lucy frowned and turned her head to look at her, gesturing between them. "Is that all this is? A sales tactic?"

Scarlett whipped her head to Lucy and looked as if she'd just been stabbed. She grabbed Lucy's hand and squeezed her fingers. "*Never.*"

Lucy let out a quiet breath and squeezed her hand back, her hand growing warm under her touch. "Thank God. It's working either way though," she said, a small smile creeping along her lips.

Scarlett mimicked her smile and stroked the back of her hand with her thumb. "Nothing I've ever seen on this ship or off could ever compare to you."

Lucy blushed *darkly* and felt her breath hitch in her throat. She stared into the other woman's eyes and tried to convey everything she was afraid to say without uttering a word. The feeling of her hand against hers was charging her in a way nothing ever had before. Lucy shuddered out a quiet breath, then let go of her hand as Gavin began walking around to talk to everyone.

Scarlett smoothed down her blazer and trousers, before walking away from Lucy to join Olive in displaying the art for each round of bidding. Lucy was trying to keep her cool and *not* pass out. Seriously, *don't* pass out. She felt like a damn teenager again.

S carlett pulled a white cloth off a piece of artwork as Olive did the same with the other easels lined up in a row next to her. She stepped out of the way and listened to the passengers sitting in the groups before her hum in awe as they chattered about what they liked most about each piece. They were auctioning four in a set from the same artist for a discounted price.

She tried to keep her gaze off Lucy, purely because she felt like she was going to implode if *something* didn't happen between them. She had never felt so compelled to risk her job and break her own heart than with this woman. They had the rest of the day to stop dancing around what was festering between them, then Lucy would be gone. The tension was so thick, she could have cut it with a knife.

She was thankful they exchanged their social media information, that way if *nothing* happened in the next 24 hours, she could at least get in touch with her. Perhaps they could meet for lunch on the Orlando port days, or maybe she'd even book another cruise. Maybe Scarlett could take some time off work and see all those fun theme parks and other attractions in Lucy's city, then they could come back to her apartment and…

Scarlett's cheeks flamed with color and she blinked away those thoughts, then cast her gaze downward.

It had been a long time since she'd been with a woman. She liked to think she knew her way around the female form from the few times she'd experienced it, and being a woman herself, but… God, she was in way over her head.

She wasn't sure if Lucy had ever been with a woman. She wanted to ask her when they bared their hearts to each other during their date-that-wasn't-a-date, but she worried it would have completely shown her hand. Given Lucy's age and length of her relationship, Scarlett was going to venture to guess she had no experience sexually with women. But she really *didn't* know. She could have experimented before Chris just like Scarlett had, or maybe they'd even brought someone into their relationship to try some new things. She grimaced at the thought. She'd rather drink bleach than see that man nude. He probably looked like a naked mole rat. Poor Lucy.

Traitorously, Scarlett let her eyes roam back over to Lucy, who was unashamedly staring at her. Scarlett's pale cheeks turned pink and she couldn't help the smile that spread across her face. She felt *smitten*. Nothing had even bloody happened yet.

She wasn't able to go back to where Lucy was sitting for the remainder of the auction. She had to mark down contact information for those who raised their bid cards and schedule time slots for those who wanted to buy artwork.

When the auction ended, she got caught up in conversation with a few passengers asking questions about the bidding process and how pricing worked. Her eyes kept flitting over to where Lucy was while she spoke, not wanting her to walk out of there without talking to her again first. Scarlett ended the conversation with her current distractions as quick as she could, and much to her pleasure, Lucy was hovering near the same spot she had been sitting.

Scarlett floated over to her and rolled her eyes. "Sorry about that. Sometimes they're relentless."

"You're doing your job, it's alright," Lucy said whilst smiling. "Seems like you got a lot of interest and bids. Do you think you'll meet your quota?"

Scarlett shrugged. "Maybe. It's so hard to tell, I don't really have access to those numbers. Not unless I ask Gavin. I'm sure Olive would know," she laughed quietly.

"Do you really think those two talk about work when they're together?" Lucy smirked.

"I know for a fact they do not," Scarlett sighed. "Sometimes our room is *occupied* when I try to come back to the cabin. Can't tell you how many times I've just put my hand over my eyes and put on noise-canceling headphones to *try* and keep my dinner down. Good for them and all, but... I don't need to see any of that."

"Nothing worse than being single or feeling lonely and having that shoved in your face on a daily basis," Lucy sighed. "I definitely wouldn't want anyone walking in on me and..." she trailed off, and Scarlett realized she must have been making a face. Lucy laughed and shook her head. "Well, you get what

I'm trying to say."

"I do. *Anyway*," Scarlett laughed, Lucy laughing again with her. "You'll come tonight to talk about that art you want, won't you? I can do the transaction myself," she said, opening her tablet again. "I have to schedule you into a time slot, but I have quite a few," she murmured, scrolling through.

"You're in total business mode, I love it," Lucy teased, leaning over to look at her screen. She stepped aside so they were standing next to each other, their arms brushing.

Scarlett's skin prickled with excitement and she blinked, pausing in her scrolling. Her train of thought had been *completely* derailed. She swallowed, then went back to tapping through the available appointments. "How's six tonight?"

"Perfect," Lucy said, turning her head to look at her. Scarlett could feel her breath against her neck.

Scarlett swallowed again and typed her name into the slot, then confirmed the appointment. "Don't stand me up this time," she murmured, turning her head to meet her gaze.

"Hey, I didn't stand you up the *last* time you said that. Never again," Lucy promised, her voice soft. "I'm so sorry about the first time."

"You'll just have to make it up to me. Again," Scarlett said breathily, her white teeth flashing in a soft smile. Lucy's quiet giggle send a shiver right up her spine and she just wanted to lean down and—

"Hey, Scar, can you come help me with…" Olive started as she came back into the room, then trailed off upon seeing she *clearly* interrupted a moment. "Oh, shit, my bad."

The spell had been broken, given the way Lucy pulled back

at the intrusion and began to gather her things. Scarlett's chest hurt, then she turned to Olive. "It's alright. What do you need help with?"

Lucy tucked her things back into her small bag, then walked up to the women. She discreetly squeezed Scarlett's bicep and smiled up at her. "See you tonight. Bye, Olive," she added, wiggling her fingers at the other woman, before leaving the room.

Scarlett let out a breath and brought a hand up to her face. "God help me," she muttered.

"She *wants* you," Olive laughed. "Sorry again."

"It's okay," Scarlett said, shaking her head. "This isn't the place anyway."

"What are you going to do? Are you going to make a move?" Olive asked.

Scarlett dropped her hand back down and shook her head. "I don't know. She's the one with the boyfriend. What am I supposed to say to her? What if she just… What if she's confused and doesn't really want me? We haven't even *talked* about that. All we've done is complain about the shitty men we've slept with. I've never tried to… I don't know, *seduce* a girl before? The girls I've been with were all drinking and ready to go. I've never *come out* or anything."

"Who says you need to come out?" Olive shrugged. "Just go for what you want. You don't have to label anything. She may not be ready for that either. You don't have to come out or anything when you're hooking up with a guy. A girl shouldn't be any different. If she says no, she says no. She doesn't seem like the type to be weird about it if you misread the signals," she went on. "But… I really don't think it'll take too much convincing on your part with her. She was looking at you like she wanted to unwrap you."

Scarlett blushed again and failed miserably to hide her smile. "She's going to come possibly buy some art tonight."

"I promise I won't interrupt this time," Olive laughed, before putting down her tablet. "But you have to help me put all this crap up. Don't worry, we'll be *extra careful* with whatever piece Lucy wants."

Scarlett put her tablet down and shed her blazer. "Alright, alright, fine," she teased, moving with her to clear the room.

ucy returned to her room to get changed for dinner and her...

Well, it wasn't a date. She was just going to a gallery to buy art from a pretty woman. It would look nice in her apartment. *Her* apartment.

She showered again, wanting to be as perfectly presented as possible. She left her curls wavy, putting in a little product to make sure they stayed pristine. She opted for a pair of black, high-waisted jeans and a solid, low-cut red blouse that flowed around her waist and arms. She pulled on her black heels and began doing her makeup in the mirror. She opted for a simple look. Eyeliner, mascara, lip gloss, and some foundation. Nothing gaudy, nothing flashy, nothing crazy.

Thankfully, she had *just* finished swiping another layer of nude gloss over her lips when the cabin door swung open and startled her. She swiveled in the chair at the vanity and met eyes with Chris.

"What are you getting all dolled up for?" Chris asked, his

voice gruff.

Lucy turned away from him and inspected her reflection once more. "I'm going to the art gallery in a little bit."

"So you can go see your girlfriend?" he scoffed, shaking his head. He walked over to what was now his side of the room — she had separated the beds back to their original places in a fit of rage after their last fight — and paced. She hated it when he paced.

"I don't have a girlfriend," Lucy said. "I barely have a boyfriend."

"Really?" Chris snapped, glaring at her. "Why are you being so mean to me? This is all *her*. We just need to get off this damn boat and everything will go back to normal. How could you have left me alone yesterday while you went off to the port? I was worried sick about you. You weren't answering any of my calls, and when you finally *did* come back to the room, you barely said two words to me. I bought this cruise so we could be *happy*, and all you've done is either bitch at me or avoid me."

Lucy frowned and turned to face him again. "Who was it that made a beeline to the fucking casino the *second* we stepped on board? You have no self-control, Christopher. You expect me to do all the work for you while you sit around and do whatever you want."

"I won money—"

"I don't *care* if you won a billion dollars. You have a problem. You were doing so well in rehab and then you ruined it. I don't know why you're *like this*," Lucy exclaimed. "I have tried to be patient and support you. I have *tried* to understand your addiction and do whatever I can to help you get better.

You don't want to help yourself. This isn't a partnership. It's a fucking *prison sentence*."

"You are a bitch," Chris swore, marching up to her. He pointed his finger in her face, his cheeks red with emotion and anger. "I don't know why I put up with this. What *exactly* is going on between you and her? Tell the truth."

Lucy opened her mouth to speak, then closed it again. She blushed and didn't say anything.

Chris's facial expression changed to something resembling acceptance. He nodded and stood up straight, away from her. "That's what I thought. Since when do you like girls?"

"I don't—"

"You don't?" Chris interrupted, then laughed incredulously. "You do nothing but hang out with her and ignore me. You're always talking about her. You're always going to see her. And now you're being mean and talking about things like *breaking up*? We don't *break up*, Lucille. We are *forever*."

It was Lucy's turn to laugh. "We are *not* forever. We're not even right now."

"You are *not* the girl I fell in love with."

"Join the fucking club, Chris," Lucy snapped. "I wish I had known this was my future, because I would've moved *far* across the room in Algebra Two back at UCF."

"I wish you had," Chris said, his voice raised. Lucy *hated* when he shouted at her. Volume was never the issue in hearing what he had to say. "I deserve someone better. Someone who loves *me*. Not some *lesbian*—"

"And I deserve someone who loves *me*," Lucy interrupted. "Not some *deadbeat* who can't do anything but sit in a pile of his own filth and scream into his video game headset all day. At least Scarlett actually pays attention to me and supports me."

"You don't even *know* her."

"I know her enough. She is kind and gentle and sweet."

"And what am I then?"

Lucy bit back her cruel response. Being mean to him wasn't going to fix or change anything and it would only make her look like the bad guy. Not that Chris ever needed any help with twisting the situation against her. She took a deep breath and turned back to the vanity, inspecting her reflection yet again in the mirror. "Just drop it, Chris."

"No, say what you want to say," Chris snapped, jerking her around in her seat again.

Lucy's eyes widened at the roughness. He'd never touched her like that before. She stared up at him, feeling hot with fury. "Don't you *ever* put your hands on me like that again."

"Or what?"

Lucy laughed. "You are something else, Chris. Truly. I've never met anyone who manages to make me so speechless on a daily basis with the sheer *idiocy* of his actions."

"Fuck you, Lucy. I don't have to listen to this shit," Chris said, throwing his hand up. "I'm out of here."

"Bye," Lucy scoffed, and in a moment, Chris had stormed out.

She raised her eyebrows to herself and exhaled heavily, then closed her eyes. Taking a few seconds to calm down, she used the thought of seeing Scarlett to put Chris out of her mind.

Lucy walked into the gallery room on the third deck and looked around. It was packed. No wonder they needed to schedule appointments.

"Hey, you," Scarlett greeted as soon as she came through the door.

"Waiting for me?" Lucy teased, adjusting her ivory purse strap on her shoulder.

"Always," Scarlett laughed, then tilted her head. "You okay? You're flushed."

Lucy's cheeks reddened at the accusation and she lifted her fingers to brush against her face. "Oh. I'm fine."

Scarlett merely arched an inky brow.

Lucy sighed, knowing she wouldn't weasel her way out of an explanation. "Take a guess."

"I'll kill him."

"Get in line," Lucy muttered. "But I'm fine. I promise. Just happy to be here. You're a welcomed distraction."

"That's me," Scarlett said in a sing-song voice. "Happily distracting miserable girlfriends from their terrible men."

Lucy laughed and covered her mouth, her cheeks heating even more. In a different way this time. She followed Scarlett to her little station in the corner of the room, wading through other passengers filling every available space in the gallery. "It's so busy in here."

"It always is on the last day. People finalizing their purchases, getting delivery information confirmed, all that," Scarlett said, pulling a chair out for Lucy. When she sat, Scarlett went around the small table and took the seat opposite her. "Alright then," she sighed, starting up her laptop. "Do you want anything to drink?"

"I'm good," Lucy said. "Thank you."

"No problem," Scarlett said, her eyes scanning the screen in front of her. "Alright, 'Spring Night...'" she hummed, clicking a few times. "I assume you want it framed?"

"Is it extra?" Lucy asked.

Scarlett glanced at her, then back at the screen. "A little. But it's worth it. There's an unframed piece," she said as she jerked her chin.

Lucy glanced back at the artwork behind her, then at one that was framed right next to it. It made a *big* difference. She turned back to Scarlett and nodded. "Framed, please."

"Good girl," Scarlett said as she clicked her wireless mouse. Lucy involuntarily blushed. *Again.*

"Have you made a lot of sales today?" Lucy asked, wanting to break the silence that had settled between them.

"A fair bit," Scarlett nodded, moving her gaze to Lucy. "You're my favorite customer though. Don't tell anyone."

Lucy grinned and mimed zipping her lips shut. Her eyes roamed over Scarlett as she continued ringing her up. The woman's red-painted lips were moving *just* enough with every word she read on her screen. Her eyelashes were long and dusted with mascara, and her skin was smooth with makeup. She had gone for a simple style around the eyes, too, and it was completely show-stopping. Her hair was pulled back into a pretty updo, and she had on what looked like a pair of black diamond earrings.

"Lucy?"

The blonde blinked and lasered her focus back to Scarlett.

"Hmm?"

"I said what cabin number are you?"

"Oh," Lucy mumbled lamely. "Two-oh-four."

"Two-oh-four," Scarlett repeated with each tap of the numbers on her keyboard. She smiled and nodded. "There you are. I have your address here, does this look good?" she asked, gesturing to the tablet poised behind her laptop in front of Lucy. At her nod, Scarlett continued. "Alright then. I've got you at... Five-hundred-forty-six dollars and... seventeen cents," she said. "Any questions?"

"That's less than you said earlier," Lucy said. "What changed?"

"I have my ways. Plus I forgot you have that voucher from the raffle you won earlier this week," Scarlett smirked. "It'll be framed and sent right to your front door."

"That sounds great," Lucy said with a smile. She had enough in savings and she *wanted* to splurge for herself. Every time she looked at the art, it would remind her of Scarlett. "Let's do it."

"Perfect," Scarlett said. "I assume you just want to pay for it outright? I'm supposed to ask if you want to open a credit card, but you and debt don't seem to mix well," she said with a sad smile.

"Ugh," Lucy groaned, shaking her head. "That's the truth. I'll just pay for it. Who knows, maybe Chris will hit the jackpot and I can get every piece in this room," she teased, her curls bouncing as she moved her head.

"If only," Scarlett said, then gestured to the small card reader by the tablet in front of Lucy. "Everything look good there?"

Lucy looked down and read through the words and numbers on the small screen, then nodded. "Yep." She set her purse down atop the table and took out her wallet, then slid her card out.

Just as she was about to swipe, a loud voice saying her name interrupted her. She looked over and her eyes widened as she saw Chris — drunkenly, she assumed — pushing past people in the crammed room to find her.

"Shit," she and Scarlett breathed in unison.

Chris downed another shot of whiskey at the casino bar, then slid the glass toward the bartender. He gestured for another to be poured, but the bartender merely slid his card back to him.

"Declined."

"Excuse me?" Chris scoffed, pushing the card toward him. "Try it again."

"I ran it twice. It declined for insufficient funds."

Chris clenched his jaw and snatched the card back, shoving it into his pocket. "Charge it to my room then. Two-oh-four." He stood up, a little too quickly, and gripped the edge of the bar counter to steady himself. Blinking away the dizziness, he stormed away from the bar, going straight to the lower floors.

"Lucy," Chris called out as he shoved past all the people inside the art gallery. "Lucille Price," he said in a tone that mimicked an angry parent looking for their troublesome child. "Where are you?"

He stopped when he spotted his girlfriend, of *course*, sitting with *her.*

"I should have known," he laughed. "What are you doing?"

"Have you been drinking?" Lucy asked, then she pulled a face. "I can smell it on you."

"Don't worry about it. Not like you care anyway," he said. "What's going on?"

"I'm buying some art for the apartment."

"You're what?"

"You heard what I said," Lucy responded. By this point, all eyes were on them. Chris hadn't even noticed.

"With what money?"

"With *my* money," Lucy said.

"We don't *have* any money," Chris responded. "Try your card."

Lucy frowned and turned back to the card reader. She swiped her card and a small, deep noise sounded from the machine, flashing the word 'declined.' Lucy tried again only to receive the same result. She whipped back to Chris and hissed, "What did you do?!"

"I didn't do anything. You're the one who's broke," Chris shrugged. "And you call *me* financially irresponsible."

"You spent all my money," Lucy said dejectedly, staring up at him. "On what? Booze? Gambling? Both?"

"Doesn't matter," Chris said. "All that matters is you can't get your stupid art from this *whore.*"

"Is there a problem here?" Gavin then asked, coming to stand next to the trio.

"No problem at all," Chris said, turning to face Gavin. "We were just leaving. We can't afford this art, no point in taking up any more of your time. Lucy, let's go."

"Lucy," Scarlett then said quietly, a pained expression on her face. "You don't have to—"

"*You* leave her alone," Chris snapped, pointing at Scarlett. "You've done *enough*."

"Chris, stop," Lucy said, her voice wavering. Blinking back tears, she rose from her seat. Glancing at Scarlett, she shook her head. "I'm sorry."

Chris's patience ran out and he grabbed Lucy's wrist, pulling her through the other people and out of the room. They walked through the hallway, passing the large ballroom filled with tables and people having dinner. Chris barreled toward the elevators or stairs — whichever came first — so they could get back down to the room. This whole charade was *over*. Lucy wasn't going to see that art dealer ever again. They were going to get off the boat in less than a day and go back to their *regular* lives. Lucy would calm down and stop being such a bitch, doing insane things like talking about *breaking up* and being with a *woman*, and everything would return to normal.

"Let *go* of me," Lucy grunted as she wrenched her arm from Chris's grip.

"We're going back to the room so we can pack and be ready to leave in the morning," Chris said, turning to face her. He reached for her wrist again. "Come on."

"I'm not going anywhere with you," Lucy said, stepping back as if she'd been burned. "You *humiliated* me in there. In front of all those people. That artwork was going to be for the apartment. It would look nice. It's something tangible, something that you won't just piss away at a blackjack table."

"Fuck off, Lucy," Chris swore, shaking his head. He couldn't believe she was being so selfish. That art woman had poisoned her brain, she wasn't thinking straight. "You're acting *crazy*."

"*You* are the crazy one," Lucy said with a condescending laugh. "You're the one who barged in there and dragged me out like I'm some sort of thing that needs to be *handled*. I can't believe you."

"The feeling is mutual," Chris said as he shook his head. "I wish we had never come on this cruise."

"I wish I'd come alone," Lucy snapped back. "You can do whatever you want, spend whatever you can find, but you better not fucking come back to our room tonight. Find somewhere else to sleep. I'm sure the bartenders won't mind babysitting you."

Chris's eyes widened and he clenched his fists together. "Fine. Wouldn't want to sleep next to you anyway," he said. She truly had gone insane. He remembered a time when she was falling over herself to be around him. They spent all their free time together, they laughed, they took pictures, they were the couple *everyone* in their friend groups envied. Now? Who would want *this*? "Make sure my shit is packed up by the time we leave tomorrow."

"Happily," Lucy said, her tone laced with venom.

Chris stared at her for a second, waiting for her to say something else or even take anything back, but when she didn't, he merely shook his head and stomped off in the other direction.

He would never want to spend his life with someone who obviously couldn't give less of a shit about him anyway.

Scarlett stared in the space where Lucy had been just *seconds* ago. She was in complete shock and disbelief at what happened.

"That was crazy," Gavin said quietly, then turned to the onlookers who seemed to be thinking the same thing. "It's alright, everyone, go back to what you were doing."

Scarlett put her head in her hands and felt like sobbing. She knew it wasn't her place to go after that idiot Chris and throttle him, but she wanted to. She wanted *Lucy* to. What was supposed to be an exciting time for her, a fun purchase that she would have to look forward to when she went home, was soured by jealousy and greed.

"You okay?" Gavin asked, looking down at her.

Scarlett lifted her head, her eyes tired. "No."

Gavin frowned, then gestured to the white purse still perched on the table. "She left this."

Scarlett's eyes roamed to the bag and she reached out to gently touch the leather exterior. "She was basically dragged out of here. Can we not report him?"

"Not our job," Gavin said warningly. "I know you care about her, but you need to remember the rules," he said quietly. He looked over, glad to see Olive was taking over the majority of the rest of the sales. He needed a few moments with Scarlett. "Why was he saying the things he did?"

"He's crazy," Scarlett said simply. "He is jealous and thinks there's something going on between me and Lucy."

"Is there?"

Scarlett didn't answer right away. The *responsible* answer would be to deny anything, to claim she had no feelings for that blonde angel. Before she could do that, she felt bile rise in the pit of her throat. How could she possibly deny what was happening between her and Lucy? It was a disservice to her, to *them*. She blinked a few times, then cast her gaze downward. "I don't know."

Gavin folded his arms and shifted his weight back and forth on both feet, swaying a bit. "We both need to get back to work."

"What about her purse?" Scarlett asked.

Gavin eyed the bag, then looked back at all the passengers needing help. He sighed deeply and turned his attention back down to Scarlett. "Finish up with your appointments then take it back to her. Be discreet about it. And don't get involved in anything you don't have to."

Scarlett nodded as he walked away, then she slid the purse toward her. Putting it down by her feet for safe-keeping, she composed herself, then called for her next guest to check out.

As they closed up the gallery, Scarlett was feeling more and more nauseated.

"What are you going to do?"

Scarlett turned to Olive and felt like crying. "Gavin told me to take her purse back."

"What if he's in the room?"

"I can only hope he is not," Scarlett said softly. "She needs this back though, and the room is the only place I can think of to find her. I just... The thought of being near *him* literally makes me want to chew through steel."

Olive gave her a sympathetic smile. "Don't do that. You'll ruin all your pretty teeth."

Scarlett let out a defeated laugh and rubbed her forehead with a few fingers. "God, what have I gotten myself into? Should I just leave the purse here or with guest services? I can't possibly go to her room and..."

"Yes you can. And you should. This might very well be the last time you get to speak to Lucy. Hopefully her boyfriend isn't there and you two can hash things out *alone*. It isn't fair on either of you to let whatever this is slip through your fingers. You *owe* each other that much."

Scarlett nodded and picked up the purse. She looked down at it. This was the only piece of Lucy she had left, the only excuse she could cling onto to warrant seeing her one last time. Was she so selfish to blow up her life for another night just to catch another glimpse of her? To tell her how she felt? To...

"Go," Olive said, interrupting her internal strife. "I can

finish up in here for you."

Scarlett blinked again, then nodded. She left the room without another word.

Scarlett held onto the purse for dear life as she waded through the hallways on the ship. This would turn utterly *disastrous* if Chris was in that room with her. She might not even be there at all. If he *was* there, she'd simply deliver the purse and walk away immediately. Gavin was right, she didn't need to get in the middle of another couple's fight, especially not on the last night of their vacation.

But Scarlett knew damn well if Chris was in there and wanted to cause a scene, she wouldn't be able to resist defending Lucy. She worried she'd ruin Lucy's purse by beating him upside the head with it.

Maybe it would be better just to let this go, let *her* go. She wasn't sure if she would ever see her again. Chris seemed to have a pretty solid vice around her, and now half the damn ship knew how controlling he was. Scarlett wished better for Lucy, but didn't know how to *help*. She would never be able to force her into anything, nor did they have enough history for her to give her any real *deep* advice. Scarlett had been the same way when she'd been in that situation.

Scarlett had never done anything like this before. She had never felt so close to someone and had never taken risks with her own job like this. She had taken up cruise life to escape all the drama of her days in London, and now here she was, right in the middle of an extremely *dramatic* situation. At least Lucy wasn't some rich prick who used his money to flex on innocent girls. Up until now, she had always wished she could go back in time to before she met Raphael and stop her younger self.

But now she was grateful for that, because without it, she wouldn't have started working on the ship, and she never would have met Lucy.

Though there were dozens of people in every corner she passed, she felt like she was the only one on that boat. Her ears rang as she continued toward the staircase, dissociating the entire way. Part of her wondered if she was overreacting with how anxious she felt. Was she overthinking? Was this too much? Had Chris ruined all the progress they'd made with one another and now Lucy would have second thoughts?

Scarlett frowned to herself. Second thoughts about *what*? It wasn't like they were *anything*. They had shared a few close moments together, but they hadn't discussed anything past being a worker and passenger on a ship. They hadn't messaged much other than confirming to meet up at the piano bar. They hadn't talked about what would happen *after*. For all Scarlett knew, Lucy had no intention of continuing contact with her after she stepped foot back in Florida.

She sighed jaggedly to herself and tried to shake those treacherous thoughts away. Assuming the worst wasn't going to help her heart rate or stomach in that moment.

Scarlett's hand slid down the railing for the stairs as she descended one floor. She knew nobody was watching her — nobody important anyway — and had to put her nerves out of her head. She prayed to a god she didn't believe in that this went well and nothing blew up in her face.

The hallway to Lucy's room seemed a thousand miles long. Right foot, left foot, right foot, left foot, again and again until she finally reached room 204. Scarlett stared at the numbers, as if they were written in another language. Her eyes roamed over the white paint on the cabin door. She couldn't believe she was there doing this. She still had time to turn around, go back to guest services, and drop the bag off like a good worker, like a *normal* worker. Yes, she could do that. She could just…

What? Lose this chance?

Scarlett huffed out a quiet breath, telling herself to get a grip. It was just a bag. She would give it back and walk away. That's all.

Her hand shook as she lifted it and rapped on the door three times.

K nock, knock, knock.

Lucy turned her head from staring at the ceiling and looked at the closed door. Her stomach turned and she ignored the knock, not moving from her position on the bed. It was probably Chris, trying to tell her he's sorry for something she wasn't even mad about. She doubted he even *knew* what she was mad about. He would never see anything wrong with his actions and figure out a way to turn it back on her, then convince her she was in the wrong and *she'd* end up apologizing.

What a joke.

Lucy was about to stare at the ceiling again when she heard three more knocks. She huffed a breath and pushed herself to sit up, then swung her legs over the side of the bed. She walked to the door and yanked it open. "Chris, I said don't come—" she started, then stopped abruptly when she met those pretty, dark coffee eyes of Scarlett Sinclair.

"Hi there," Scarlett said with a shy smile. "I, um... You forgot your purse."

Lucy looked down at the purse she held up, then glanced over her shoulder at the room. After a quick scan, she turned back to Scarlett. "I left that?"

"You did," Scarlett nodded, handing it to her. "Understandable, of course."

Lucy sighed and looked down at her purse clutched between her fingers. "I feel like I left more than my purse back there."

"I'm sorry," Scarlett said quietly from the doorway. "He was out of line."

"I don't think he's ever been *in* line," Lucy said sadly, her voice small. "I'm so embarrassed. I hope I didn't cause too much trouble for you. And I'm sorry about the whole artwork thing and my card declining, I didn't—"

"Lucy," Scarlett interrupted, reaching out to touch her shoulder. "Stop saying sorry. It's alright. I didn't think twice about it. Are *you* okay?"

Lucy cut her eyes back up to look at her and felt the back of her eyelids burn with that question. She said nothing.

Scarlett frowned and stepped forward, pulling her in for a hug. The door swung shut behind her. "I'm sorry," she whispered, cradling her head against her chest and neck. "I'm so sorry."

Lucy's dam burst and she broke down into tears against Scarlett, her arms enveloping her in a hug so tight, Scarlett's breathing nearly ceased. Lucy dug her fingers into the material of the back of Scarlett's blazer and her body shook with the force of her crying. She didn't even know what she was crying about anymore. It wasn't like any of this was a surprise: Chris's behavior, his jealousy, the downfall of her relationship, the loss of her money. She had been living this way for years now.

The only difference was the woman she was holding onto for dear life.

After she calmed down, she slowly pulled back from Scarlett, her cheeks red and damp with tears.

"Poor thing," Scarlett cooed in a whisper, bringing a hand up to gently wipe her face clean. She smiled slightly and kept her hand there, her thumb gently caressing her cheek. "I much prefer you happy, Lucy."

Lucy laughed weakly under her breath and held her gaze. Something shifted in Scarlett as they continued staring at each other, and Lucy felt a jolt go *straight* to her core.

Rising on her tiptoes, Lucy leaned up and crushed her lips to Scarlett's.

The taller woman melted in Lucy's embrace and immediately returned her kiss with just as much enthusiasm. Lucy gripped onto whatever she could of Scarlett and deepened their kiss immediately, their bodies swaying with the force of their union. A small moan of desperation and elation escaped Lucy's lips, Scarlett swallowing it in earnest. The blonde moved one hand from Scarlett's back up to her hair, her fingers pulling loose the bun she had twisted atop her head. Scarlett's raven hair tumbled down over her shoulders, and Lucy took the opportunity to weave her fingers through her straight, soft locks.

Scarlett, meanwhile, was touching every inch of Lucy she could, their kiss never breaking. One hand stayed holding Lucy's face as their lips melded together, her fingertips brushing against some of her golden curls. Her other hand was stroking down Lucy's waist against her blouse, then slid around to cup one of her asscheeks over her jeans.

Lucy moaned again at the contact and arched her hips toward Scarlett, trying to get some form of relief. She tugged the woman's lower lip between her teeth, experimenting with what she could get away with. Chris was so *vanilla* in bed and never wanted to be adventurous; however, when Scarlett moaned — a sound Lucy would never forget — and answered her action by biting her lip back, Lucy knew this woman wouldn't give her any such problems.

"Overdressed," was all Lucy could rasp out.

Scarlett nodded quickly in agreement and moved her arms out of her blazer as Lucy hurriedly pushed it off her. The offending garment dropped to the floor and Scarlett quickly kicked off her heels. The dark-haired woman paused her task of undressing to taking Lucy's face in both her hands, their tongues dancing with the intensity of their kiss. She took several moments just kissing Lucy, as if breaking apart would kill them both.

"I only have the small bed," Lucy whispered between kisses, her breathing labored.

"Won't stop me from making you scream," Scarlett breathed back, her hands leaving Lucy's face and traveling to the ends of her blouse. She pulled it over Lucy's head and tossed it aside, then immediately leaned down to begin peppering her neck and chest with more hot kisses. Lucy moaned and held the back of Scarlett's head against her, tilting her own head back at the feeling of it all. Her jaw fell slack as Scarlett's nimble fingers moved against her back, and her bra was soon loose as her lover undid the clasp. Lucy shrugged out of her bra and let it fall to the floor, and Scarlett wasted *no* time in showing each of her breasts and nipples ample attention.

Lucy felt like she'd died and gone to heaven. Her knees gave way and thankfully Scarlett kept her upright.

"I've got you, darling," Scarlett whispered as she held onto her.

Lucy could have sobbed. She was overwhelmed with both pleasure and emotion, things she had *never* felt before. Kissing boys, Chris, had never felt so right. It hadn't felt wrong, necessarily, but this brought her entire world down.

Hands shaking, Lucy carefully unbuttoned the blouse Scarlett had on, then pulled it untucked from her suit trousers. Scarlett helped get it off her, then Lucy moved her hands around to undo Scarlett's bra. Her breasts came free and Lucy dipped her head down and did the same thing Scarlett had done to her.

All of this was happening so fast that Lucy didn't have time to worry about whether she was doing everything right. She just followed her instincts and listened to Scarlett's moans of encouragement. Scarlett's grip on her curls tightened when Lucy flicked her tongue over one of her nipples, her fingers toying with the other one. She took that as a good sign and continued, then it was *her* turn to keep Scarlett on her feet.

"Bed," Scarlett rasped, kissing Lucy again as they shuffled over to the tiny twin bed. Lucy went down first and pulled Scarlett atop her, the feeling of their chests pressed together nearly sending her over the edge. Lucy matched every movement the other woman made, their hands blurred with the speed at which they were trying to touch each other. Scarlett rolled her hips against Lucy's and the blonde was on the verge of losing her mind with the friction.

Scarlett broke the kiss and sat up, staring down at Lucy. Scarlett's chest heaved and her hair was disheveled.

She was *radiant*.

Lucy's breathing was so heavy, she was worried she'd have some kind of asthma attack. Scarlett moved off her and began unbuttoning her jeans. Lucy felt a little nervous, only because she had never done this with a woman before, but trusted Scarlett implicitly. Lucy arched her hips off the bed as Scarlett curled her fingers into the waistband of her jeans and panties and pulled them down her legs in one motion. Lucy moved her legs out of the garments and let Scarlett toss the clothes to the floor.

"So beautiful," Scarlett breathed as her palms spread across Lucy's knees and pushed her legs apart.

Lucy blushed and for once, believed that compliment.

"Have you ever done this before?" Scarlett whispered, looking up at Lucy with hooded eyes. "With a woman."

"I haven't," Lucy admitted, knowing better than to lie. "Is that okay?"

"Yeah," Scarlett laughed breathily, tilting her head. Her fingers were still tracing little patterns on the sensitive skin of Lucy's inner thighs. "Of course it's okay. I just wanted to make sure. I don't want to do anything that makes you uncomfortable. You let me know if you want me to stop, alright?"

"Sure," Lucy said with a nod, propping herself up on

her forearms. "Does everything look… okay down there?" It was different for her to experience this with a woman who was familiar with the anatomy and what wouldn't look right. Men didn't really care about that sort of thing, at least in her experience. They didn't *know*.

"Trust me," Scarlett laughed, her voice ragged, "everything looks *perfect*."

Lucy blushed again — something she'd been doing a *lot* lately — and nodded bashfully. "Okay," she whispered.

Scarlett glanced up at her and smiled, crawling over her to give her a few more kisses. The clinch was languid and drawn out, making Lucy's toes curl with every passing second. Her lips parted in a gentle gasp as she felt Scarlett's fingers explore between her legs. Lucy nodded in encouragement and lost herself in their kiss once more.

Scarlett inserted one finger inside her, then another, until Lucy was panting against her lips. Their moans sounded together in the room and Lucy was rocking her hips in earnest against Scarlett's expert hand, wanting more, more, *more*.

"You're enjoying yourself," Scarlett whispered.

"Yeah," Lucy barely managed to squeak out. She couldn't even fucking think straight. Was this how it was supposed to feel?

Scarlett laughed quietly, a sound that Lucy could only compare to velvet chocolate, and she slowly removed her fingers from her body. Lucy crooned with the loss and opened her eyes, Scarlett's right there in front of her. Their noses brushed together. "Aww," Scarlett murmured, pecking her lips once, twice more. "Don't worry, darling. I'll give you what you want.

I just had to see if you were ready."

"Are you always this hot?" Lucy asked, her chest heaving and her lips parted. *"Jesus."*

"Talking about a man while I'm about to fuck you, rude," Scarlett grinned, kissing her ear, then down to her jawline, then her neck. "Thank you for the compliment, though. I do hope you'll call out my name instead of God's," she whispered. "It's nice to have the challenge."

"I don't think that'll be a— problem," Lucy moaned, her breath hitching in her throat as Scarlett's blazing trail of kisses seared down her body.

"Lie back and enjoy yourself," Scarlett murmured, nipping the skin of Lucy's stomach gently. Lucy did *just* that and rested her head against the pillow, her gaze downward. Scarlett settled between her legs and wrapped her arms around Lucy's thighs, squeezing tightly to hold on. Scarlett leaned down and shifted just her eyes up so she could watch Lucy as she took her first taste.

When her tongue stroked up her center, Lucy decided she would pursue religion and worship Scarlett Sinclair.

"Scarlett," Lucy breathed, her voice a bit higher and raspier than usual. The other woman hummed smugly in response and continued licking her in all the right places. Lucy's eyes fluttered closed as she gave into the warm feelings shooting through every crevice of her being. Her fingers tangled in Scarlett's hair and she held onto her head, letting her do all the work.

After what couldn't have been more than two or three minutes, Lucy's orgasm ripped through her body like a freight train. She tugged Scarlett's hair, holding her head firmly against her center as she rode wave after wave of pleasure. Scarlett didn't seem to mind with the way she was lapping at her like a woman starved.

"Okay, okay," Lucy giggled breathlessly, her nerve-endings shot with ecstasy. She slowly pushed Scarlett away and tried to catch her breath, her chest and stomach heaving with the exertion. Her skin was flushed and she felt like she'd just been reborn.

"I'm open to any and all feedback," Scarlett said from above her. Lucy opened her eyes and focused on the woman, then simply answered her by pulling her down for a kiss. She moaned as Scarlett's tongue darted into her mouth and she tasted herself.

"You've done that before," Lucy whispered against Scarlett's lips.

"Once or twice," Scarlett responded, pecking her lips between every few words. "But you're easily my favorite. And the only one who's ever meant something."

Lucy smiled against her kisses and slid her hand up to cradle her cheek. "You're so sweet."

"I mean it," Scarlett pressed, trailing the tip of her nose up her cheek.

Lucy smiled wider and pecked her lips, then her nose, then her cheek. "It's your turn now."

Scarlett moved onto her back as Lucy switched positions with her and began showering her with kisses *all* over. Tears pricked her eyes as Lucy was distracted loving on her. She would not cry. She would *not*.

The tears that threatened to spill over were not sad ones. They were over the top *happy* ones. She had waited so long to find someone to make her feel this way. She had never believed in something as silly as love at first sight… until now. Scarlett had spent years guarding her heart after everything that happened with Raphael. She had told herself she'd never let anybody in and give someone that power over her ever again, but with Lucy, she wanted to bare her soul.

Lucy's hands ran over the belt locked around her waist and she arched her hips so the woman could slide it through the loops and toss it to the floor. Lucy quickly followed suit by undoing her trousers and pulling those down, along with her knickers. Her skin prickled along her arms and back of her neck as she lay exposed before Lucy.

She felt *seen*. She wasn't being leered at, she was being admired, treasured, *worshiped*. Scarlett soaked in the feeling of Lucy's lips brushing against her skin lower, and lower, and lower…

"Taking your time?" Scarlett teased, only if just to get away from her own inner monologue.

Lucy looked up, resting her cheek on Scarlett's inner thigh, her arms wrapped around her legs like Scarlett had done to her earlier. "I want to remember every second of tonight. You are so beautiful."

Scarlett now knew what it meant to swoon. Was this how Lucy felt when she had complimented her just before this? Did she feel the same flames burn through every cell under her skin?

"You're going to help me, right? I don't want to do it wrong," Lucy said, trailing her finger along the apex of Scarlett's thighs — not *quite* where Scarlett wanted her to be, but it was obvious she was enjoying taking her time and teasing.

"Of course," Scarlett responded. "I doubt you'll do anything wrong."

"I've never done this before," Lucy said with a small frown. "I just want to make you feel as good as you made me feel."

"You already are," Scarlett reassured. "Just do what you like to have done to you. I guarantee I'll enjoy myself," she laughed softly.

"Promise?"

Scarlett stared at Lucy and saw insecurity rearing its ugly head behind those enchanting blue eyes of hers. She pushed herself to sit up and gently pulled Lucy to come closer so they could share another kiss. "My love," Scarlett whispered, holding her face gently with her hands, "I promise that you are all I want. I'm going to enjoy myself no matter what because it's *you*. Don't be nervous. I'm right here and I'll tell you if I want you to do something different, okay? Would that help?"

"Yes," Lucy said, nodding. She rested her forehead against hers and sighed shakily. "Sorry."

"Don't be," Scarlett murmured. "I'm yours."

Lucy smiled slightly and kissed her again, making Scarlett turn inside out. They returned to their earlier positions and Scarlett was about to coach Lucy on how to make her come when she felt a finger gently circle her clit. Scarlett's jaw hung open and she tilted her head back against the pillows. "*Fuck*," she blurted out.

Lucy looked up and smiled proudly. "Even you *cussing* is hot."

"I'm a woman of... many talents," Scarlett breathed, her head still thrown back. "That feels so good."

Lucy's smile grew and she continued rubbing gentle circles against Scarlett's center, watching how every inch of her body reacted. Scarlett reached down to gently stroke Lucy's forearms as she touched her. She hadn't a clue why Lucy had been worried about being good at this; it was obvious she was a *natural*.

Lucy used the moisture built up between Scarlett's legs as an invitation to go further. She copied Scarlett and slipped two fingers inside her, making the woman beneath her moan out a guttural noise she'd never heard before. The sound must have spurred Lucy on, because she started pumping those gorgeous fingers in and out, making Scarlett's breathing more and more shallow with each movement. Lucy curled the digits inside her and Scarlett shivered, her nails digging into Lucy's forearms.

"Minx," Scarlett muttered to herself, spreading her legs even wider for her lover. "Taste me," she begged.

Lucy stopped her hand and smirked. She removed her fingers, then sucked them clean, causing Scarlett to moan again. She was thankful she'd been looking that time and not letting her eyes roll into the back of her head. Before she could make another flirty quip to the woman between her legs, Lucy dove down to get *properly* acquainted with her body. A long sigh escaped Scarlett's mouth and she stared down at those blonde curls bobbing as Lucy went down on her. Scarlett moved her hands from Lucy's arms to her hair, pulling it up and out of her face. She twisted it atop her head and held it there.

Lucy was *devouring* her.

Scarlett had never felt so good in her entire life. This woman didn't even need any bloody direction, she knew exactly where every sweet spot on her body was. Scarlett kept quiet — aside from her moaning — and let Lucy go to *work*.

In the middle of her feast, Lucy began fingering her again, and Scarlett was sure her body was about to spontaneously combust. She moaned out another string of curse words and dirty nothings as Lucy grew more and more determined to ruin her for any other person on the planet.

Lucy's tongue eventually tore pleasure through her and Scarlett was seeing stars. Her eyes closed and she gripped tight onto Lucy's head as the blonde sucked her clit and made her legs shake. After a few moments, Scarlett panted and eased Lucy off her. Her arms fell limp by her sides and she was *exhausted* with pleasure.

"I'm open to any and all feedback," Lucy teased in a whisper, suddenly laying beside Scarlett. It was a tight fit on that bed, and Scarlett was surprised they hadn't fallen off yet, but it was all the more reason to stay close to her. Scarlett laughed quietly at her words and turned on her side, their limbs and bodies tangling together.

"You are so good at fucking me," Scarlett whispered against her lips, before they shared a deep kiss. Her hands roamed down Lucy's back and to her ass. She squeezed one of her cheeks again and pulled her hips to press against hers. "I can't get enough of you."

"That makes two of us," Lucy murmured, wiggling to try and get some sort of friction and release. "I've never wanted to come twice before. Usually I barely make it to the first time, but I don't want to *sleep*."

Scarlett laughed again — she'd never *laughed* during sex so much. She'd never *enjoyed* herself so much in all her life. "I'll make you come as many times as you want, darling."

"I like it when you call me that."

"What, 'darling?'"

"Mhm."

Scarlett smiled and kissed her again. "My darling Lucy."

"The accent *really* does wonders with that pet name, too," Lucy giggled, running her tongue along her lower lip. "Not sure what pet name a Southern accent sounds good with."

"Mmm… anything that comes from your mouth is good," Scarlett grinned.

"You're too sweet to me. Like honey," she whispered. "Do you like the name 'honey?'"

"Not sure… Use it in a sentence," Scarlett murmured.

Lucy smiled and kissed her way around Scarlett's cheek and to her ear. From there, she whispered, "I want you to make me come again, honey."

Scarlett felt a *deep* shudder crawl down her spine and she clenched her thighs together to try and still the throbbing between her legs. "I like 'honey,'" was all Scarlett could get out.

"Good girl," Lucy said, nipping her earlobe gently with her teeth.

Scarlett was glad Lucy had grown in confidence in the last hour, because this woman was a goddamn siren. She had never been so turned on in all her life, and she'd, regrettably, had a *lot* of sexual partners in her promiscuous past. After a while, none of that seemed to make her feel better or numb any pain, so she'd signed off hooking up and dating for a long time. Lucy was the first one to break the curse and Scarlett wanted to *live* between her legs.

"Lie back for me again and I'll give you what you want," Scarlett murmured, planting a harsh kiss on her neck. She wasn't sure if it would leave a mark, but she couldn't bring it in herself to care.

She *hoped* Chris saw it.

Lucy held Scarlett as close as she could against her chest, their legs tangled. They were languidly kissing, neither of them in a hurry to do much more. Scarlett had given her *three* more orgasms after the first and Lucy felt like she was going to disintegrate. She had never felt *so* worshiped before. With

Chris, she couldn't wait to get things over. There were a few times where she would be excited to hop into bed with him, but she usually only got off by thinking about something else. Chris was the only person she'd ever had sex with, so she didn't know it was *supposed* to feel like this. Her night with Scarlett made her completely understand why people raved about fucking.

It also made her a little sad that she had been missing out on something so mind-blowing for the last six years of her life.

She also didn't know when she was going to get it again after tonight. But she couldn't think about that and ruin the moment.

"Tell me about these," Lucy murmured, coming out of her turmoiled inner thoughts. She ran her hand gently along Scarlett's inked left arm, her fingers tracing every design she could. "It's a little bit of everything, huh?"

"Yeah," Scarlett said, holding her arm up so they could see the tattoos better. "I started when I was eighteen. This was my first," she said, rotating her arm to reveal a snake on her inner forearm. "I got it on my birthday. I was so excited to get a tattoo. Mum wanted to kill me." Scarlett and Lucy both laughed quietly. Lucy continued tracing her soft skin. "It doesn't really mean anything, I just wanted a snake. I thought it looked cool. I picked it from one of the booklets at the front of the shop. But once I got one, I couldn't stop. I was getting them as soon as I got the extra money," she explained, turning her arm over slowly. "This one took the longest," Scarlett continued, adjusting in the bed to show off the upper half of her arm. From elbow to shoulder were winding flowers creeping up her arm: roses, sunflowers, lavender, tulips, dandelions.

"Why these flowers?" Lucy asked quietly, her fingers moving up to inspect each one.

"Well, roses are my favorite. Red roses, specifically." Scarlett turned her arm as Lucy's fingers explored. "I have always loved gardening, ever since I was young. It's something me and my nan used to do a lot when I'd be out of school. She taught me everything I know about flowers. I loved spending time with her. She was my favorite person in the world."

"Is she…?"

"She's gone," Scarlett said simply. "She died when I was nineteen."

"That must have been devastating for you. How old was she?"

"She had just turned sixty-nine. She had a heart attack."

"That's awful," Lucy frowned, moving her hand from her arm to squeeze her waist. "I'm so sorry."

"Thank you," Scarlett murmured. "It was definitely difficult. It was my first real experience with loss. I was in uni at the time and it was almost impossible for me to get out of bed. I still harbor guilt for that time frame because my mum lost her mum. She was grieving too and I wasn't there for her. I was too wrapped up in my own shit."

"Grief doesn't choose sides, Scarlett. It's okay. Your mom knows that. I promise she does."

"I know," Scarlett sighed. Her voice wavered with those two words, then she soldiered on, clearing her throat. "It took about six months for me to get back to normal. I spent too much of my time partying and drowning any feelings I had. I graduated from Sotheby's and got an internship at an interior design firm near Cambridge. Things were a bit easier after that."

"So you always wanted to work in interior design?"

"Pretty much," Scarlett nodded. "I was always rearranging furniture in the house — especially my bedroom — when I was younger. Making a room look good always just made me happy. Kind of weird, I know."

"Not weird at all," Lucy reassured. "That's how I felt about fashion. Clothes. I wasn't super confident growing up and there were things I couldn't exactly control: my face, my weight, for the most part, my personality... but I could control what I wore. I began to explore different styles and found what I was comfortable in, I experimented with makeup, and eventually fell into my niche."

Scarlett turned over on her side and furrowed her brows. "Lucy, you are the most beautiful thing I've ever laid eyes on."

Lucy's lips parted and she blushed *darkly*. "I..." she trailed off, her brain mush.

Scarlett put her out of her misery and kissed her so deeply, Lucy worried her brain was going to go from mush to seeping out her ears. Lucy's hand traveled down Scarlett's waist and she palmed her ass, crushing her against her. They kissed for what felt like hours, and only pulled away to get more air.

"So... flowers?" Lucy rasped.

Scarlett laughed again and turned on her back once more, holding up her left arm. "Yes. Flowers. These are all the ones I used to plant with Nan. Then I have two cardinals here, one for Nan and one for me," she said, turning her arm so she could see the red birds. "And a duck because I like ducks."

"Ducks are cool," Lucy giggled.

"A garden tattoo wouldn't be complete without bugs, so I have a few ladybirds, a—"

"A few *what*?"

"Ladybirds," Scarlett repeated, shifting so she could get her other arm out from under Lucy. She pointed to the small group of tiny red, yellow, and orange bugs with black spots on their backs. "See?"

"You mean a *ladybug*?"

Scarlett looked over. "Is that what you lot call them?"

"That's the *correct* word for them, yes."

Scarlett rolled her eyes and tapped the insects. "Fine. *Ladybugs*, a few bees surrounding the roses, and there's a beetle somewhere... ah, there it is," she said, pointing to a dark blue beetle just above her elbow. It was walking along one of the flower stems.

She had similar designs on her other arm, different flowers and insects. Lucy wanted to call them sleeves, but they were *just* different enough that she wasn't sure it would be the correct terminology. She didn't know much about tattoos. She'd leave all that to Scarlett, she pulled them off way better than Lucy ever could.

"What about down here?" Lucy asked as she sat up and crawled down to the base of the bed. The frame and mattress creaked with the movement. "These?" she breathed, skimming her tongue up Scarlett's inner thigh.

Scarlett whimpered quietly and spread her legs. "Those... are a bunch of nonsense," she managed to croak out, Lucy's tongue going further and further up her skin. "There's another snake down there and a large vase of flowers…"

"Mhmmm," Lucy hummed against her thigh, moving agonizingly slow in her journey upward. "Which flowers?"

"Lilies," Scarlett said softly, the last syllable hitching in a gasp as Lucy's mouth was suddenly on her center again.

Any other talk about tattoos, flowers, varying insect dialects, dead grandparents, or how beautiful Lucy was were postponed until further notice.

ucy slowly blinked open her eyes, unsure of what on earth happened to her. Why was she so sore? What was this weight on top of her—

Oh.

A small smile crept its way onto her mouth and she slowly stroked the masse of dark hair away from her face. Scarlett was sleeping soundly, draped across her chest. They were both under the covers, melded together due to the small size of the bed. Lucy languidly ran her hands over Scarlett's perfect body, her fingers brushing her smooth skin and curves.

That movement caused Scarlett to stir. Lazily, the other woman moved and looked around, then met eyes with Lucy. She smiled tiredly and settled in her embrace. "Morning."

"Hi," Lucy said, searching her eyes. "How did you sleep?"

"Good," Scarlett sighed, turning so she could stretch out. She kept one arm firmly around Lucy though, just in case she moved too much and she went flying off the mattress. "I'm so sore, what did you do to me last night?"

Lucy laughed quietly and nodded. "I'm sore, too. Looks like we're even," she smirked, not wanting to leave the warm cocoon they'd made for each other.

Scarlett leaned over and pressed a kiss to Lucy's lips, causing the other woman to let out a soft moan of pleasure. Lucy returned her kiss, pulling her slender body to press even harder against hers. She could feel her body properly waking up and responding to every touch. A huge part of Lucy wanted to lean into this and just let go, allow herself to feel all the wonderful things Scarlett had shown her *all* night long.

But… she couldn't.

Slowly, Lucy pulled away and broke their kiss. Scarlett opened her eyes and looked at her in a way that pulled Lucy's heart right from her chest. It was as if she knew. As if she'd feared this. And now Lucy was making all those fears a reality.

"Scarlett, I…"

Something in Scarlett's eyes shifted that caught Lucy off-guard. Her sweet, adoring eyes that she'd woken up to just moments ago had frosted over and become distant. Lucy swallowed and rested her forehead against hers, keeping Scarlett close. "Chris can't come back and find us," she whispered.

"Leave him," Scarlett said against her lips.

"It's not that simple…"

"It *is*. Leave him and I'll love you more than anyone has before. I'll show you the happiness you crave. I'd *never* hurt you like he does. You'd only smile with me. No more tears, no more nights wishing things could be different, just *us*," Scarlett said pleadingly. "Don't make me beg for you."

"We have an apartment together. I have to handle things

when we get off this boat. Things with Chris will never be how they were, especially now that I cheated on him," Lucy said sadly. She had never considered herself unfaithful, but she couldn't say that anymore. "I don't regret anything of what happened," she then added quickly as Scarlett started to pull away from her. She kept her close, forcing her to stay pressed against her. She needed to hear this. "I wish things could be easy. I wish I could just stay here with you and not have to worry about anything else in the world. But I have to go back home, I have to get my life together. You helped me make a big decision," she said, staring into Scarlett's eyes. "But now I have to do the rest of the work. I hate that I'm hurting you, honey," she whispered, feeling tears form at the utter *sadness* plastered across Scarlett's face. She looked *betrayed*.

"I'm never going to see you again, am I?" Scarlett whispered, a few tears rolling down her cheeks.

"I never said that," Lucy said, shaking her head. She kissed the salty droplets away from Scarlett's face and breathed shakily against her skin. "I just said I need to handle things back home. Handle *him*. I can't do that if I'm here. It's going to be difficult and a big headache, and it will take time, but it's going to happen one way or another. It's not fair that I drag you in the middle of it."

"I'm *already* in the middle of it, Lucy," Scarlett said, pushing gently out of her embrace. She sat up and climbed out of bed so she could get her clothes back on. "I understand you have to break up with him properly first, but... I don't know," Scarlett sighed, shaking her head. "I don't know why I expect some sort of happily ever after."

Lucy frowned and got out of bed, reaching for one of the robes the ship had provided her that was hanging up on the bathroom door. She wrapped it around herself and tied a knot in the waist to keep it snug. "Our story is not over."

"Isn't it?" Scarlett said sadly, looking down at her. "You'll get off the boat in just a few hours and that'll be it. You'll go back to your regular life, I'll be here stuck on this ship, and we probably won't talk again. You'll forget about me."

Lucy closed the distance between them and brought Scarlett down for a kiss that made the taller woman dissolve against her. Lucy tried to kiss all the worries out of her, but she wasn't sure she succeeded. The blonde slowly pulled back, keeping hold of Scarlett's cheeks in her hands. "You are *unforgettable*. I need you to trust me. Our story is *not over*," she repeated firmly, her voice soft.

Scarlett held onto her and a few more tears escaped, dripping onto the floor. She sighed shakily and nodded. "I've never felt this way before. Can you fall in love in just a week?"

"Yes," Lucy answered immediately, their noses brushing against each other. "Yes."

Scarlett kissed her again, holding onto her wrists. After a few tantalizing moments of their mouths becoming one, Scarlett broke the kiss and kept her forehead pressed against Lucy's. "Go handle your shit."

Lucy smiled and let out a quiet, dejected laugh. "I'm not going to forget about you."

Scarlett hesitated for a moment, just long enough for Lucy's stomach to turn over inside her. Long, slender fingers tenderly traced over Lucy's cheek, and Scarlett kissed her forehead. She held her there for a moment, and Lucy couldn't help but feel like it was more of a goodbye than a promise to see her again. Slowly, Scarlett pulled back and met Lucy's eyes. "I'm not going to forget about you either."

Lucy blinked back some tears and let Scarlett trail from her grasp as she backed off and put on her heels. In a moment, Lucy was alone in her room again. She stood there, wondering if the last 24 hours had actually happened. What was she supposed to do?

She gently brought her fingers up to touch her lips, which were still puffy from all the kisses from the night before and that morning.

Grief consumed her.

Lucy crossed the small room and flung the door open, rushing to look out into the hallway.

But Scarlett was gone.

She let out a quiet cry to herself and leaned back against the wall next to her door, sobs threatening to overtake her body. She knew she could have run after her, she could have messaged her, she could have *stopped* this awful goodbye, but her feet weren't moving. She wrapped an arm around herself, her other elbow propped up against her forearm as she held her face with one hand. Tears came and went against her palm.

"Lucy?"

She looked up to see a very concerned Chris standing near her. She felt like she could throw up. Was she a horrible person? Her relationship was over, yes, but... not *officially*. She had slept with someone else. Where had he been all night? Where had he found to sleep? Had he done the same thing she had?

"You didn't come back last night," Lucy said quietly, wiping her cheeks.

"You told me not to," Chris said. "I just slept in one of the sitting areas on the main floors. Why are you crying?"

"Because I'm sad," Lucy said weakly. Why else?

"Anything I can do to help?"

Lucy looked at Chris for what felt like ages. She swallowed thickly, her throat tight with indecision. She sighed deeply and nodded. "I need you to move out."

S carlett stepped into her cabin and was thankful Olive wasn't in there. She really didn't think she could explain where she'd been, why she was in the same clothes as last night, or *anything* that happened between her and Lucy Price.

She shed her clothes as if they would harm her. It felt like thousands of tiny insects were swarming her skin. As she flung the garments haphazardly into a corner of the room, she saw Lucy Junior sitting on her nightstand.

Scarlett's walls broke and sobs overtook her. She picked up the alligator and stared down at it, droplets falling and merging with the short green fur. She pressed the toy against her forehead and tried to stop crying, but the tears kept falling.

Putting Lucy Junior back down in her spot, Scarlett walked into the small bathroom and started up the shower. She immediately stepped in without waiting for the water to warm up. She tensed at the ice-cold jets hitting her skin, soaking her to the bone. It helped her come back to reality. As the water began slowly warming, she just broke down into sobs.

Lucy had done everything right. She hadn't been cruel to her, she hadn't told her to get away from her, she hadn't told her she would never talk to her again, she had merely said she needed to handle her business and then she'd be back. Scarlett didn't know *why* she was having so much trouble believing her. Wouldn't it end the same way it always did? This was exactly why she didn't allow herself to grow close to anybody. Something or someone always had to come and get in the way of her happiness. It was always a mirage, a cruel joke played on her at the expense of her heart and body.

She thunked her head against the shower wall in frustration, *knowing* deep down that this line of thinking was unfair toward Lucy. She couldn't control it within her. The fear from Raphael's abuse infected her like a smog within her body and her thoughts became casualties of war. She began frantically scrubbing at her skin with soap, wanting to wash off *every* trace of Lucy. Of *feeling*.

When she exited the shower, the water having run cold again, she wrapped herself in a towel. On her way to her bed, dripping as she went, she realized she was no longer alone in the room.

"I heard you crying in the shower," Olive said from her bed. "Are you okay?"

Scarlett turned to the woman and clutched her towel even tighter around her body. "No."

"What happened? Is it Lucy?"

At the sound of her name, tears began flowing yet again, and before she could even wipe them away, Olive was by her side comforting her. Olive gently moved her to sit down on the bed, then the mattress dipped beside Scarlett as her roommate sidled next to her. After a few moments of silence and Scarlett calming down, she was ready to speak. She always appreciated that Olive never pushed her to open up before she was ready.

"I went to give Lucy her purse back last night and we ended up sleeping together," Scarlett murmured.

Olive regarded her thoughtfully and laced her fingers together on her lap. "You don't sound happy about that."

"It was great," Scarlett sighed. "Perfect. More than perfect. But this morning… it was just different. She said she has to get her life together, figure things out with Chris…"

"That makes sense," Olive said softly. "You wouldn't want to be with her when she's in a relationship. It sounds like she's trying to make that happen for you both. What else did she say?"

"A lot of beautiful, thoughtful things," Scarlett said, her voice wavering again. "I understand that *we* can't happen straight away, but it didn't make me feel any less dirty. Maybe I should have just controlled myself. Now she's confused and has to deal with him when she gets back…"

"Did she say anything about not wanting this to continue?" Olive asked.

"No," Scarlett murmured, looking at her. "She told me to trust her."

"Then stop making things up in your head," Olive said, rubbing her back. "If she says things are going to be okay and that she'll handle them, then you *do* need to trust her. If she's lying, well… you'll just have to go through that. But sabotaging something before it even begins isn't going to help anything.

It's just going to make you even sadder, and then you'll spend the rest of your life wondering what would have happened if you'd just gone for it."

Scarlett looked down and closed her eyes. "I'm scared."

"I know, but… that's life. That's *love*. You have to be vulnerable. You have to take those risks. Otherwise you won't experience anything. Being with Gavin is a risk, and if anyone higher up found out, we'd both be fired, but I love him," she shrugged. "And that's worth anything we have to face."

Scarlett looked over at her and gave a small smile. "That's the first time I've ever heard you say you love him."

"Don't tell him," Olive laughed. "It'll go straight to his head." The women laughed more with each other, then Olive folded her arms. "What are you going to do?"

Scarlett blinked a few times, then turned her gaze back down to her feet. "I have no idea."

Scarlett got ready for the day and went to the gallery to try and find Gavin. It was technically her turn to get off the ship and visit the port, but she had given it to Olive instead. She didn't feel like exploring or potentially running into Lucy again. She wouldn't even know what to say, and she wasn't overly confident she would be able to hold herself back around Chris.

She walked into the gallery, seeing Gavin at his desk, typing something on his computer. "Hey, Gavin?" Scarlett greeted, tapping her knuckles against the open door. "Can I talk to you for a minute?"

"Sure, Scarlett," Gavin said, glancing up. "Everything go

okay last night?"

For a moment, she was a bit taken aback, but remembered the gallery incident. She nodded. "Yeah, I gave her purse back no problem," Scarlett responded. She took the seat opposite his desk and crossed a leg over the other to keep from fidgeting. "I want to buy some art."

Gavin stopped his typing and gave her his full attention. "Do you? Where are you going to put it?"

"Not for me," Scarlett said. "A gift for someone else."

Gavin regarded her thoughtfully, then leaned back in his chair. "Do I even have to guess?"

"Probably not," she said. "Please? She wanted it so badly and she wasn't able to get it. I want her to have it. I'll buy it right now and we can ship it with the others that are scheduled to be ordered today."

Gavin stared at her, pressing his lips together in a thin line, then he sat up and started typing again. "You know how much it is?"

"Yes. It's fine," Scarlett said, reaching into the pocket of her blazer. She pulled out her wallet, then handed him her card. "You still have her address on file?"

"Yes," Gavin said, taking the debit card from her. He swiped it on the device by him, then a beep signaled the transaction went through. He handed the card back to her and clicked through a few more screens. "Alright, it'll be delivered to her house in a few weeks. What a nice surprise for her," he said. "Maybe she'll come on another cruise *without* that guy and she can actually buy something," he laughed. "At least you won't be so distracted on the next cruise."

"Actually…" Scarlett winced, forcing herself to look at him. "My contract ends in a month. I don't intend to re-sign. So this next cruise and the one after will be my last."

Gavin rolled his chair slightly to the side so the computer wasn't blocking his view of her. "What? You're quitting?"

"Yes," Scarlett said. "I want to go back home. I need to… start fresh."

"I thought you loved this job. We love having you here. You perform so well."

"I do love this job, but… it was something new for me when I started. It did what I needed it to do. Now I just want to go back home to my family. I have loved traveling and seeing the world, but I can't live like this forever."

Gavin frowned and rested his elbows on the desk. "You're sure about this, Scarlett?"

"I am," she said, her heart pounding in her chest.

"Alright," Gavin sighed. "I can't stop you. I'll let corporate know you won't be renewing your agreement."

"Thank you."

"They'll be in touch with you about next steps: returning your key cards, resetting your log-ins, your transportation home, your last paychecks, and whatever else they need from you during the exit interview."

"Okay," Scarlett nodded. "Thank you again for teaching me so much, Gavin. We'll stay in touch, I promise."

"You're making this so sad," Gavin laughed, standing up. He moved around the desk and gave her a quick hug. "We still have a few weeks to get some last memories in. Olive won't be happy."

"She'll be okay," Scarlett chuckled, squeezing him back. "She loves you, you know."

"I know," Gavin smiled, pulling back from her. "She hates to admit it though."

"So stubborn," Scarlett grinned. She felt like the weight of the world had been lifted from her. She could finally stop running. She could go back where she *belonged*.

Scarlett sluggishly returned back to her cabin. The ship was empty as workers turned everything over to get ready for the new batch of passengers. When she walked into the room, Olive was sitting on her bed, staring down at her phone. The woman lifted her head when Scarlett entered and turned her phone around to show her the screen. "Gavin says you quit?"

Scarlett sighed and gently let the door swing shut behind her. "Do you two discuss everything the second it happens?"

"Not the point. Is this true?"

"Yeah," Scarlett said, leaning her head back against the door. "I'm going to finish out the next two cruises and then fly back to London."

"You're doing all this because of Lucy?"

"No." Scarlett sighed and pushed herself off the door, then sat down next to Olive on the bed. "I have been thinking about this for a while. I started working here because I was running away from something terrible. I wanted to be a different person. But this isn't me." She shook her head and folded her hands in her lap. "I miss my family. I miss England. I've had so much fun and learned *so* much, but..."

"You're not happy."

"Not completely." Scarlett looked into Olive's brown eyes and frowned. "I will miss you so much though."

"That makes two of us," Olive said, hugging her tightly. After a few moments, they parted. "What are you going to do when you get back home? Go back to interior design?"

"I don't know for certain, but… I don't think so. I like art. I may stay in this field. Chroma's main office is in London. Maybe I'll transfer."

"That's true. I'm sure Gavin could make that happen for you. Did you talk to him about it?"

"No. Our conversation wasn't that long. It was all very spur of the moment," Scarlett laughed quietly. "But I will run it by him when we see each other again. Maybe I'll just go work in a museum or something. I haven't even had a chance to tell my mum what's going on."

"You definitely owe her a call."

"Yeah," Scarlett agreed. "God, I'll miss you, Olive. Is there any way I can convince you to drop everything and come with me?"

Olive laughed and shook her head. "I'll *definitely* come visit you, but I'm good where I'm at as far as permanent living arrangements. Plus Gavin hasn't *quite* pissed me off enough yet for me to move continents."

"Let me know if he ever does." Scarlett smiled and squeezed her hand. "You always have a place to stay with me no matter where I end up."

"Hopefully Lucy won't mind," Olive smirked.

Scarlett rolled her eyes. "Wishful thinking."

"No, *manifesting*. If you're willing to go back to your past life — no matter how much you deny it's because of Lucy — then you're down *bad* for this girl. I have full faith that you'll get the happily ever after you want so bad. Nobody deserves it more. I *will* miss having someone to annoy though. I doubt your replacement will be as fun."

"Excuse me? I'm irreplaceable," Scarlett scoffed, flicking her hair back over her shoulder. Olive was the queen of turning her mood around.

"That you are, babe," Olive said, gently tugging one piece of Scarlett's hair. "Now let me get dressed for work before I get chewed out."

Lucy scrolled through photos from the cruise on her phone. It had been a month and a half since she'd walked off that boat and seen Scarlett Sinclair. She had returned back to her apartment in Orlando with Chris and despite his protests, had convinced him to pack up all his things and move out. Her name was on the apartment lease and she was the only one paying rent or utilities anyway. There had been a time when Chris had mostly supported them, but that part of her life was long over. She wished him the best and didn't want him to have a miserable life, but she hadn't wanted *her* life to be spent with him.

It had been a difficult conversation. She had not told him about Scarlett, purely because that wouldn't change anything and would only add salt to the wound. She was sure he had come up with his own conclusions anyway. She didn't mind being the villain in his story, so long as she was written out of it. She had had to get his family involved, unfortunately, and the situation had been dragged out far more than she'd wished.

They had been on her side though and helped cart him out of her apartment. She didn't know if he would move back in with them or if they would buy him an apartment of his own, but either way, she was finally alone again.

Her parents had offered to help her move out of the apartment she shared with Chris, but a part of her wanted to see out the rest of her lease. She only had a few months left on it, then she could go somewhere new and start fresh. She had worked hard on the interior decor of the place, but even so, she needed something that wouldn't remind her of the downfall of the longest relationship of her life.

She spent many days crying over something or another. Sometimes it would be Chris, mourning those years and her time with him, and other times it would be Scarlett, and how much she missed her but just didn't know how to contact her. Her social media had been deleted, or at least, she didn't answer it. Lucy wasn't sure if she just… didn't want to be bothered. Maybe she didn't have any Wi-Fi on the ship.

Lucy's scrolling stopped when she came across a photo of her and Scarlett together in bed. They had taken them after their first time together while they'd been catching their breath and processing what just happened. Her cheeks warmed as her eyes scanned over the skin hidden under the covers. Their hair was all over the place and they…

Well, they looked in love.

She swiped to the next photo, smiling sadly to herself at the memories. She should have worked harder to go after Scarlett when she walked away. She should have just done *more*. But she knew that she had made the right decision when it came to

Chris, and that she owed him the courtesy of a clean breakup.

She just hoped she wasn't too late for fate to give her and Scarlett the ending they deserved. They had barely gotten a beginning.

Ding!

Lucy looked over as her doorbell sounded and she frowned. Tucking her phone in the pocket of her jean shorts, she got up and walked to the door. Upon glancing out the peephole, she saw what looked like a delivery person. She pulled the door open and leaned against the frame. "Hello?"

"Are you Lucy Price?"

"Yes…" Lucy answered slowly. "Can I help you?"

"Delivery, I need you to sign," the person said, handing her a small clipboard with a paper and pen attached to it.

Lucy was about to ask what she was signing for when she saw a rather big box leaned up against the wall by her front door. Her eyes scanned over the logo stamped to the side, then she looked down at the paper. The logo for the actual studio Scarlett worked at, Chroma Gallery, was plastered on the top. Lucy's breath caught and she signed without another thought.

"Can you get it in yourself or do you want some help?"

Lucy shook her head. "I've got it, thanks," she said, watching as the deliverer nodded and went on their way. She took a deep breath and grabbed the ends of the box, sliding it over the threshold and into her apartment. She walked around to the other side of it and pushed it into her cleared living room. She carefully set it down flat, then went to fetch a box-cutter.

In a few moments, the box was open and there was 'Spring Night,' framed and beautiful just like she remembered.

She swallowed thickly and gently ran her fingers over the canvassing, then pulled the art out of the tightly packed and secured box. A piece of paper fell out as she did so, and she picked it up with one hand, the other still propping up the artwork.

It was a receipt.

She scanned over it, half-wondering if her card *had* gone through that last night on the boat and she was five-hundred bucks poorer, but... no, there was another name there for payment. Scarlett's. Lucy smiled bashfully to herself, and put the receipt down, before properly pulling out the artwork. She carried it with a small grunt of exertion and angled it against the couch. Spinning around the room, she tried to find the perfect spot for it.

Eventually, she had it hung front and center in the living room.

She backed off to admire her handiwork. It pulled the entire space together. Her heart swelled as she thought about Scarlett, about their night together, about how she *of course* had done something so damn thoughtful it made her want to cry. Lucy knew Scarlett had been telling the truth that night when she said she'd love her more than anyone else could. She knew she would treat her better than Chris ever had.

Lucy walked over to her phone and picked it up to take a picture of her new decoration. She opened up one of her social apps so she could send what would probably be another unopened message to the woman of her dreams, when said woman's post popped up at the top of her feed. Lucy paused to read.

It was a picture of a busy streetscape, people bustling down cobblestoned roadways, and the weather looked rather dreary. There was a huge building in the center, one she assumed was some sort of museum. Lucy looked over the post and saw 'London' tagged at the top. She looked down at the caption, which read, '*Home sweet home. Glad to be back.*'

Lucy blinked. Scarlett was back in England? How was she supposed to go talk to her now? This explained why she hadn't been answering her, she was probably too busy flying across the entire ocean to bother opening her messages. Lucy sank dejectedly onto the sofa and stared down at the picture, feeling hopeless.

Zooming in, Lucy spotted a few landmarks. There was a big fountain in front of the pillared building. It almost looked like the White House, despite her *knowing* it wasn't. There were other light-colored buildings surrounding it.

She frowned to herself and locked her phone, not wanting to think about how far away Scarlett was now.

After a few minutes, she opened her phone again and clicked one of the contacts on her recent call list. She needed advice *now*.

"Tell me what's wrong, angel," Lucy's mom cooed as she sat on Lucy's sofa with her. "And what was so important that I had to stop yoga?"

Lucy sighed and pointed to the giant piece of artwork on the wall. "*That* is what's so important. And that is what's wrong."

Lucy's mother looked over at the artwork and tilted her head, then turned her attention back to her daughter. "Looks beautiful to me. You don't like it? Did Chris leave it? I don't ever remember you having that before."

"I didn't have it before today," Lucy explained. "It was a piece of artwork I really liked on the cruise. I was going to buy it, but you know what happened with all my money on that ship," she muttered, the older woman across from her huffing under her breath. "Apparently... Scarlett bought it for me and had it sent here."

"That was generous of her," her mom said.

"Yeah," Lucy sighed. "I don't know what to do, Mom. I tried messaging her after Chris left, but... she hasn't answered. She just posted that she moved back to London. I miss her so much. I want to *be* with her, but I don't know how that would be possible now, especially when she's an ocean away. She probably hates me."

"I don't think someone who hates you would have bought you a piece of fine art," the woman next to her said. "What *exactly* happened on that boat with her, Lucy?"

Lucy hesitated, unsure of what to say. She took a deep breath and finally steeled her nerves. "Scarlett and I... spent the night together. It was... Oh, Mom, I don't want to talk about this with you," she cringed, putting her hand up to her face.

"Why not?!"

"Because you're my mom," Lucy laughed. "Listen, it was good. I miss her more than anything and she's all I can think about. But now she's so far away, it's pointless to try."

"Why is it pointless?"

"Because… well, it could never work, Mom."

"Why not? Crazier things have happened."

"But she's in *England*. I'm way over here in Florida."

"Planes exist, sweetheart."

"I don't have *money* to just go off to London. And how am I supposed to find her? All I've got is this stupid picture she posted," Lucy groaned, shaking her head.

"Let me see the picture. I've been to England before," her mom said, holding out her hand. When Lucy pulled up the picture, her mom zoomed in, then scoffed. "Oh. This is the National Gallery."

"What's that?" Lucy asked.

"It's a big art museum there. She deals art, so… that all makes sense," she said, handing the phone back to Lucy. "I'd start there."

"What?" Lucy gawked, taking her phone back. "What do you mean?"

"I *mean*…" her mom started, pulling out her phone. "Your birthday is coming up soon. Maybe you can get an advance on your present," she murmured, tapping a few things. Lucy's phone buzzed after a moment and she looked down at it, seeing a notification from her banking app. She unlocked the alert and saw a *big* deposit into her checking account.

"Mom, I… What?" Lucy spluttered, looking up at her. "What is this for?"

"For you to go make things right."

Lucy blushed and looked down at the money again. "All by myself?"

"You have a passport and money, and hopefully you'll have a girlfriend who can show you all the tourist traps when you get there," her mother teased. "You've always been begging Chris for more romance. Doesn't get more romantic than this, crossing the world to save a love. You're writing your own happily ever after, Lucy. I'm happy to be a part of it."

Lucy grew emotional. She scooted across the empty cushion between her and her mom and pulled her in for a huge hug. She breathed deeply against her hair, trying to get herself in check. Crying wasn't going to help anything. "Thank you," Lucy whispered into her mom's light curls. "For everything, Mom."

"You're welcome, my angel," she murmured back, hugging her tight. "Go be wildly happy."

"Absolutely, let me know if you need anything else."

Scarlett smiled at the person who walked away from her to go explore more art inside the museum. She'd picked up a job as a design expert for the National Gallery in London. Though she had wanted to stray from the world of interior decor and focus on the art industry, this career allowed her to dip her toes in both. It paid much better than the ship had so she didn't need to move back in with her parents upon returning.

Working on a cruise allowed her to save up a good chunk of money, even with her minimal wages. When she left DreamWave, she had enough to put a deposit on a small studio flat in the heart of the city, near Soho, and pay for Lucy's art.

Lucy.

She sighed to herself as she thought about the woman. She had seen a few of the messages that had come through, but hadn't brought herself to answer them. What was she supposed to say? She wasn't in the States anymore, she couldn't just hop off the ship and go find her. She had run away *again*, despite coming back to the place she called home. It had been the right decision and she didn't regret leaving the ship, but she still didn't feel happy. Perhaps it had been naive of her to think things would magically go back to normal when she went back across the pond.

Lucy had given her no real reason to believe she would hurt her, but Scarlett wanted to beat her to it. She wanted to be in control of her own heartbreak. Lucy couldn't shatter her if she didn't give her the chance to.

This was where she was meant to be. She wasn't traipsing around the oceans and seas and gulfs, she was landlocked and glad for it. She didn't need to go parade with Floridians who she fell into bed with after a week. She didn't need to continue falling in love with pretty blondes with icy blue eyes. She didn't need to *think* about Lucy Price any goddamn more.

Scarlett strolled through the galleries and different rooms, making sure everything looked good. She wasn't in charge of security or informing guests on pieces, but sometimes she liked to roam away from her office and get her legs moving. She liked interacting with people, and she *did* know quite a bit about the artwork. It was an ever-changing rotation and it was a challenge to keep the interiors up to snuff, but she loved it. She liked to think she was good at her job and could handle any challenge thrown her way.

Scarlett wore one of her signature suits, this one a deep royal blue with a black blouse tucked in underneath. She was taller than usual in a pair of black stiletto heels and her hair was down her back and straight. She was trying to let it grow out some more.

She turned a corner and went into a contemporary-themed room, gazing at all the canvases and statues on offer. She crossed the room and stopped in front of a piece hung on the wall, lit up with spotlights. She stared at the bright reds, greens, blues, oranges, yellows, and all the other colors blended between. Her eyes roamed down to the two splotches for people walking along the sidewalk scattered with reflections of puddles. She imagined her and Lucy being those two splotches, doing something as simple as walking through a park on a rainy day in April.

"That one's called 'Spring Night' by Daniel Wall. I have it at home."

Scarlett's eyes widened as she heard the voice that had been taking residence in her dreams right behind her. She slowly turned around and came face to face with Lucy.

"Some cute girl bought it for me then skipped town. Didn't even give me time to thank her. I had to run around the world to find her," Lucy said with a smile, her lips painted red. She was in a long, flowing cream-colored dress and a dark brown cardigan. She wore a simple, wide-brimmed brown hat to match the color of her cardigan, and some dark brown ankle-boots. Her white purse — that damned purse — was slung over her shoulder, and for lack of a better word, she looked like a masterpiece.

"What... What are you doing here?" Scarlett breathed, her heart pounding. She didn't even have enough time to process what was happening. Lucy was there in front of her, in the flesh, smiling as if the last two months hadn't happened.

"I just told you. I wanted to thank you for the artwork. And let you know I got my shit together."

"You..." Scarlett trailed off, her cheeks red. Though the museum was bustling with people checking out the work, she felt like they were all alone in that big building.

"You're usually more eloquent than this," Lucy teased, taking a step toward her. She dropped her playful tone and reached out to take Scarlett's hands, which were trembling. "I told you our story isn't over. I came here to find out the end. Or... hopefully the beginning," she said with a small smile. "If you'll have me."

"You came all this way..." Scarlett said dazedly. "All this way for... for me?"

"For you," Lucy said gently. "I love you, Scarlett. You're who I want to be with. You're everything I want. You are worth every mile, in the air, on the water, on the road, *anywhere*. I'm yours until you send me away."

"How could I possibly send you away, darling?" Scarlett whispered, before closing the distance between them to give her a kiss. Lucy wrapped her arms around her and they held each other like they were the air they needed to breathe. Scarlett deepened the kiss and glued her body to the other woman's, her entire *soul* lit up.

Eventually, they broke apart and Scarlett looked around. People who were staring quickly busied themselves with pretending to look at art. She blushed and laughed under her breath, before looking at Lucy. "I... I don't get off for another two hours," she whispered.

Lucy smiled and pecked a small kiss to her lips again.

"Occupational hazard, right?" she teased. Scarlett laughed and nodded, remembering their first conversation. She had known from the second they met that something was different about this woman, and now here they were, *together.* "Mind if I keep you company? I can go into puppy mode."

Scarlett couldn't stop her giggles. She felt lightheaded with happiness. "Of course, of course. I don't think I can let you out of my sight ever again." She brought her hand up to gently cradle Lucy's cheek, her eyes wide. "You're really here. Really, really here."

"It wasn't easy," Lucy said, leaning into her touch. "All I had was a vague picture on Instagram to go off of. My mom actually recognized the building and helped me. I just hopped on a plane and hoped for the best. For all I knew, you could've been off today."

"What was the plan then?"

"Find a hotel and keep coming back until you weren't off."

"You don't have a hotel?"

"Like I said, hoped for the best." Lucy smiled sloppily and brought her hand up to gently rest over Scarlett's against her cheek. "I was hoping I could maybe shack up with a hot brunette while I was here?" she asked in her best, pitiful English accent.

Scarlett, again, laughed and nodded adamantly. "I believe all of that can be arranged."

They kissed again and eventually pulled apart so Scarlett could show Lucy around the rest of the museum.

After they walked around the entire museum, Scarlett brought

Lucy back to her office so she could see everything. The dark-haired woman leaned against her desk, her arms folded as she watched the blonde pace around, taking everything in. It was a big room and separate from other offices. Scarlett's eyes followed Lucy as she circled the room, then stopped at the door. Slowly, Lucy pushed it shut and turned a small mechanism on the handle to lock it. Scarlett's brown eyes darkened to a shade of espresso and she didn't move.

Lucy prowled toward her and stopped in front of her, standing between her legs. Scarlett's expression dripped with lust as Lucy planted her hands on her thighs and squeezed. It made Scarlett's breath hitch. "Sorry I don't have a more comfortable venue," she murmured.

Lucy leaned forward, her lips brushing against Scarlett's ear and hair. "Won't stop me from making you scream."

Scarlett's entire body caught fire and the deepest shudder she'd ever known ripped her in half. Their lips met in a flurry of movement and Scarlett moaned the second Lucy's tongue prodded her mouth, begging for entry. Scarlett's hands shot out and began clawing at any part of Lucy they could. Lucy's hands deftly pushed the blazer off Scarlett's shoulders, the garment pooling on the desk behind her. Lucy's fingers pushed buttons through holes one by one while Scarlett swiped the hat off the woman's head and treated her cardigan the same as Lucy did her blazer. Both things fell to the floor with a quiet noise and Scarlett greedily ran her hands up Lucy's bare arms. "Fuck me," she moaned.

"That's the plan," Lucy teased as she trailed her kisses from the corner of her mouth, down her cheek, her jawline, her neck, her collarbone…

Scarlett had died. She was in heaven. Actual heaven. It had gone from being a boring work day to the best fucking day of her life. She tilted her head back as Lucy's firestorm of kisses moved down her sternum. Scarlett's shirt was hanging open now, half-tucked into her trousers, which were still buckled and buttoned up. Lucy paused her kisses and instead palmed Scarlett's breasts over the black, lace bra strapped to her chest. She unhooked the front clasp and Scarlett was finally exposed. The small snake tattoo in the center of her cleavage wriggled with every breath.

"I missed these," Lucy whispered, and whatever clever quip Scarlett had died in her throat as Lucy's lips were immediately caressing her hardened nipples. Scarlett tangled a hand in Lucy's curls and held her tightly against her chest, Lucy's mouth moving back and forth, left to right, giving each of her boobs so much attention it made her stomach muscles clench.

Scarlett was too focused on Lucy's talented mouth, she didn't even notice one of the woman's hands unbuckling her belt. She undid the button to her trousers swiftly after and Scarlett's thoughts ceased the second Lucy shoved her hand into her knickers and against her pussy.

"Fuck!" Scarlett blurted out again, her voice high-pitched. She was *trying* to be a little quiet, but Lucy was making it nearly impossible.

Lucy looked up at her with a feral grin. "Here? Now?" she teased, her tongue poking between her teeth. Scarlett's eyes glazed over as Lucy continued stroking her clit, building her orgasm slowly and deeply. She alternated from the bundle of nerves to swiping down the slit of her sex. Then she dipped inside, coating her skin with Scarlett's desire, removed it again, and went back to circling the top of her pussy.

"Please, darling," Scarlett breathed. "*Please*."

"Such a good girl, begging for me."

Scarlett twitched in response and clenched around Lucy's fingers. Who was this *siren* and what had she done with the shy, lesbian-virgin Lucy Price? Her soft, Southern voice washed over every one of Scarlett's nerve endings like melted candy. She craned her neck down so she could kiss Lucy again. She didn't even want to *know* what her face looked like, given how much red lipstick was smeared around Lucy's mouth. She found she didn't bloody care, so long as Lucy made her come.

One of Scarlett's hands stayed tangled in Lucy's locks while the other stretched back to hold onto the edge of the desk. A few things clattered to the ground with the movement and Scarlett made a quick mental note to keep her desk free of *any* breakable things to prepare for this exact scenario hopefully *many* times in the future. Her blouse slipped down her shoulders, along with her bra, and eventually settled at her elbows. Scarlett rolled her hips against Lucy's knuckles, gasps of air growing shallower under her chest. "I'm close," she panted, her pupils almost as big as her eyes.

"Come for me then, honey," Lucy whispered against her lips, her hand working the same constant rhythm and speed. She curled her fingers inside her, and with a few strokes of the *exact* spot she wanted her, Scarlett saw stars. The woman quaked violently into Lucy's hold, tugging harshly on her curls as she gave over to every moment of rapture this goddess fed her. Lucy moaned quietly at the harsh movement and moved with her pull, her lips parted in a way that made Scarlett want to lick her head to toe.

Lucy's hand stayed in Scarlett's trousers, teasing her lazily with her fingers. Scarlett quivered with every touch and let go of the desk. Sitting up properly, she pushed one loose sleeve of Lucy's ivory dress down her shoulder. Scarlett lost count of the freckles dotting her tanned skin. She still looked like she came straight from a beach in her dreams.

"I love making you come," Lucy breathed, her cheeks flushed with a pale pink hue that traveled down her neck and disappeared beneath her dress.

"I love *you*," Scarlett sighed happily, her eyes pricking with moisture. "I love you so much, Lucy Price."

Lucy's dazed look of ecstasy turned into an emotional smile. "I'm not going anywhere. Ever again."

"You better not," Scarlett laughed tearfully.

They kissed again and Scarlett resumed her task of getting that dress off.

Lucy's heart was *pounding*.

She told herself over and over on the plane ride to London that she would exude confidence, make Scarlett fall in love with her, and secure the happy ending she promised them. She thought about everything she was going to do, what she was going to say, how she was going to stand, and how to make the woman melt under her.

She *liked* to think she was successful, given the way Scarlett was staring at her and breathing like she just ran a marathon. Lucy felt parched.

Lucy's eyes fluttered shut as Scarlett pushed her dress sleeves further down until the top half of the material bunched up at her waist, the rest of the dress still hanging down. Cold air bit at her chest, leaving her nipples hard and aching with anticipation. Scarlett moaned and looked up at her. "No bra?"

"Is that a complaint?" Lucy breathed, words barely forming.

The other woman laughed and shook her head. "No. Not at *all*. I'm loving this new cocky Lucy."

"Don't say 'cock,'" Lucy groaned, making Scarlett cackle. Scarlett apologized quickly and made up for it by swirling her tongue around Lucy's right nipple. The blonde moaned deeply, the sound morphing into croon as Scarlett's fingers pinched the other nipple. Lucy stumbled forward as Scarlett used her free arm to reel her closer. Scarlett squeezed her ass over the dress and kneaded her fingers into the muscle. Lucy moaned again, coherent thoughts a thing of the past.

Scarlett mumbled something and it took several seconds for Lucy to register the sound. Only when Scarlett stopped touching her completely did she come back to Earth and look at the woman in confusion.

"I said go sit in my chair," Scarlett said. It was not a request.

Unable to do anything else, Lucy nodded and went around the desk. She sat in the chair, her breasts still full and on show, her dress bunched around her waist. Scarlett closed in on her like a panther stalking its prey and Lucy practically melted into a puddle. Scarlett kneeled on the floor and grabbed the bottom hem of her dress, pushing it up her thighs. Lucy arched her hips and trapped the material between her and the chair, giving Scarlett a full view.

"I missed you," Scarlett breathed while holding Lucy's legs apart. Back when she'd been with Chris, she had shied away when he tried to look at her in a similar fashion. She worried she wouldn't be good enough or he'd find something he didn't like. With Scarlett, Lucy felt like she was Aphrodite reincarnated.

"Show me how much you missed me," Lucy purred. She didn't even *know* where all this conviction came from. It was just so easy to be confident with Scarlett. She felt comfortable, loved, and *safe*.

Scarlett hummed lowly in response and trailed her hands up Lucy's bare thighs, her skin prickling in their wake. Lucy's mind was racing. She wanted this teasing to both last forever and end immediately. She was trying to calm herself down, force herself to focus on the *moment* and not whatever the future may hold for them. She had no reason to believe Scarlett would love her and leave her, but she was taking a huge risk being there. Eventually, she would have to go back home and figure out her job, her *life*. With her career, she could move to London and get a job at a fashion magazine or company there. She would miss her family, but maybe leaving the U.S. would be good for her. She wouldn't have to feel anxious going to the grocery store or *anywhere* else in Orlando. She wouldn't have to worry about running into Chris when she went out with her friends at a bar they used to frequent. She would change her number to a U.K. one and Chris wouldn't have it. She could start *fresh*.

"Lucy."

Her eyes flipped open and she looked down at Scarlett.

Scarlett smirked as they made eye contact and shook her head. Lucy smiled sheepishly. Scarlett knew her too well, better than a man who had spent more than half a decade with her. Lucy suddenly registered the cold air against her wet folds and realized Scarlett had stripped her of her light pink, lace panties without her even noticing. Just as Lucy was about to apologize for being so spaced out, Scarlett's tongue was flat against her clit and anything she was about to say dissipated in a proverbial puff of smoke in her mouth. Lucy groaned loudly, unable to hold her eyes open anymore. She tilted her head back against the chair and weaved a hand into Scarlett's hair, holding her firmly between her legs. Warmth spread throughout her belly as she melted beneath Scarlett, who was *feasting* on her body.

"Oh, God," Lucy groaned out, her throat bobbing.

"Nope, just Scarlett," the other woman mumbled against her pussy. Lucy laughed and gave a warning tug on Scarlett's hair, before her giggles turned into more moaning. Desire coiled in her chest, stomach, arms, legs, fingers, *toes*. She had almost forgotten how expert Scarlett's touch was. Often, Lucy thought about that night on the cruise, the awakening Scarlett had provided her. She thought about the way her tongue ran over her clit like she'd been born to do it, how her fingers curled in just the right spot, making her beg for more, how her breath hot against her ear was nearly enough to send her over the edge regardless of the touching. She thought about it in the shower, in bed, at work, in shops, on the street, *everywhere*. Scarlett had completely overtaken every synapse in her brain.

Lucy clamped her thighs around Scarlett's ears, holding her head right where she wanted — no, *needed* it. Scarlett's tongue circled the bundle of nerves in her core, making Lucy croon with pleasure. Gently, Lucy guided Scarlett's head up and down, the other woman's tongue coating every inch of her sensitive skin. Scarlett nuzzled her head between Lucy's legs, her fingers digging into the flesh around her.

"Missed you," Scarlett repeated in a moan, her voice muffled.

"Missed *you*," Lucy responded, her voice barely above a

whisper. "I'm so close, baby. Keep going, *please*. I *need you*."

Scarlett seemed to take the encouragement in stride and doubled down her efforts. A few seconds passed of her wonderful tongue and fingers doing all the work and Lucy's body went taught, then snapped like a bowstring. She shuddered violently, half-worried the iron grip her legs had around Scarlett's head would pop her skull open. Every part of Lucy was trembling by the time Scarlett pulled away.

"Did you come?" Scarlett teased, her lips and chin glistening in the low light of her office.

Lucy answered with an incredulous look, lifting her head from the back of the chair. Her chest heaved with exertion. The sight of Scarlett kneeling there, looking up at her like she was the most important being in the world was too much for Lucy. She hooked Scarlett around the back of her neck with her hand and pulled her up for a kiss. Long and languid, Lucy's tongue met Scarlett's in a dance of dominance. She could taste herself and despite never having achieved nor desired multiple orgasms with Chris, felt flames of desire being stoked within her once more.

After an age, they broke the kiss and stared at each other. Lucy smiled emotionally and pressed her forehead against Scarlett's, the tips of their noses brushing. "Take me to your place?"

Scarlett nodded and kissed the few tears that managed to escape away from Lucy's cheeks. "*Our* place."

Epilogue

"**D**on't be nervous. You have worked so hard on this gala and it's going to go off without a hitch. Okay?" Lucy reassured Scarlett as they stood just outside her office. Lucy rubbed her arms, her palms swiping over the smooth material of Scarlett's dark red blouse. "I won't be far at any point. If you need me, just look around and I'll be there. I promise."

"Okay," Scarlett said with a shaky breath. She had organized a fashion gala at the National Gallery to promote a new Greek exhibit they had just received. Lucy had helped her nail everything down and co-organized the event with her new job as a photographer with *Iconic London*, a cutting-edge fashion magazine that was quickly finding its place among the household names within the city.

Lucy had gotten everything rolling pretty much immediately upon reconnecting with Scarlett. She had only left her once to go gather her things from the United States and say goodbye to her family. Lucy's family had been happy for her for following her dreams, but of course, sad to see her go. Lucy had reminded them it was just an excuse for them to come abroad any time they liked and save money on hotels. Her mother had jumped at the opportunity.

This gala was Scarlett's last big hurdle to holding her own within the art scene of England. She told Lucy that if this went well, there would be no more questioning within the community if she was still as good as she'd been when she left to go overseas. Raphael wouldn't define her anymore. She'd make a name for herself and finally move on from *everything* her past tried to remind her of.

"I have to go out there and get ready for the first guests," Lucy said, bringing her hand up to cradle her girlfriend's cheek. "I love you. Remember to breathe, honey."

At that, Scarlett took a deep breath and nodded. "I'm good."

"I know," Lucy smiled, pecking a gentle kiss to her lips. In a moment, she had disappeared to the front of the building, cameras strapped around her and ready to go. Scarlett leaned back against the wall and twisted her hands together, then flattened them against her thighs. She was in a black suit, black stiletto heels, and a dark red buttoned blouse. Her hair was down her back and pin-straight, and she'd let Lucy do her makeup for her — a smokey eye look, but nothing over the top to where she looked clownish. She looked as good physically as she possibly could, but mentally was another story. She was so bloody thankful for Lucy's support.

It had been a year since Lucy had come to take the risk and see if Scarlett wanted to *do this*. Lucy had moved into

Scarlett's flat in downtown London and put her own touch on the place. She had completely transformed it and despite Scarlett's background with interior design and art, she never thought her home looked more like a *home* than with Lucy's influence. Things had been a little stressful at first with the adjustments and culture shock on Lucy's end, but when she landed her job at the magazine and got her things over to the United Kingdom, the couple settled into their routines. This gala was the first time they had ever properly worked together on something and to Scarlett's surprise, they hadn't fought once. It had been as easy as breathing to craft this event with her. She felt somewhat guilty for assuming the worst, but it was just her trauma from Raphael and working with him. There was always something wrong with *something* when they'd do things together. She hadn't wanted to step on Lucy's toes with the project, but she still wanted to have her own voice since the National Gallery was her responsibility. Thankfully, Lucy had seen her vision from a mile away and rolled seamlessly with it. It made Scarlett love the woman even more.

"Get a grip," Scarlett muttered to herself, her eyes closed. After counting to ten, she pushed herself off the wall and walked toward the front. She could do this.

Lucy held one of her cameras up and snapped a few shots of a group of people coming in with dresses the Met Gala would be jealous of. She glanced down at her camera's screen to check the composition of the photos, then quickly pulled her phone out to take notes and names. She had a team with her to cover this, considering the event was too large for one person, but she was taking the lead.

She was a senior editor for *Iconic London*, both a promotion and hefty pay raise from her last position in Orlando. Scarlett had had a connection within the community to help get her foot in the door for an interview and work visa to live in the United Kingdom. Lucy had smashed the interview and was offered the position before she even got off the bus ride back to Scarlett's flat. That night had been one of the best of her life, jumping and squealing excitedly with Scarlett, knowing that things were going to be fine and she was able to stay with her. She was able to get that fresh start she'd been searching for for so long.

This event was a big deal for both of them. Scarlett was cementing her place in the world of design and art, and Lucy was going to use this success — because she couldn't afford to think otherwise — as a jumping board into making a name for herself in a cutthroat and huge city full of people just like her. Lucy and Scarlett had spent countless nights together staying up late to plan the finer details of the gala, and Lucy couldn't feel both prouder and more relieved that it was off to a good start.

Lucy caught sight of Scarlett across the room, standing in front of a camera giving an interview. She couldn't help but smile to herself as she watched her girlfriend conduct herself with the utmost poise and class. She was *hers* and Lucy still found herself giggling with pure elation that she got to come home to her, that she got to love her with everything she had.

Lucy sighed to herself, then snapped back into work mode.

She had the rest of her life to gawk at her beautiful partner, for now, she needed to lock in and get the content she needed to come back to the office a hero.

Flashes of cameras, a dull roar of chatter and interviews, and clicks of heels filled the large ballroom that was decorated with the finest art Lucy had ever seen. The floor was lined with a velvet red carpet leading through the room and into the restaurant area that had been kitted out and made over for the event. Lucy loved looking at all the creativity the best designers in the city showed off for the event. Greek history was one of her favorite time periods to learn about, both in school and out, and seeing the inspiration in the clothes in front of her was like eye candy. Some of these models and celebrities might as well have been Grecian statues or gods or goddesses anyway.

When everyone settled for dinner, Lucy took it as a break and went to go find Scarlett. After wading through the edges of the room, she found the woman absorbed into the tablet in her hands, her fingers tapping rapidly. Lucy smiled to herself and made a beeline for her. "You look frustrated."

"The sodding Internet is acting up again, nothing's loading for me," Scarlett grumbled as she kept tapping the screen.

"What do you need?" Lucy asked as she moved around her to stand by her side. "Hmm…" Lucy looked down at the seating chart that was glitching. She could understand her frustration. "Look," she said, getting Scarlett's attention. She jerked her chin toward the crowd of tables. "They're all sitting down, they're all happy, they're all about to eat. I know you want to double-check, but it looks like you don't need to. Okay?"

Scarlett's dark eyes scanned over the room and she finally

let a breath out. "Okay. Okay. You're right. I'm sorry."

"No need for sorries. You're wanting this to go well, I get it. From someone who has just as much staked in this as you do, I think it's going as well as possible. The hard part's over, really. They'll eat, we'll snap a few more pictures and get some last-minute interviews, then it'll be time for clean-up. Hopefully nobody tries to steal a billion-dollar necklace like *Ocean's 8*."

"Ocean's what?" Scarlett asked, furrowing her brows.

Lucy laughed and shook her head. "It's a movie. I'll show you later. Honestly, I've been thinking about it all week, but I didn't want to bring it up and make you watch it and it freak you out. Basically, the whole main plot is surrounded by a group of female criminals burgling an expensive necklace. They use the Met Gala as the scene of the crime. It's really good, actually. One of my favorites. Plus it has Anne Hathaway in it."

"Oh, *that's* why. But you're right, that definitely would have freaked me out," Scarlett laughed, shaking her head. "I love you, Lucy. Thank you so much for always being here for me, *with* me."

"You'll have me forever, Scar. I promise. I love you, too." Lucy squeezed her hand, then leaned in for a quick, but loving kiss. "I'm so proud of you."

"I'm proud of *you*," Scarlett said, pecking her again. "After this is over, what's next?"

Lucy pulled back and rested her head on Scarlett's shoulder, heaving a large sigh. "You mean after we're super famous for putting on the party of the season? Maybe we can go on a cruise."

Scarlett covered her mouth to hide her laughter and shook

her head. "I think I'd honestly sooner jump off the boat and let sharks eat me."

"I'm going to *not* take that as an insult, thanks," Lucy said with a small laugh. She stood up straight and turned to face her girlfriend fully. Shrugging her shoulders, she tilted her head. "We can do whatever we want."

"Maybe get married?" Scarlett asked, worrying her lower lip with her teeth.

Lucy blushed and reached forward, her thumb gently urging Scarlett's lip back where it was supposed to be. "Not if I ask you first."

"If you get down on one knee right now…"

"You've ruined the surprise!" Lucy laughed, a grin spreading into her cheeks. "You really think I'd do it at work?"

"Well, you showed *up* to my work to confess your undying love to me last year, so…"

"Okay, fair." Lucy scrunched up her nose, then kissed Scarlett's cheek. "I promise you'll love what I have planned."

"You've planned it already?" Scarlett asked, moving to look into her eyes.

"Don't even act like you haven't. Going on a date to try on rings 'just for fun' isn't exactly super subtle."

"I needed to make sure!"

Lucy smiled, a content smile that made her feel like everything was falling into place. "Whenever the day comes, I can't wait to call you my wife."

Scarlett beamed and nodded. "Me, too."

ABOUT THE AUTHOR

Kerrigan Bailey Casimir is a former journalist-turned-author with a passion for romance and all things weird. She grew up in Panama City Beach, Florida, but moved to New Orleans, Louisiana in her twenties with her wife, Amber. Though she has a background on the sandy beaches of the Florida Panhandle, she grew up attending Saints games and exploring the French Quarter in New Orleans with her family.

An Ole Miss graduate (Hotty Toddy!), Kerrigan has dedicated most of her life to honing their craft and delving into the nuances of storytelling. She started her literary journey by writing fanfiction with her best friend, Becca Prince; that love for stories led her to a career in journalism, where she was trained in formal writing, photography, videography, and auditory storytelling.

Outside of the writing realm, Kerrigan can be found running around New Orleans with a camera in her hand, capturing all the best moments for tourists and locals alike. When she's off the clock, she enjoys a yummy cocktail and dinner with her wife, and coming home to all her animals.

ACKNOWLEDGEMENTS

To my beautiful, supportive, I-can't-believe-you're-real wife, I want to thank you first and foremost. Amber, you are my life blood and without you I wouldn't be able to stand upright or function. You are always cheering me on in every corner, even when I want to give up. I never knew how wonderful life could be until I met you. You are the brightest light in an otherwise very dark world — I am lucky beyond comprehension to get to call you my partner.

To my mom, Wendi, thank you for your unwavering support in my professional and personal life. You have always nurtured me to be the best person I can be, and I hope I make you proud with everything I put into the world. You are always the first to give me feedback or read something I send you. You lose sleep making sure everyone and their brother knows about my work, from writing to photography. I am so blessed to have you as my mother.

To Ashley, Shelby, and Nathan, Lauren, and Elizabeth, my closest friends and confidantes. Your support is unmatched, unwavering, and most of all, more appreciated than you could ever possibly know. Your opinions mean everything to me, and I know you'll always ground me when I need it. I couldn't do life without you.

To my sweet Becca, gone far too soon and forever 29, I miss you sorely. You are every bit to credit for my writing skills and any and *all* of my authoring prizes. I miss you so much it makes my bones ache. I hope you're sleeping well. I miss your hugs and laugh.

And lastly, to you, my lovely reader, without you this simply would not be a reality. Your support keeps my dreams alive and I am so beyond grateful for your attention. Thank you, thank you, thank you.

- Kerrigan xoxo